The Center Piece

The Center Piece

Larry A. Nielsen

The Center Piece Larry A. Nielsen

Also by Larry Nielsen

Fiction

Dead Man on Campus (2022)
(A Des White-Elena Bertoni Mystery)

Non-fiction

Provost--Experiences, Reflections, and Advice From a
Former "Number Two" on Campus (2013)
Nature's Allies--Eight Conservationists Who Changed Our
World (2017)
Wolfpack Ramblings--A Thousand-Mile Walk Across NC
State's Campus (2021)
Speaking Skills for Graduate Students (2022, ebook only)

To Sharon,
the Centerpiece of my life

Thursday

Elena Bertoni leaned against the table at the far end of the conference room. Once again, she was lost in the painting on the room's back wall. It was a simple painting, just two great blue herons flying across a clear blue sky. The birds flew in scientifically accurate form, the wings in a gentle arc, long necks folded into a tight "s," feet trailing behind. As a wildlife biologist, Elena appreciated the artist's technical accuracy.

But she also sensed the poetry in the forms. These weren't just generalized abstractions of birds, like the drawings in a bird guide, accompanied by little arrows to point out the clues to their identification. These birds felt real to her, going about their lives just as she did. In her mind she could hear the beat of the birds' broad wings, feel the rush of air as they passed, react to their rusty-hinge call. "We're going to the other side of the lake," she imagined them saying, "get out of our way or pay the consequence."

The painting drew Elena in and transported her away. Away to a small lake, the shoreline ringed with cattails where red-winged blackbirds roosted. Where lily pads with pink flowers stretched into deeper water, frogs jumping from leaf to water and back again, avoiding predators from both above and below. Where dragonflies sketched their erratic flight through the morning mist. Higher on the shore she imagined stands of white pines, their soft five-needle tufts waving gently in the breeze and filling the air with the cleansing aroma of northern forest. Across the pond, she saw a ring of forest trees with low, time-worn mountains completing the background.

"So, that's what the fuss is all about, huh?"

Elena jumped to attention and spun around. "Good lord, Aaron, you about scared me to death."

"Sorry, my dear," he said. "Didn't mean to frighten you. I'm just a little early for the meeting."

Aaron Schmidt would never have purposefully scared Elena. They were colleagues in the Department of Renewable Resources at Virginia Western University. Not colleagues really, more like kindred spirits. But it wasn't their scientific specialties that made them close—he an expert in wood identification and she a wildlife behaviorist—but rather their overall love of the university. They had been friends since Elena joined VWU nearly six years earlier. An unlikely pair, a casual observer might think, a crusty old professor remembering fondly the scholarly refuge that campus used to be and the young, vibrant associate professor aimed purposefully at the future. But they would be wrong.

Aaron had been at the university for decades, gaining worldwide fame as a wood anatomist and physiologist; a narrow niche, to be sure, but well respected within it nonetheless. At the same time, he became one of the university's most loyal citizens, devoted not only to his own specialty but also to the diverse life of the campus. He was, to put it tritely, the epitome of a gentleman and a scholar.

And Elena, in her brief tenure so far, was following in his footsteps. Their boss, department head Ted Graham, lectured her regularly on the reality of getting promoted to full professor—grants, publications, graduate students, that was the ticket, and the only ticket. Save all your other interests for after you get promoted, he told her, then you can be the new generation's Aaron Schmidt.

It didn't work. Of course she was building her resume for eventual promotion, but the university was so interesting that she couldn't help herself from getting involved all over campus. Study abroad, club advising, task forces on undergraduate learning, campus environmental team—she was deep into all of it. She was what the provost once described as faculty members who worked with their heads up, curious about what was happening across the hall and across the campus. Ted told her to ignore the provost, to work with her head down, avoiding all those fascinating distractions. At least until she could drop the "associate" from her title and just be called "professor."

The meeting that Aaron had arrived early for was an example of her head-up problem. Elena was chair of the university's art and environment program. This was one of her favorite projects. It linked the university's arts and environment majors. One of the ways to interest students in conservation was through the arts, from painting to sculpture to dance and music. And one of the ways to get biology majors out of their focus on environmental problems was to engage their creativity. If ever there was a topic that used both the right brain and left brain, art-and-environment was it.

Elena had recruited Aaron as a member of the steering committee. Their monthly meeting was set to begin at the top of the hour.

"Yeah, well, just quit sneaking up on me like that, old man. The least you could do is groan or wheeze when you get close."

Aaron smiled and pointed to his feet. "Can't help it. These new walking shoes are so quiet I scare myself sometimes." He was wearing a pair of green and gold sneakers, the colors of the university, tied up incongruously with neon orange laces.

Elena returned the smile. "So, you've finally given up those old leather brogues that sounded like a platoon of storm troopers sent by Darth Vader. Welcome to the 21st Century."

"Me thinks that these shoes are the high point of the century, at least so far."

She ignored both his rhetoric and opinion, and turned back to the painting. "Yes, my friend, this is what the fuss is all about. It's beautiful, isn't it?"

Aaron walked up beside her and considered the piece. "Sure. But don't those birds look a little lonely up there all by themselves? Wouldn't it be a better painting if it had some other details with it? Some trees maybe, around the edge of the lake or pond or whatever they're flying over. See, we don't even know where they are. They could be flying over Iowa for all we know."

Other members of the committee started arriving, so time for art criticism was over. "I'll explain it all to you later," Elena said.

"Great," Aaron said, "a grog at The Hawk's Den after work?"

"You got it," she said, and called the committee to order.

She adjourned the meeting after precisely one hour. Her colleagues often complained that Elena was obsessive about getting things right and following the rules, but no one objected to the way she ran a meeting. Start on time, follow the agenda, quit on time. She gathered her materials as her colleagues quickly abandoned the room.

"See you after work," Aaron said.

"Yeah," Elena said, "but after my work day, not yours. That's six o'clock, not three-thirty."

Aaron faked a hurt look, then gave her a wink. "I'll take a little nap so I'm refreshed." He silently glided out the door, except for a few exaggerated groans.

Elena turned and looked at the painting again. The herons were still there, still winging across the undefined sky. She laughed at Aaron's complaint that there weren't any trees in the background. Typical for a wood products guy, she thought, just like the Lorax, speaking for the trees, or at least for the things you could make when you cut the trees down.

She loved this room, combining her passions for art and the environment. That the biological sciences library at Virginia

Western University had a conference room filled with wildlife art was a marvel. It was called the Fuertes Room, named after Louis Agassiz Fuertes, who had painted those herons well over a century ago.

And it was all due to the generosity of the Dean of Biological Sciences, Ralph Vukovic. Vukovic had been dean for nearly two decades, an eternity in university administration, and over the years had donated several important paintings to the university. He had collected wildlife-related art throughout his life, and every few years he moved a painting from his own collection to the university. It was selfish, he would say with each donation, to keep these great works of animal art to himself when the whole world should have the chance to enjoy them.

Elena let her gaze follow around the room. It was a rectangular space, just inside the entrance to the library. A glass door, flanked by floor to ceiling windows, opened into the library's foyer, across the aisle from the library service desk. A dozen works of art lined the walls, but five stood out (the "Big Five," as Elena liked to think of them). Along one long side hung a study by Albert Bierstadt of deer wading in shallow water for his master painting of Yosemite Valley, and then a whimsical pen-and-ink drawing of an owl by humorist James Thurber. On the other long wall hung a group of alligators in a swamp painted by John Singer Sargent and a bald eagle painted by Charles Bull that had been the original for a long series of World War I savings-bond posters. And the prize of the exhibit was the Fuertes painting of herons, hung by itself on the short wall at the far end of the room.

Most of the art in the Fuertes Room came from Dean Vukovic, including the Big Five, and two other smaller, less noteworthy sketches. But the dean's generosity had attracted other gifts of animal art by alumni and donors. Several of those were in the Fuertes Room, and others were hung in the atrium that ran through the building's first floor, separating the library on one side from the teaching rooms on the other.

All told, it was an impressive collection. Travel sites that listed things to do typically had the Fuertes Room as one of the top ten for Stone Valley. It couldn't compete with the Hawks' Sports Hall of Fame or the hiking trail up to Cooper's Overlook, but it held its own against the model railroad museum.

Elena liked to schedule meetings in the room, but it had gotten more difficult to find available times since the start of the fall semester. During the summer, the university announced that the Fuertes painting would be moved to the American Museum of Natural History in New York, as part of a major exhibition in celebration of Fuertes. Since then, visitation to the library's art collection had risen substantially. The room had always been reserved for visitors on Friday afternoons, when alumni and other visitors were most likely to be around, but it was now reserved for viewing every afternoon, including Saturdays and Sundays.

Elena was glad that people were enjoying the artworks, but she was equally glad that around Thanksgiving, when the painting moved to New York, everything could go back to normal.

She usually enjoyed the art-and-environment meetings, but this morning she was just happy to call for adjournment. She was eager to get back upstairs to her office in the Biological Sciences Building. She had a pile of work waiting for her. Ever since she had helped solve the murder of Drew Robbins and then was tasked to untangle his years of research fraud, her life had been a blur. Extra research projects to run, extra graduate students to mentor, extra classes to teach.

Her willingness to undertake the job of correcting the misdeeds of Drew Robbins was welcomed by the university and applauded by her departmental colleagues, but she hoped that the work would translate into positive additions to her resume. So did Ted, who quizzed her regularly about what she was producing. When it all comes together, she told him over and over, the results will be spectacular. Well, then, she could hear him say, get it all together.

She walked up the back steps to the third floor and headed to her office. Standing by her door were three students who needed her advice, desperately they said. Stuck to the door was a note asking her to see the department's research accountant, ASAP. And she could hear the phone ringing inside.

Normal, she mused, what's normal?

3

Des White pushed the off button on the table-top speaker and took a deep breath. "Well, that crisis is over. The toxic waste spill has been contained, and all campus personnel—students, staff and faculty—are safe."

"Jimmy," she continued, "please have the duty officer inform all field units that they can return to normal patrol."

"On it, boss." Jimmy pushed his chair back from the conference table, stood up, stretched and gladly hurried out the door. Sitting around a table coordinating the response to a mock campus disaster was not his idea of police work.

"Jessie," Des said, "you stay with me, so we can work on the post-exercise report." Jessie was just as glad to stay as Jimmy had been to leave. She loved the chance to work closely with the person she most looked up to in the world.

Des stood and moved to the door. "The rest of you can return to your regular duties. Thank you for your work this afternoon. You all did great." She smiled and gave each of her officers and administrative staff a high-five or a pat on the shoulder as they left the room.

"Jeez, I'm glad that's over."

"We did good, though, didn't we, Des?" asked Jessie.

"I guess. But who knows how this would go if there had actually been a train full of toxic waste that derailed on the edge of campus. I'm exhausted, though. Keeping up the pretense of a disaster response might be harder than actually responding to a real problem."

Desdemona White was the chief of police for Virginia Western University, a job she loved. Even during disaster drills. Law enforcement at a university matched what Des felt should be the job of police. The old mantra that she learned as a child—the policeman is your friend—never left her, as a kid growing up in the rougher neighborhoods of Richmond, as a marine MP in Afghanistan, or during her years on the Richmond police force. You had to get the bad folks off the streets, of course, but keeping the community together, safe, and confident of that safety, was the work she preferred.

That's what university police did most of the time. Be a presence on campus to remind everyone that they were all friends and needed to look after each other. Handle little problems so they didn't become big problems. Take charge of a bunch of big kids when their parents dropped them off as freshmen, and help them grow up before they graduated and went off to lead the world. In her five years as the university's police chief—and the first African-American and the first woman to hold the job—that task occupied most of her working hours.

Last spring had been different, though. A famous faculty member had been murdered on campus, sending shock waves not only through the university, but also throughout the world-wide conservation community. With the help of Elena Bertoni,

Des and her folks had solved the murder within a week. But the effect of the violence itself, and the bizarre circumstances underlying it, still lingered. Every time an emergency vehicle turned on its siren, it seemed the entire campus tensed, bracing for a frightening unknown.

Fortunately, nothing serious had happened in the intervening months. The summer had been calm, as usual, and the fall semester started uneventfully. Just the usual spate of misbehavior as eighteen-year-olds escaped adult supervision for the first time. And, of course, the even worse misbehavior of so-called adults who couldn't accept a loss at the football stadium without banging heads with fans from the winning side.

And, so, given the relative calm, the vice-president for health and safety had decided that early October, when the football team was playing two consecutive away games, was a good time to simulate a campus disaster. Des had wanted to wait for a week, until fall break, so students wouldn't be around. But, the vice-president reminded her, the state's protocols for emergency preparedness required these exercises to be done during normal operating times. So, she said, let's get it done.

And it hadn't been so bad, Des had to admit. All the groups with specific responsibilities had performed well, and the rest of the campus had paid attention to notices that a disaster drill was happening. Most of campus, at least. Des's patrol officers had to field anxious calls from a few students and staff, but tamping down those fears was actually good practice. The drill started after lunch and was over by—Des checked her watch—4:55. The budget office must have lobbied for the schedule so they didn't have to pay overtime.

Des looked at her watch again. "Tell you what, Jessie. Let's leave the reporting until tomorrow. Go home. You earned a free evening."

"Thanks, Des. See you in the morning."

Des was tired, and she knew what she needed. She texted Elena: "You up for a cold one?"

The return text came almost immediately. Urgently, maybe, thought Des. "You bet. Meet me and Aaron at The Hawk's Den at six."

Des sent back a thumbs-up. She walked back to her office and sat down behind her desk. Doggone it, Elena, she thought, don't you know when the work day is over? She punched her computer back to life and called up the post-exercise report template.

4

Aaron was waiting when Elena walked into the bar. The Hawk's Den was a favorite campus hangout, named for the university's mascot. Elena still grimaced every time she came through the door, under that absurd name. Hawks didn't have dens, they had nests. But no call for scientific accuracy was going to get that changed. As the sign by the door proudly announced, the place had been called the Hawk's Den since it opened in 1952. It was the university's unofficial "sports headquarters," the walls filled with team photos, signed jerseys, and faded front-page stories of bygone glory. The clientele was mostly graduate students, staff and faculty, except on game days when two opposite ends of the misbehavior continuum—alumni and undergraduates— took over.

The weather was warm for October, so Aaron had snagged a table on the outdoor porch. He stood as Elena approached, always the gentleman. "Good tidings, fair maiden."

Elena grinned. Aaron loved to play with words, and he reserved his most fanciful rhetoric for her. She played along. "Likewise, Sir Galahad. Thank you for saving me from the fire-breathing dragons of faculty life."

"Anything for a lovely damsel in distress."

The bar had been buzzing, but all at once it became nearly silent. Elena and Aaron stopped sparring and looked around. Des White was standing at the door, in her police uniform, scanning the crowd. The silent, watchful, curious crowd. She saw her friends, waved, and strolled to the table. "It's okay, folks," she said loudly to no one in particular, with a broad smile, "just here to see my friends." The buzz started again as the relieved, but perhaps also disappointed, patrons got back to their beer and barbecued Hawk's wings. Des liked being seen both on and off campus when she wasn't handling someone's problem. But when a police officer walked into a bar, the effect was generally like this.

Elena and Aaron greeted their friend. "So," Aaron said, "a wildlife biologist, a wood technologist and a police chief walk into a bar..."

Des gave the required grin and then led them away from the probability of an arcane joke she was unlikely to understand. "Catch me up, guys. Which of the world's problems are we solving?"

"Haven't gotten there yet. But let's get you a beer."

Des shook her head. "Not when I'm in uniform, I'm afraid."

"But you're off duty, right?" Elena asked.

"When you're in uniform, you are always on duty. Perception, remember?"

"But didn't you tell me you needed a cold one?"

"Yes, but in this case it'll be sweet tea. What I really need is some friendly companionship."

"Tough day for the gendarmes?" Aaron asked.

"Brutal. We saved the university from the dangers of a derailed train carrying toxic chemicals."

"Ah, yes," he said, "you were playing war games today. Did our side win?"

Elena raised a mock salute. "With Des White on the case, of course we won!"

With two cold beers, one sweet tea and a basket of nachos, they settled into their usual cross-generational banter. Wildlife versus forestry, yellow legal pads versus thumb drives, solar versus wind, black-and-tan versus lager. But the real topic this evening would be the painting.

"So, Elena," Aaron said, "tell us the sad tale of that lonely pair of birds, flying through eternity to find a tree in which to roost."

"Help me out here," Des said. "What are you talking about?"

"We had a meeting today in the Fuertes Room in the biological sciences library, and Aaron wants me to tell him about the painting that the room is named for." Aaron knew all about it, but he loved to watch Elena as she told the story. She visibly glowed when she talked about the painting.

"The American Museum of Natural History in New York created a pair of exhibits for the 1892 Columbian Exhibition in Chicago. One depicted the built-up urban landscape of the city itself, but cleverly showing the wildlife that managed to co-exist with people."

"The other exhibit portrayed the natural resources of rural New York. For the background of the exhibit, the museum hired a young, little-known ornithologist and artist to paint a large mural of a lake surrounded by forests and mountains, highlighting native birds, mammals and reptiles. The artist was Louis Agassiz Fuertes, only eighteen years old at the time."

"Imagine that," Aaron quipped. "Today's eighteen-year-olds can scarcely lace up their shoes. In fact, most of the time they don't."

Des gave him a disapproving glance. "You don't wear exaggeration well, Aaron. Go on, Elena, this is interesting."

"The mural was nine-feet square. Because it needed to be transported from New York to Chicago, the exhibit designers instructed Fuertes to paint it as nine separate panels, each three-feet on a side, that could be disassembled in the studio and then reassembled in Chicago. The completed display was a diorama with the Fuertes mural in the background and various stuffed specimens in the foreground."

"I'll bet there were trees and other plants in that diorama," Aaron said.

Elena conceded. "Of course. The display was meant to emphasize that habitat—including trees—was essential for the wildlife to thrive."

"So where are the trees for those birds?"

"Do you want to tell the story, or me?"

Des watched them bicker as she sipped her tea. She had known Aaron since she first came to the university, as he was one of VWU's most senior and distinguished professors, often speaking to donor events and board of trustees' meetings where Des provided security. But since his expertise helped crack the Drew Robbins' murder, they had become closer friends. To her, Aaron was everything a university should be. "Do I need to de-escalate this situation?"

Elena laughed. "I think we'll be okay, chief. But watch him, he might be carrying a concealed toothpick. Anyway, when the fair ended, the mural was disassembled and returned to the museum. The panels got stuck in a back room somewhere, and they forgot all about them."

"And then Fuertes got famous, right?" Aaron asked.

"Right. Most people consider him second among American wildlife artists, next to John James Audubon."

"Where do our flying birds fit in?" he asked.

"Getting there," Elena said. "For the centennial of the Columbian Exposition, in 1992, the museum decided to feature its original exhibit. However, when they searched for the mural, they could only find three panels—the top row, that had just plain sky or a bit of foliage from overhanging trees. The other panels, those that included birds, other animals and plants, had been sold during the depression to raise money to keep the museum afloat."

Aaron winced. He knew well the perils of trying to maintain a collection in the face of competing demands, money or otherwise. He had accumulated what was arguably the world's largest repository of wood samples, built slowly and methodically over his forty years at VWU. Along the way, he encountered numerous attempts to dislodge him from his space, the most recent attacks from his now dead and disgraced nemesis, Drew Robbins.

He wagged a finger at Elena and Des. "If you don't respect the past, you can't protect the future."

"Right, got it. So, the museum had to give up on an exhibit for the one-hundredth anniversary of the original display. But they didn't give up on the idea. For nearly thirty years now, the museum has been on a quiet mission to find and recover the six missing panels. They have five of them back at the museum now, to join with the three they already had, making eight in total. And…"

"And the ninth one is ours, that pair of birds, right?" Aaron asked, although he knew the answer.

"Right. The university has agreed to make an indefinite loan of the painting to the museum, as long as it is on display."

It was Des's turn to join in. "I need to get over and see this thing. The head of university development is all over me about the safety of the painting as it gets transported up to New York. She wants an armed entourage to accompany it."

Aaron chuckled. "Hard to put hand-cuffs on a painting, no?"

"I don't know," she suggested. "Just poke a hole in the corner and slip a cuff around the frame."

"Don't even joke about such a thing," Elena scolded, and then smiled. "It's valuable, you know."

"I figured that," Des said. "How valuable?"

Elena tilted her head, as though calculating. "There aren't many Fuertes' paintings out there. Most of what he did was to paint large murals on the walls of museums. A free-standing painting is rare."

"So, how much money are we talking about?" Aaron asked.

Elena shrugged. "I don't know. A hundred grand? Maybe two?"

Aaron wouldn't give up. "Imagine how much it would be worth if it had some happy trees in it, the kind that curly haired guy put in his paintings. You remember, on PBS. What was his name? I loved that guy."

"Bob Ross," Elena said, exasperated.

"Yeah, Bob Ross. He was great. Happy little trees all over. Not just a couple of silly birds."

"The reason there are no trees is that this is what the museum is calling 'The Center Piece.' It's the panel from the middle of the mural, showing just the two herons against a pure blue sky."

"And just before Thanksgiving," Des said, "I guess I'll be escorting those birds up to New York to be reunited with their buddies."

"Back to their natural habitat—isn't that what you ecologists would say?" Aaron saw the excitement in Elena's eyes and heard it in her voice.

"Exactly," she said, "exactly."

5

Friday

Elena finished her Friday class, and the students began to leave the lecture hall. It was one of her favorite presentations, "Three Heroes" as she titled it in the syllabus. She covered the life stories of Chico Mendes, the Brazilian rubber-tapper who worked to save Amazon rain forests and was murdered for his efforts, Wangari Maathai, the Kenyan woman who planted fifty million trees and won the Nobel Peace Prize, and Billy Frank Jr., the Native American who defended Indian fishing rights in Washington state and brought about a revolution in fisheries management.

The students were usually enthralled by these inspiring stories, but today they had been restless. Their rush to the exits verified to Elena that their heads were elsewhere. The beach, probably. Fall break started at the end of the day, and most students would be heading out of town as soon as their last class ended.

Elena motioned to her graduate assistant to come to the front of the room. "Would you do me a favor, Ara?"

"Sure, what do you need?"

"Please take my book bag back to my office and leave it on the chair outside my door. I need to take a long walk rather than rushing back. I need to tramp this class out of my head."

"Sure thing," she answered. "They weren't being very attentive today, were they? Such a shame when your lecture was so good. You're an amazing, teacher, Elena. But the students are looking forward to a week off, I guess."

Ara Sun had turned out to be Elena's best teaching assistant in recent memory. Originally from South Korea, she was a graduate student in Elena's department, studying natural area protection, and her expertise complemented Elena's specialty in wildlife behavior. They had met during the aftermath of the Drew Robbins murder case. And now Ara and Jimmy Nesbitt, one of Des White's two investigative assistants, were dating. They were all starting to feel like a family to Elena, so she was delighted when Ara requested to be assigned to Elena's class for her fall teaching.

"They sure didn't care about the three heroes today. Remind me to schedule something dull, like how EPA toxicity levels are set, for the day before break." Ara grinned at the wisdom of Elena's comment. "But thanks for doing this." Ara grabbed Elena's bag, and they headed out the door together. Ara turned left, waved, and disappeared between two buildings on her way back to the Biological Sciences Building.

Elena stood on the steps for a few seconds, deciding on a route and saying goodbye to the few students who weren't hurrying away. This day, she headed to the right through the grove of sweetgum trees behind the student union, their star-shaped leaves blazing yellow against the blue October sky. Then past the main library, virtually deserted before fall break, and onto the playing fields, where she followed the outlines of the intramural soccer pitches. Only a few players were there, as most of the students were getting ready to leave town.

She walked through what most of campus called the international village. The low-rise apartment buildings had been put up in the 1950s, for veterans returning to school after tours in Korea, but now they housed mostly graduate students from other countries, many with young families. This place was alive with activity—most international students didn't get to travel for fall break—and Elena always loved seeing the children playing, un-phased by what country their friends came from or the languages they spoke. Children spoke one language, Elena thought—kid. As a product of American and Italian parents and having lived in both countries, she appreciated the richness of blending cultures.

Eventually her path took her back to the Biological Sciences Building, situated on the south edge of the main campus. The building was the hybrid style of most university buildings, a 1960s era utilitarian box with a new addition that tried to look trendy, all glass and metallic panels. It was waiting for a donor to serve up a hefty gift as a naming opportunity, so now most of campus just called it the BSB.

BSB had several features to recommend itself, including the large multi-story atrium that separated the old half of the building, filled with labs, offices and teaching rooms, from the new half, occupied by the library on the first floor and modern labs for modern sciences like molecular genetics on the upper floors. But the feature that Elena really cherished was the pollinator garden. Most new university buildings endeavored to be environmentally conscious, outfitted largely from recycled materials or with a rooftop rain garden. BSB had all those things, but the pollinator garden always lifted Elena's spirits. Not only were the native flowers and grasses of the garden a delight, but it was an insect metropolis, bees and butterflies of dozens of species never out of sight. The warm September and early October had kept the insect population at an unusually healthy abundance. Elena stood still in the middle of the garden for a few moments, letting curious bugs check out the rainbow of colors in her scarf, and then fly off disappointed at the lack of nectar.

As she walked towards the building entrance, she noticed a police car parked in the service vehicle spot at the center of the building's parking lot, near the main door. Nothing unusual about that, but as she walked closer she realized the identifier behind the rear wheel was PC01. Police cruiser 1, Des White's vehicle.

As she went through the big double doors into the atrium, she saw Des.

"Hi, Des," Elena said, grinning, "having a look at the painting already? Beautiful, isn't it?"

Des turned and walked toward Elena, but her usual smile when she saw her friend didn't come. "Not funny."

"What do you mean?"

"It's gone, Elena."

"What do you mean? What's gone?"

"The painting."

"What paint...you mean the Fuertes painting?" Des nodded. "What do you mean, gone?"

"It's been stolen."

6

Elena couldn't believe her ears. "What, say that again? The painting's been stolen?"

Des frowned and nodded. "Yeah. Taken right out of the library in broad daylight and gone, just gone."

"That's terrible, Des, just awful. How could that happen?"

"Well, that's what we're trying to find out. And I'm glad you're here, because maybe you can help us calm down the girl at the library desk. She's pretty hysterical."

"Who is it?"

"A student who was working the desk. Her name is Hannah. Hannah Maddox."

Elena's hand went to her mouth. "Oh, my god, she's one of my advisees."

"Let's go see her," Des said. "I'm sure she'd like to see a friendly face."

They walked the few steps down the hall to the library and through the double glass doors of the entry. Jessie Hunt, one of Des's investigators, was talking with the girl, mostly trying to settle her down.

The student looked up and nearly shrieked when she saw her advisor. "Dr. Bertoni! I'm so glad you're here. I...I...I don't know what's going on. This is terrible."

Hannah ran to her, and Elena hugged her tightly. Hannah's face was blotchy red, streaked with black where tears had washed her eye makeup down. "It's okay, Hannah. We'll get this all figured out."

"Thank you, Dr. Bertoni. Thank you for being here." Elena didn't let on that it was just a lucky accident that she had walked through the door.

Des took over the situation. "Jessie, please stay here at the desk and keep anyone from touching anything here or in that room." She pointed across the hallway. "Elena, that's where the painting was, right?"

Elena nodded. "Yeah, that's right. It was hanging on the back wall, all by itself. It was the focal point of the room." The wall looked glaringly empty to her with just a pair of hooks where the painting used to hang. It seemed almost obscene to Elena, naked and exposed. The effect was lost on Des.

"Let's go sit at one of the study tables, Hannah, so we can talk this out," Des said and led the way. They walked down the hallway that ran perpendicular to the atrium, the Fuertes Room on one side and the library desk on the other. A few feet beyond the desk, the hallway opened into a large area filled with tables where groups of students could work together. Beyond that were rows of bookshelves that ran to the far end of the building.

Elena walked with an arm across Hannah's shoulder and she sat next to her, opposite Des.

"Okay, Hannah, just tell us what happened in your own words."

Hannah tried to get words out between sobs. "He was so nice. And I just let him take it. Oh, god."

Elena asked, "Who was so nice?"

"The boy who came to take pictures."

"Okay," Des said, "maybe we're going to have to go at this a little differently. I'll ask some questions, and you do your best to answer, okay?"

Hannah looked to Elena for support, and seeing her smile and nod, Hannah forced her own version of a smile.

"You were working on the library desk, is that right?"

"Yes," Hannah said. "It's just my second day. I'm supposed to work on Mondays, Wednesdays and Fridays, from noon to five."

"Who else was working with you today?"

Hannah shook her head. "No one. I had someone here with me on Wednesday, when I was training, but not today." She looked at Elena. "No one else wanted to work today. They're all leaving for break."

"And why were you willing to work?" Des asked. "Aren't you going away?"

Hannah shook her head again. "I live in town, with my parents. This is just my first year, and my folks wouldn't let me just run off somewhere for a trip. They're pretty strict. I was supposed to work all next week, full-time, sort of." She looked startled. "Oh, no, do you think I'll get fired? I don't want to disappoint the dean."

"What about the dean?" Elena said. "Why would he be disappointed?"

"He recommended me for the job. I met him during new student orientation, and he was really nice."

Elena got the picture. "I forgot, you're in the CSC, right?"

"Yes," Hannah said, "and the dean is my mentor." The Campus Success Cohort was a special VWU program to help first-generation college students make a successful transition from high school to the university. Along with special advising and workshops, each student was assigned a faculty mentor for their first year. They also got preference for campus work-study jobs, like Hannah's, if they needed the money.

Des tried to get the interview back on track. "Was anything unusual going on at the library today?"

Hannah shook her head for the third time. "No, nothing. Only a couple of students came to turn in books. I'm not sure there was anyone in the library, really."

Des nodded. "And when did the boy come in, the one who was so nice?"

"Not long after I started. Maybe around 12:30." Elena looked at her watch. It was just after 1:00. She'd taken a longer walk than she had planned.

"And what happened when he came in?"

"He told me he worked for university advertising, something like that." She sobbed again. "I don't remember exactly."

Elena tried to help. "University advancement, maybe?"

"Maybe," Hannah said. "Anyway, he said they had sent him to get some good pictures of that painting. He told me the painting was important, and the big shots needed really good pictures of it. He had an id card around his neck, and everything."

"Did you look at the id card?" Des asked.

Hannah looked sheepish. "No, not really. I noticed it had his picture on it and the university logo, but that's all."

"Then what?"

"He asked if he could leave his back-pack on the desk—it's still there, I think. Then he went into the room and started to set up his camera and stuff. It looked like a really fancy camera, you know with one of those big lenses. And he had one of those stands to put the camera on."

"A tripod?" Elena offered.

Hannah nodded. "Yeah, that's it. A tripod. But then he came back to the desk and told me it wasn't going to work."

Des frowned. "What did he mean?"

"He said he couldn't get far enough away from the painting to get a full shot because the big table was in the way. And besides, he said, the light wasn't good enough in the room. So he asked me if he could just take the painting out onto the patio to take the picture."

Des was about to yell when she caught herself. Settle down, she said to herself, she's just a scared little girl. "And you let him do that?"

"Not at first, no. I told him that I wasn't sure he should do that, seeing it was a special painting. But he told me that's exactly why he needed to get a great photo of it." Hannah started to cry again.

Elena intervened. "It's okay, Hannah, just tell us what happened."

"He was so nice. He told me he'd like to take photos of me, too, because,...because..." She shivered.

"Because why?" Des was trying to be supportive, but it was getting to be ebb tide for patience.

"Because I was so pretty." Hannah started crying again. In normal circumstances, she would have been pretty. Petite, with long blonde hair tied in a ponytail, dressed in a long tunic top and black leggings, checking all the required style boxes. Elena remembered her bright smile when they had met for advising earlier in the semester. But not this afternoon. "And he invited me to a party tonight at his fraternity."

Elena saw where this was going. "I understand. He was being really nice. So you let him take the painting outside, right?"

Hannah kept sobbing and nodded. "Yes, I did. He told me he'd leave his student ID, you know, just like when you want to use one of the reserve books we keep behind the desk."

Des perked up. "Do you have his ID?"

"Yes. Well, no, the other police officer has it."

Got him, thought Des. "Keep going, Hannah. You're doing great."

"He took some white gloves out of his back-pack and put them on, joking about how he wasn't supposed to touch it, and a white sheet sort of. He went back into the room and took the painting down. He put the sheet over it. He took his, uh, tripod with the camera and the painting and went out the door. He told me he'd be back in a few minutes."

"Then what?" Des asked.

"Nothing," Hannah said.

"Nothing?"

"No. He never came back. After a while I got worried, and I went out on the patio to look for him. He was gone. I started shaking and came back in. I called the supervisor's number and told her what happened, and she told me to stay here, she would call the police. And then the other policeman, uh, policewoman came."

For a minute, the three just sat there, Elena and Des trying to take it all in, Hannah shaking in terror.

Finally, Hannah broke the silence. "Am I in trouble? Am I going to jail? Oh, god, what will my dad say."

Des reassured her. "No, Hannah, you're not in trouble. Unless we find out that you're lying to us. You aren't lying, are you Hannah?"

"Oh, no. It happened just like I told you."

"You don't know the boy who took the painting? He's not your boyfriend? Or someone who you owe a favor to?"

For once, Hannah seemed confident. "No, I never saw him before, ever. I swear."

7

Des told Hannah she could go, but that she needed to tell the police if she were going out of town or if she remembered anything else about the theft. The girl seemed confused about what to do next, so Elena took her up to her office, where they could talk more.

Des watched them head up the elevator, and she thought how good it was to have Elena around. Every professor should be like that, Des thought, not just a fountain of obscure facts and theories, but someone who truly cared about others, especially students. Des loved her job as VWU's police chief, but sometimes the faculty were a little much, more concerned about what was in their test tubes or on their "graphic interfaces" than the condition of the students or staff who did their bidding.

She went back to the library desk to catch up with Jessie. "Everything under control here?"

"Yes, boss," Jessie said. The library was all on one floor, with the usual racks of books and journals, along with computer stations and study tables. "There isn't anyone here, except the supervisor Hannah called. Friday afternoon before fall break, the library's not a big draw."

"Hannah said you have the thief's ID card."

Jessie held up an evidence bag. "Right here."

Des looked through the bag. "James Shipp. Should be easy to track him down."

"If it's a real ID," Jessie said. "It looks real, but I doubt he would be dumb enough to give her his real ID."

Des nodded. "You're probably right, so let's hope it has fingerprints. Hannah also said the boy left his backpack on the desk."

Jessie pointed to the far end of the wide desk. "I haven't touched it yet."

Des slipped on gloves and picked up the back-pack. It looked new, and it was filled with wadded up pieces of newspaper to make it look full. She set it back down. "Wrap this one up, too, Jessie, and call our crime scene team to dust down this desk and the area of the room where the painting was hanging. I'm going to talk to the librarian. Where is she?"

Jessie pointed to a door around the corner from the library desk. "In the office back there. I told her to wait for you."

Des walked the few feet to the door and knocked. She looked in to where an obviously distraught woman sat. "I'm Des White, the university's police chief."

"Hello," the woman squeaked. "My name is Yvonne. Yvonne Michaels." She was trembling.

"It's okay, Yvonne. You can relax."

"Thank you, but I can't relax. This is terrible. How could this happen? In the library? We never have any trouble in the libraries."

Des knew that wasn't true. Her officers got calls from the libraries all the time. Nothing major, typically. Students having sex in the far corners of the stacks, backpacks setting off alarms as students tried to sneak reference books out of the building, an occasional vagrant sleeping in a bathroom. But correcting her wasn't important now. "It's okay. No one got hurt, and the building didn't burn down. Just a theft."

"Just a theft?" Yvonne cried out, shattering the silence of the empty library like glass breaking. "That painting was really valuable, and it was such a big deal that it was part of a nationwide project to restore the original. This is terrible, just terrible."

"I understand. So, let's try to figure out what happened and try to get this thing back where it belongs. You were the supervisor here today?"

Yvonne shook her head. "The supervisor, yes, but not here."

"Better explain."

"This library is one of the university's branch libraries. Along with the main library, we have three branches—this one, one for art and design and one for veterinary medicine. I, or one of my colleagues, supervise all three at the same time. We are all stationed at the vet medicine library, which is the largest. We just have students running the other two."

"So is it usual that one student would be working alone at this library?"

"No, not really," Yvonne continued. "Usually we have at least two student workers on duty, three if we can schedule them. One handles the desk, checking books in and out, and the other one or two are shelving books, filling on-line requests, those sorts of staff jobs."

"Why was Hannah here all by herself today?"

"Fridays are really low use days in general, especially the afternoons, and the day before break there is almost no one in the libraries. And we have trouble getting students to want to work on those days, too. So, today, we just had one student at each of the branches."

"But Hannah had just started this week?"

Yvonne's voice began to break again. "I know. She never should have been allowed to be here by herself. That's my fault. There just wasn't anyone else we could get to work. It's terrible."

"So, why weren't you here to help her?"

"I should have been," Yvonne said. "But the other two branch librarians had both taken the day off, leaving town just like the students. So, I thought I needed to stay at the veterinary library. That one is always busier than the others, and the use doesn't drop off as much during breaks."

There will certainly be new staffing protocols after this, Des thought. "Well, too late to worry about that now. What about security cameras?"

Yvonne shook her head. "We have cameras at the main library, but not at the branches. We've had requests in for camera systems for several years, but they keep getting delayed." Then she looked up and pointed towards the doorway. "But, wait, we did put something up here a few weeks ago."

They walked to the desk. A portable camera sat on one end of the desk, pointing into the Fuertes Room. Yvonne explained, "When the announcement about the painting came out and people started coming around more to see it, the library director decided we needed something. So, the IT folks rigged up this temporary camera. See, it sits on the desk and points directly into the room, straight at the painting." She faltered. "Well, at where the painting was. We should have everything recorded."

But Des was doubtful. The thief's backpack had been right in front of the camera.

8

"So what do you think?" Des sat behind her desk, with Jimmy and Jessie opposite her.

Jessie was the first to speak. "That girl at the library, Hannah, was almost hysterical about the theft. I can't believe she's involved."

"I agree," Des said, "but we do need to check into her a little more. She said she lives at home, with her parents, but check that out. And dig into her record at the university. She's in some special program that Elena mentioned. The Campus Success Cohort. Find her friends and talk to them."

Jessie nodded. "Will do."

"Maybe it was a frat prank?" Jimmy offered. He hadn't been involved so far, having been working on a rash of car break-ins during the week. Minor thefts like that always picked up just before the end of the semester or the beginning of a break, as students got more careless and distracted. "Didn't the girl say the thief asked her to a frat party?"

Des smiled. Jimmy usually blamed any campus misbehavior on fraternities. "A prank would be great," Des said. "That would mean we'll get the painting back soon, maybe hung somewhere it doesn't belong, like on the door of The Hawk's Den."

"I don't think it's a prank," Jessie said.

"Why not, kiddo?"

"Everything seems so calculated. It's like a perfect storm for a perfect theft. The timing was perfect. No one around on the day before break starts. The library was understaffed. And the girl at the desk was brand new, and, frankly, as naive as a daffodil. And then the thief puts his backpack in front of the camera and wears gloves when he's taking the painting out. And he had some kind of fake staff identification and a fake student ID card. It's all too organized for a stunt."

Reluctantly, Des had to agree. "I'm with you. And the ID card had been wiped clean of fingerprints, right?"

"Yes, nothing on the card at all. And the card was issued to James Shipp." Jessie had been working to identify the student after she left the library. "He graduated four years ago. When I talked to him this afternoon, he said he had sold his ID at a party the night before graduation. Twenty bucks he got for it."

"So, next week, Jimmy, I want you to do some digging about who's buying and selling old ID cards on campus."

"I'll try," Jimmy said, "but I doubt I'll get far next week. No one is going to be around."

Des knew he was right. "So," she asked, "if it isn't a prank, why do you steal a famous painting?"

Jessie shrugged. "Revenge, love or money. Aren't they the three things crimes are always about?"

"Okay, let's try it in order. Revenge?"

Jimmy spoke up. "Somebody doesn't like the university. VWU is getting all sorts of press, and he wants to stomp all over it. Steal the painting and destroy it."

"Okay, but who hates the university that much?"

"Easy. Someone who just got thrown out. We should check with admissions to see if there have been any particularly ugly suspensions lately. Or someone who just got fired."

"Good idea," Des said. "Get on that as soon as you can, Jimmy." Jimmy nodded yes, but inside he frowned. Another bunch of administrative tasks.

Des continued, "How about love?"

It was Jessie's turn. "Some guy's girlfriend told him she really loves that particular painting, so he steals it for her. That might work in some circles, but I don't think it's the sort of thing that would motivate college students. They steal the road sign for Love Drive all the time." She was right about the sign. Signs, actually, that marked the street that ran between the football stadium and basketball arena, named for the university's first president, Howard K. Love. "But not a painting."

"But what about love of the painting itself?" Jimmy asked.

Des was intrigued. "What are you thinking, kiddo?"

"Well, maybe someone wanted the painting for himself, or herself? And maybe the idea that it was leaving was just too much, so he, or she, took it to keep it."

Des laughed. "The most likely suspect for that would be Elena Bertoni. She really does love that thing. But I don't think she did it."

"What about the woman who gives all the money to the university, and is a big art fan, too?"

"You mean Michele Richards?"

"Yeah," Jimmy said, "that's her. I could imagine her getting someone to steal the painting, so she could have it on her private yacht, or in her castle in, uh...."

"Spain?" Jessie finished his sentence.

"Wherever."

Michele Richards was one of the university's prominent donors, an alum who was an All-American tennis player during her undergraduate years and who had made it big in the world of cosmetics after getting a chemistry degree. She had diversified with a chain of designer hotels, including one in New York City where she kept a penthouse apartment. She lived part of the year there, and part still in Stone Valley. But she was just as likely to be in Milan or Singapore as anywhere else. Her major passions in life were tennis, art and Virginia Western University. Never married, she lavished time and money on those passions. Most recently, the Richards Indoor Tennis Pavilion had been dedicated, making Stone Valley competitive with schools farther south and west that had good weather all year round.

"Well, that would be a great true-crime podcast," Des said. "I think we can discount love and drop Ms. Richards from the suspect list. So, what about money?"

That's the obvious motive," Jessie said. "Steal the painting and sell it. I bet it was worth a lot of money. But how could you sell a painting that everyone in the world knew was stolen?"

"Black market," Jimmy said. "You can sell anything. You just need to know who's buying."

"So, kiddos, there's your agenda for next week. Track down all the loose ends about this thing, including where you'd fence a famous painting."

"On it boss," they said in unison.

9

Elena sat in her office, finally alone, and totally depressed.

The theft of the Fuertes painting had really gotten to her. It had happened in her own building, and her advisee Hannah had been involved. No, not involved. Victimized. The poor girl had cried in Elena's office for more than another hour as Elena tried to calm her down. Hannah would have stayed the whole afternoon if Ted hadn't barged in the door. The presence of an angry department head was finally enough to get Hannah to hug Elena one last time and then slink out the door.

Ted Graham was fuming about the consequences of the theft. As head of the Department of Renewable Resources, he wasn't in the direct line of fire. The library space on the first floor of BSB was officially assigned to the dean's office, and the functioning of the library was a university responsibility. But he knew that he would be dragged into discussions and recriminations about what had happened.

So, he, too, needed someone to calm him down. He and Elena were close—she had been his first hire after arriving at VWU six years earlier—and he treated her as much like a daughter as an employee. Sometimes it was tough love he gave her, but they both knew the underlying feeling was fatherly affection.

"How does someone just walk into a building and walk out with a painting?" Elena asked, more thinking out loud than seeking an answer.

Ted slapped the desk. "Forget the stupid painting. Do you realize what this will mean for me? Tighter security for everything. More layers of approval on everything, more forms, more oversight, more times I'm going to have to sign that so-and-so is trustworthy." Listening to him took most of what was left of the afternoon, and absorbed whatever emotional energy Elena could still summon. When he left, she closed the door, turned off the lights and just sat still to think.

She loved that painting. Aaron had objected to the simplicity —just two birds against a blue sky—but Elena loved it for that very reason. The birds were just flying, free, strong, no destination in sight. Seemingly without care. She could get lost in that feeling of weightlessness, separated in time and space from beginning or ending, from obligation and consequence. The scientist in her knew that the birds were part of their habitat, and she knew the other panels of the mural gave that context. But the romantic in her could get lost in the pure untroubled, unconstrained existence she sometimes longed to share with two great blue herons flying over a clear blue sky.

But just like for Ted, there was consequence from the theft for her, too. She was linked to the painting in a direct and tangible way. When the news of the painting's provenance had broken over the summer, Elena had decided to create a special interdisciplinary course around the work. The university's general education program included a requirement for one course that linked at least two disciplines (multi-disciplinary perspectives, the catalogue stated), and Elena had long wanted to teach such a course. Ted would never approve it, though, reminding her that she needed to concentrate on the things that really counted for promotion to full professor.

But last spring, after she had taken on the job of fixing the mess that Drew Robbins had created, he had to give her something she really wanted. So she was now teaching a course that linked wildlife art with environmental science. She limited enrollment to twenty students, half from humanities disciplines and half from the sciences.

It was more fun than she had ever had teaching. The energy that the students brought was amazing, the continuing shift from science to art and back again keeping everyone engaged.

And, when she was organizing the course, she came up with what seemed like a brilliant major assignment. Pairs of students, one from a humanities and one from a science background, were assigned to create a triptych with the Fuertes painting—the center piece—between two of the students' artworks. No holds barred, she had told her students, except that the three had to form a sequence with the flying herons in the middle.

Elena had arranged a special evening at which the students' art works would be displayed. Judith Heinz, a retired art instructor at VWU and her new friend from the Robbins case, would judge the students' work, along with a local artist whom Judith had recruited. Judith had helped introduce the painting and the concept of a triptych—three independent paintings that made a coherent whole—to the class.

Stacked against one of the bookshelves in her office were ten full-sized copies of the Fuertes painting. All Elena could think as she looked at the stack now was that they were mocking her. Should have listened to Ted, they seemed to say, but, no, now you're stuck with an event starring a phantom. A brilliant assignment, indeed.

The special exhibit was scheduled for the Wednesday after fall break, and Elena had invited many university officials, including her department head and dean, as well as community arts leaders, to attend the event. Alice Crutchfield, the university's president, and Michele Richards, loyal Hawk alum and art lover, had both agreed to come. And Hans had agreed to host the event at his Scandia Cafe, complete with complimentary appetizers and soft drinks (no alcohol, Elena had told him, at a student function).

Good old Hans, she thought. Hans Kjer, who most people would call her boyfriend as long as she wasn't in hearing range, had emigrated from Denmark several years earlier and built his Scandia Cafe into a Stone Valley institution. Elena rejected the boyfriend label, although she knew Hans liked the idea. No commitment, she had told him time and again, let's just enjoy the moment.

But now was one of the moments when she needed him. She took the back stairs out of the building and drove to the cafe. Hans looked up from behind the counter when she walked in, surprised to see her. Friday evening visits weren't her usual. He came from around the counter to greet her.

"Hey, baby," he cooed, "how you doing?"

Elena looked like the proverbial whipped puppy. "Not so good, I guess."

"What's wrong?"

"There was a problem at school today."

"Okay, okay. Sit down out there," he said, pointing to an empty table on the patio. "I'll bring you a beer."

"What's Danish for ASAP?" He risked a kiss on her cheek—she didn't like his amorous attention in public—and hurried off.

He returned with a lager in a tall glass, a perfect inch of foam above the golden liquid. She took a long drink and sighed.

He sat down and rubbed her arm. "So, what's wrong?"

Elena described the theft of the painting, her student's involvement, Ted's ranting. Hans was a good listener, and just talking about it all calmed Elena down. As the cafe got busier, she knew that Hans needed to get back to work.

"Thank you, Hans. I feel better now. I'll see you tomorrow afternoon."

"Listen, baby, I know you're upset. I don't think you should be alone tonight. How about I come over?"

Normally Elena bristled at his "hey, baby" talk, and his condescending attitude might have sunk his plan. But today she was prepared to overlook his pandering. She really didn't want to be alone.

"Please, Hans, yes. Please come." He beamed. "And bring something good for dinner." If possible, he beamed more.

10

Saturday

Elena slid quietly from the bed, hoping to leave Hans asleep. She succeeded, and then tip-toed into the kitchen. She liked Hans. A lot. He was fun, much more than her colleagues at work. He was generous with his time, even though he had a busy bakery and cafe to run. Too generous, she thought. Hans wanted more from the relationship than she did, more time than she was willing to give.

He was always there when she needed someone, though, and she appreciated his company when she was worried or stressed. Or even just hungry. The trouble was he wanted to be around more than that. Elena didn't allow him as far into her life as he wanted, but he didn't really try to push his way in. Damn him, she thought, he was just too nice.

And so here he was, asleep in her bed on Saturday morning. She had invited him, of course, and, she smiled, they had had a very good Friday night. Hans was an honors student at bedtime.

But Saturdays were for her, not for her-and-him. At least Saturday mornings. So she made coffee and toasted the bread he had brought with him last night. She topped it with the Danish butter and raspberry jam that he had also brought. God, she thought, he makes good bread.

She retrieved the *New York Times* from the front porch and opened to the crossword puzzle. The Saturday puzzle was part of her me-time routine. Harder than Friday, but still straightforward, no silly themes like on Sunday, no tricks like on Thursday.

She was concentrating on the puzzle when she felt two hands on her shoulders, fingers lightly tracing her collar bones, and a light kiss on the back of her neck. "Good day, my darling."

"Hello, Hans. Did you sleep well?"

"Of course," he answered, and kept kissing her neck. His hands slipped slowly down from her shoulders "Would you like some Danish for breakfast?"

"I had some of your Danish bread and jam already," Elena answered, purposefully deflecting from his real meaning and gently brushing his hands away. "It's ten already. I think you need to get going. You've got a restaurant to run."

"Yeah, and I've got a whole staff of people there to run it for me. I have all the time in the world for you."

There it was again, the Hans-problem. "Well, I don't. I have a ton of work to do this morning before I come to the cafe later."

"After the crossword, you mean?" It was a subtle form of protest, but it registered nonetheless.

Elena put the puzzle away. "I was just killing time until you got up," she said. And they both acted like they believed her.

Hans gave up easily, like the gentleman he was. She was right, of course, he did have a restaurant to run. Within a few minutes he was gone. "Later, baby," he crooned as he walked out the door.

Elena got to the Scandia Cafe about two that afternoon, as usual. She sat down with her friends and soon was absorbed into their chatter. The painting was a main topic of discussion, having been reported on the news that morning, but the others also had their own weeks full of tales to share, and Elena found herself able to relax and push the theft into the background.

A waiter brought her Tuborg, and she ordered the koldt bord, Danish equivalent of a charcuterie (we invented the charcuterie, Hans liked to say, just like we discovered North America). Pickled herring, smoked salmon, tiny meatballs, blue cheese and tilsiter, pickled cucumbers, onions and beets, roasted walnuts, and hard rye crackers. For a while the food occupied everyone's attention.

Eventually the talk swung back to the stolen painting. Her friends at the cafe had all been invited to the special exhibit, and they wondered if it would still be held.

"Probably," Elena said. "Well, I hope so anyway. I don't know what the brass might think. But I'm planning on having it. The students are working very hard, I can tell from the emails flying around, and they're super excited."

Her friends were all for having the event. Some were university faculty members, and they worried that it might be cancelled because the university's administrators were notoriously conservative. Others worked in private business around Stone Valley; they were all on Elena's side. The show must go on, they reasoned, and so should the education.

"It's only been a day, however, and we're going to have wait and see." Elena suspected that the art and environment event hadn't crossed the minds of Des White or her bosses. They had a theft to solve.

11

Wednesday

For Des White, fall break was turning out to be just a frustration. The students and faculty were having a week off, and usually it would be a relaxed time for the police as well. Get caught up on some paperwork, service as many patrol cars as possible, complete a few overdue on-line training courses.

This fall break, though, was a series of dead-ends for the theft investigation. As predicted, Jimmy was getting nowhere with tracking down the black market in ID cards. Jessie had found nothing to incriminate Hannah in the theft. The hope that it was all a prank had vanished as the days ticked by.

The admissions office had given them a list of students who had recently been put on suspension or dismissal, about a dozen in all. They tracked each of them down, but found nothing worth following up. The most likely candidate was the child of a state legislator who had made a big stink over his son's treatment, but, alas, the son had beat it to Fort Lauderdale the day after his appeal was refused, a full week before the theft.

They had the same negative luck with the human resources office. A few individuals had been fired in recent months, but none of them stood out as a possible art thief.

And now the big boss wanted to talk. Alice Crutchfield, VWU's president, didn't get involved often in police business, a credit to Des's competence and the university's low-crime profile. Stone Valley was still a small town in the Virginia mountains, and Virginia Western University was a place where students went to avoid the issues that often crept onto the campuses of big-city universities. Low crime had been one of Des's reasons for taking the job, to get away from police work on the much meaner streets of Richmond. But the murder of Drew Robbins and the associated crimes had raised VWU's public profile in undesirable ways, and a summons to the executive suite in the wake of the art theft was inevitable.

"Come in, Des," President Crutchfield said when Des knocked quietly on the open door of the office. Alice got up from her desk and motioned to the sitting area in the alcove that jutted out from the main office. "Let's sit over there."

The alcove was semi-circular, with windows all around. The shape was mimicked outside by an arc of ginkgo trees whose leaves glowed a brilliant yellow in the October sunshine. "They aren't quite quaking aspens," Alice said, looking out at the trees, "like on my parents' farm in Colorado where I grew up, but they're pretty close."

Des grew up on the wrong side of the tracks in Richmond, so the comparison was alien to her. But she did appreciate what was here. "Yes," she said, "they are beautiful."

They sat down on the leather bench that followed the contours of the alcove. Alice asked a few questions about the theft, and Des filled her in on the state of the investigation. It didn't take long.

"I'm pretty sure this was a professional job," Des said. "We've ruled out the obvious possibilities, like student pranks or vengeful ex-employees. It seems to have been carefully planned, not the sort of off-hand thefts that we're used to with students."

Another soft knock at the door interrupted their conversation. "Ms. Richards is here," one of the president's assistants announced discreetly.

"Send her in, please."

Michele Richards came through the door and smiled. "Good to see you, Alice. It's been a few weeks." She was the picture of elegance, tall, tanned and obviously fit, dressed in an off-white suit complemented by a brilliant green and gold scarf. Ever the Hawk booster, Des thought.

"Please join us, Michele. This is Des White, our police chief. I assume you know each other."

Michele shook hands with Des. "Of course. Nice to see you again, too, Des." Then she frowned. "But not such a happy occasion today, to discuss the theft of the Fuertes painting."

"No, not a happy occasion," Des answered. Her internal threat meter switched from routine-update-with-the-boss to what's-going-on-here.

Michele sat with them on the bench, and Alice turned to Des. "You may not know that Michele is on the board of the state's art museum in Richmond, along with its local branch in Stone Valley." Des didn't know that. "She's also very well connected with the art community in New York City. She thinks she can help move the investigation along."

"What? How?" Des blurted, sounding more defensive than she intended.

Alice smiled. "I know. Don't worry. This is just an opportunity, and I think we should take advantage of it."

"Sorry. I didn't mean to react that way."

"It's okay. I understand. Let's listen to her idea."

Michele replaced her smile with a serious face. "Please understand, Des, that I'm only trying to help, not get in your way."

Des nodded. She thought about Jimmy's idea that Michele might have been behind the theft, then willed herself to dismiss it. Drop the Agatha Christie crap, she said to herself, and listen; you need some help.

Michele continued. "I work with a man in New York who is one of the top art authenticators and appraisers around. He also works for major insurance companies on fraud and the like. He's helped me in many situations over the years. He has his ear to the ground, and he knows just about everyone in the art scene on the East coast. I know you think this was a professional job."

How do you know that, Des thought. A little too interested in this, maybe? But, of course, she was right, and Des admitted as much. "Yes, Michele, I'm afraid we've run the table on anyone at the university or in the local community who might have done this, and we've come up empty."

Alice took over. "So, we need some help, and Michele tells me her friend is willing to meet with you to discuss the situation."

Des relaxed. Maybe this was a good idea. She and her folks weren't getting anywhere. Maybe Michele's colleague could help.

Or maybe not. "Okay, that sounds promising. If you give me his contact information, I'll see what we can set up."

"That's the sticky point," Michele said. "He's scheduled to fly out West somewhere, Vancouver, I think, next Monday for several days of work out there."

"I guess we'll have to wait."

Alice smiled, the kind of smile that the boss gives when she's going to make life difficult. "No, I don't think we should wait, and neither does Michele. He can meet with you in New York on Friday."

"Friday? It's already Wednesday afternoon. That's pretty short notice."

"Yes, well, sometimes things have to happen when they can happen, right? Can you go up tomorrow to meet with him on Friday?"

Des knew the only answer that would be acceptable. "Of course."

"Great," Alice said, "I knew we could count on you. Michele has already booked a complimentary room at her hotel for tomorrow through Sunday."

"That's very kind of you, Michele. Thank you."

Michele pulled an envelope from her purse and handed it to Des. "His name is R. V. Tremblay, and he's set to meet with you on Friday at 10, at the hotel. I think you'll like him. All the details are in here." She handed the envelope to Des and then stood. "I'm sorry, Alice, but I have to go. Playing tennis with the coach in a few minutes."

After Michele left, Alice gave Des a pat on her hand. "I know that seemed a little strange. Michele is pretty intense, and she expects to get her way. But she means well."

"I understand," Des said, wondering if she really did.

"So, go up there and meet with him on Friday. See what he has to say. It can't hurt. And then enjoy yourself on Saturday and fly back on Sunday. My assistant has made tentative plane reservations for you. Check with her on your way out."

Alice rose, signaling the meeting was over. Des confirmed her plane reservations with the president's assistant and headed back to the office. When she arrived, Jimmy and Jessie were just preparing to head out on the remaining tasks that Des had assigned them for the week. "Not so fast," she told them. "Come in here."

They gathered in her office, Des behind the desk and her two deputies in their usual chairs opposite. "Plans have changed for the next few days," Des said, explaining her new travel plans.

Jessie was intrigued. "Cool, New York. I've never been there, how about you, Jimmy?"

"Never been north of Richmond," he said. "I have no interest in going any farther away than that."

Jessie giggled. "Ara will be changing all that. I'll bet you're off to Korea real soon."

Jimmy reddened at her teasing, but he didn't really mind. Since he'd met Ara Sun in the Drew Robbins case, Ara had become the center of Jimmy's world. She was the most serious girlfriend he'd ever had, even though they seemed an unlikely pair. She a doctoral student from South Korea, he a local boy who always wanted just to be a cop in his hometown.

"Enough of that," Des said. "You two are in charge while I'm gone, okay? So cancel any plans for the weekend, you're both on call. Got it?"

They got it. Truth was that they would do anything for their boss. Each of them admired Des White, albeit for different reasons. For Jessie Hunt, Des was a role model, exactly the kind of person Jessie wanted to be. Efficient, professional, but with a caring soul that never let up. When Des wasn't working, she was volunteering or helping out her family in Richmond. An African American woman with a big heart, just like Jessie. Someday, she thought, I'll be the next Desdemona White.

Jimmy's thoughts didn't run that deep. He just wanted to learn from his boss. True, he used to fantasize about something more, but he had Ara now, and that was enough. But he knew that, as a police detective, he was still a beginner. Getting better all the time, Des liked to tell him, but he knew he was still as likely to get things wrong as right. Go too fast or too slow, say too much or too little. He needed to master all the little things that made an investigator successful, things that Des White taught him, little by little, every day. Someday, he thought, I'll be the next Desdemona White.

12

Thursday

There's nothing like a public-relations nightmare to prod a university to action. The football coach gets caught drinking with cheerleaders after a big win, and new ethics clauses are added to all athletic contracts. A black bear escapes from the wildlife faculty's experimental pens, and new standards are handed down for all animal holding facilities. A famous painting is stolen from an unsecured library room, and new camera systems get installed.

The long delayed CCTV cameras were in place before Des White landed in New York. One camera each in the special collections rooms of the art and veterinary libraries and a third in the Fuertes Room.

But not without quite a bit of finger-pointing for why the cameras hadn't been in place already. The special meeting that the library director held on Thursday afternoon was a study in innocence and recrimination. The branch libraries supervisor, Yvonne Michaels, claimed that she had left the project in the hands of the technical and facilities folks many months earlier, assured that it would get done pronto. The IT specialist for the branch libraries, Will Morales, said it took a long time before the cameras and other electronic equipment arrived, citing a manufacturing backlog for the only devices that were permitted under state purchasing rules. The purchasing officer claimed that no one had ever asked for an exemption, which she would have been glad to issue (everyone else in the room rolled their eyes at her assertion).

The library's facilities manager said he hadn't gotten a request for installation until last month, and that it was just a routine request, with no special instructions or timing requested. As with purchasing, he said they could have given this a rush priority and had it installed immediately, like they had done this week.

Jessie had attended the meeting, as a police representative had been requested by the library director. She didn't know if it was to keep peace or because the theft was still under active investigation. But the talk around the table raised her antennae. The IT guy seemed particularly tense during the meeting, showing all the mannerisms of a suspect under questioning. His argument for delay also seemed the flimsiest of the bunch. He's been sabotaging the camera installation, Jessie thought, and I want to know why.

She checked him out when she got back to the office. Will Morales had been with the university for nearly a decade. He had moved up gradually in the IT system, transferring often from office to office, as IT staff were prone to do. There was always a shortage of qualified techs, and they took advantage of it. He had come to the library from central purchasing two years earlier, so

Jessie assumed he should have known the right people to ask if he needed some help with a supply-line snafu.

His undergraduate degree was a joint major between library science and computer science. His resume was on file from his interview for the library job; it stated his career goal was to combine his majors to make libraries and their materials more accessible to everyone through advanced digital technology. A perfect fit for the library's strategic plan, the notes in the hiring decision said. He had been assigned as the sole IT technician for the three branch libraries for the entire two years. Most of his work was routine, just keeping everything on-line and working from day to day. But he had led a couple of projects to upgrade wi-fi in the branches.

His performance reports were above average (although Jessie knew that nearly everyone at the university got high ratings; just like grade inflation, the HR chief often complained). The only issue seemed to be that he often couldn't be found when needed. His explanation was that when you worked for three libraries, two of them were going to be looking for you, unsuccessfully, all the time.

Jessie talked her suspicions over with Jimmy as Des was flying to New York. "He's the perfect suspect, Jimmy. He had control over the new cameras, and their installation hit every road-block possible, road-blocks it looked like Morales had either put up or was happy to leave in place."

Jimmy agreed. "He was probably the guy who installed that temporary camera on the library desk, so he would know to tell the thief how to cover it up with his backpack. I'll find out to-morrow if he was the one who got the temporary camera going."

"The only problem with him is the timing."

Jimmy frowned. "Why? What about it?"

"The cameras have been delayed for a long time, months and months. But the painting just got really famous over the summer. I can't imagine that Morales would have known in advance that the painting would become such a big deal so long ago. Doesn't make sense."

"Well, I don't care. I think he belongs on our list of suspects. We need some suspects, Jessie."

'Yeah," she agreed. "With him, that makes one."

Des got out of the taxi in front of The Placide. She thought the name was a bit of an oxymoron for the busy location in New York's garment district. But that was what Michele Richards called each of her several boutique hotels around the world.

And Des understood once she entered the lobby. Calm took over from the hustle-bustle outside. The decor was understated and comfortable. The space was small, suitable for the relatively few rooms in the five-story hotel. The furnishings were plain but luxurious, in soothing shades of pale blue, green and cream. But one wall was dominated by a huge abstract painting in seemingly every color of the rainbow. Des decided that Judith Heinz, the retired art teacher who had helped her in the Drew Robbins case, would love the feel of the place. Big splashes of color punctuating plain surfaces, that was Judith's style.

The desk clerk smiled when Des introduced herself. "Oh, yes, Ms. Richards told us to expect you. We have you in the Picasso Suite."

Sweet, Des thought to herself.

The Picasso Suite was a smaller version of the lobby, the same colors and textures, along with a smaller but equally colorful painting on the wall. She looked out the window, surprised that the building opposite looked like a working garment factory. It was called the garment district, of course, but Des hadn't expected that any real manufacturing still went on in the middle of Manhattan. Keep observing and learning, she always told her cops; now she reminded herself of the same lesson.

Even though it was late on a Thursday evening, lights were still on and workers were still present. Des could see bolts of cloth in a rainbow of colors piled high on tables and suspended from wooden dowels, the bright lights above and behind them making a living canvas like the one hanging in her room.

She had eaten before leaving Stone Valley, and now all she wanted was a good night's sleep.

The phone on the nightstand buzzed. The desk clerk said, "Sorry to bother you, Ms. White, but you have a message. A Mr. R. V. Tremblay just called to confirm his appointment with you at ten tomorrow morning."

Well, Des thought as she shut off the light, I wonder what Mr. R. V. Tremblay has up his sleeve.

13

Friday

Des was sitting in the lobby at 9:45. She was dressed conservatively, black pants suit and a purple crewneck sweater. To add some brightness, she wore a multi-colored scarf loosely tied around her neck. Rather like the lobby itself, she mused, all muted palette except for a splash of color.

She had no idea how an expert on art crime would be dressed. Could be all black, could be all flamboyant. She surveyed people as they moved in and out of the lobby. Observe and learn, she had reminded herself last night. So, she did, just like a good cop would do.

An elderly man entered the lobby. His shock of white hair and white whiskers seemed promising, either as the art expert or Santa Claus. But a young woman immediately jumped up from a chair, yelled "Grandpa!," and gave him a long hug.

A somewhat grimy beatnik type was the next possibility. He wore faded, distressed jeans and a grey leather vest over a t-shirt with a Mick Jagger picture. His hair was tied in a long salt-and-pepper ponytail. An artist, maybe, but certainly not one that the ever-elegant Michele Richards would tolerate.

Des was tiring of the guessing game when he walked in. That is the most gorgeous Black man I've ever seen, she thought. He was tall and squarely built, not gym-rat bulky but obviously fit. His hair was neatly cropped, slightly graying at the temples. He was dressed casually, but carefully, with grey trousers, a white linen shirt and a navy blue blazer. Not all black, not all flamboyant, she thought, too bad he isn't the highly anticipated Mr. R. V. Tremblay.

He spoke to the desk clerk who nodded Des's way. The man turned, smiled at Des, and walked toward her. "Ms. White?" he asked. "I'm Remy Tremblay."

Des stood, wobbled a bit and croaked out an answer. "Yes, I'm Des White." She cleared her throat and recovered her composure. "Nice to meet you, Mr. Tremblay." Nice indeed, she thought. Michele was right, I like him already.

"Nice to meet you, also," he said. "Do you mind if I call you Desdemona?"

"Well, yes I do mind." He drew back slightly, looking concerned at the offense. Then she smiled. "Only my mother calls me that. Please call me Des."

Now his smile seemed to light up the entire lobby. He chuckled. "You had me there for a minute. Please call me Remy. Shall we sit down?"

They sat opposite each other in over-sized chairs with an over-sized low table between them. The furniture was as conducive to conversation as a parking lot is for a picnic. "This isn't going to work," he said. "I know a coffee shop just down the street. Perhaps we should go there to get acquainted?"

"Wonderful," Des said.

"Do you have a coat?" he asked.

"No, I'll be fine like this. It was a little chilly when I ran this morning, but it is already warming up." Or is it me that's overheating, she thought.

They walked north, up two short blocks to a tiny coffee shop. "Hey, Remy, good to see you," the man behind the counter said. "And hello to your lovely friend."

"Good morning, Carmine," Remy answered, and turned to Des. "How do you like your coffee?"

"Black, with sugar," Des answered. She didn't allow herself to complete the thought, either out loud or to herself. "You're a regular, are you?"

Remy smiled. "I come here often. Michele, um, Ms. Richards, has me meet clients regularly at the hotel. But like we saw, the lobby isn't made for private conversations. So this is 'my office' in midtown."

They sat at a small table near the front windows. "Remy— that's an interesting name," Des said. "Like Des, I assume it is short for something else."

"Oh, yes, indeed," he said. "My full name is Rembrandt Vincent Tremblay."

Des couldn't keep a small laugh from escaping. "Quite a name, Rembrandt. But so appropriate for an art expert."

"So now you know why I insist on Remy. My parent were both art lovers, hence the name. And I was surrounded by art and artists from the time I can remember."

"It was fate, then, that brought you to this business?"

"Fate, yes," Remy said. "That an an early realization that I was lousy at creating art, but quite good at judging what others produced." Des thought of all those how-to-run-an-effective-meeting workshops she had been through: creating and evaluating are different kinds of tasks, you have to separate them.

Carmine brought their coffee, along with a small plate of biscotti. "My mother just baked these this morning. She told me I'd have special customers today, so I needed something special for them." He smiled broadly, looking back and forth at his two guests. "As always, Mama was right. Enjoy."

They sipped coffee and dipped biscotti for a few minutes. "So, tell me about this painting," Remy said.

Des filled him in. The painting had been made by a famous wildlife artist, Louis Agassiz Fuertes, but long before he became famous. It was featured in the 1892 Columbian Exposition in Chicago, then brought back to the American Museum of Natural History, long forgotten, parts lost in the warehouse or sold. The museum had recovered eight of the nine panels of the original work, and VWU had the ninth. It was to be brought back to the museum in late November, but had been stolen from one of the university's libraries, where it had been on display for years.

"And no one had ever paid much attention to it," Remy asked, "until the news broke about its return to the museum. Right?"

"Right," Des said. "All of a sudden, lots of people were coming by to look at the painting. Campus and local folks mostly, but out-of-towners, too."

"Tell me about the theft itself."

Des went on to describe the specifics of the theft, the security —or lack of it—at the site, and the beginnings of their investigation. "We're getting nowhere," she said. "That's why Ms. Richards thought you could help. I hope she's right."

Remy looked at Des and smiled, "I hope so, too."

His glance held her eyes a little longer than it should have. Eventually, Des broke the trance, took another biscotti and dipped it in the remains of the coffee. She took a bite and chewed for a moment to reset the mood. She held the remainder of the biscotti between her fingers like a cigar and waved it in his direction. "Okay, Colombo," she said, "what next?"

14

Remy finished his coffee. "What's next is time to learn a little more about our friend Fuertes, at the American Museum of Natural History."

He hailed a taxi and they rode north, skirting the edge of Times Square and traveling up the west side of Central Park. When they reached the museum, he led her around the work zone where the formerly famous, but now infamous, entry statue of Teddy Roosevelt was being removed. Inside, he flashed some sort of identification at the entry desk, and the clerk opened a side gate to let them pass. Des didn't ask; by now she was getting the idea that Remy moved around New York's cultural world at will.

They walked up the stairs to the next floor, where they entered the Sanford Hall of North American birds. Dioramas of birds, lots of birds, stretched along the walls. He led her down to one that featured wading birds.

Remy said, "This is the world created by Louis Agassiz Fuertes and another ornithologist, Frank Chapman."

Des was stunned. She had seen dioramas before, of course, they were a staple of museum displays. But these were, well, stunning. The land stretched from foreground into the distance without any apparent transition from real to painted. So did the birds. A few stuffed specimens filled the front, but then transformed into painted birds in the background. At least that is what Des thought must be happening. She really couldn't tell.

"My god," she said, "these are remarkable."

Remy agreed. "Yes, they are. And they are about a century old. These displays were revolutionary at the time. Most exhibits then had birds grouped together randomly, just mounted on a stand or a tree branch, without any reference to where they might actually live. It was more for aesthetics and curiosity, not for science."

"And Fuertes did all of these?"

"No, not all of them. But the best are his. Chapman, who was in charge, took Fuertes into the field with him when he went on collecting trips. That allowed Fuertes to sketch or use water colors to quickly paint what he actually saw—the colors, shapes, movements of the birds. All of it."

"They are just beautiful."

They walked back up the aisle, and now they could see the massive flamingo mural on the front wall of the hall. "This was once in a diorama with taxidermy specimens, but was saved when the museum was remodeled and is now presented as a mural. It is instructive because we can get closer to Fuertes' actual work."

They moved right up to the painting, and Remy pointed to a flock of flamingos standing near each other. "Look at the birds carefully, Des. You'll see that each one is different. The eyes, feathers, legs, feet. The way that each bird is standing. That is what Fuertes could do because he had observed the birds in the field. They are more like portraits of people, each one individual."

Des was trained to observe people and situations carefully, but it took all her concentration to begin to see the details in the birds. But as she focused on the individual birds, her appreciation for the artistic skills of the painter rose. "I had wondered why Fuertes was so special, but I think I'm beginning to understand."

They went down to the museum shop, and Remy picked out a book about Fuertes art. "Take this home so you can look at his work when you have more time. You'll find that his paintings are even more remarkable than his murals." He flashed his card at the check-out station, and once again the clerk nodded without taking payment.

"I think I should pay for this, Remy," Des said.

He smiled and shook his head. "No need. I do some favors for the museum director from time to time, and he provides me a little account here that I can draw on. But, tell you what, you can buy lunch. I know a place."

"I'll bet you do."

He led her out of the museum and across to Central Park. A short walk brought them to a street vendor. "Hey, Remy, my man. Good to see you. And where have you been hiding this splendid creature?"

"Cut the crap, Joe. But this is my new client, Desdemona White."

"Lovely to meet you, Desdemona. Very lovely indeed." And she was. The day had been an adventure so far. Remy. The coffee shop. Fuertes. Central Park. Her face glowed from the crisp fall air. Her eyes flashed with the stimulation of it all. Defying gravity, she thought, just like in the play, that's what I'm doing.

Remy turned to Des. "Let me apologize for this cretin. He doesn't know a lady when he sees one."

Des smiled, opened her jacket and flashed her badge. "I think I'll survive. Joe, make whatever Remy usually has and do the same for me. And I'm paying."

"Yes, ma'am!" Joe put two Polish sausages on steamed buns, squeezed on a generous line of brown mustard and topped them with sauerkraut. He cracked the lids on two bottles of unsweet tea and added two packs of corn chips. Des paid—an exorbitant amount, she thought, but it is New York—and the pair made their way to a nearby bench.

They sat quietly and ate their lunch as part of a perfect October day. Remy took the remnants of lunch to a nearby trash bin. When he sat down again, he said, "So tell me a little about Police Chief Desdemona White."

She demurred. "Not much to tell."

"I don't believe that. You came from somewhere."

"Richmond, Virginia. My family still lives there."

"Big family?"

Des beamed. Talking about her family always made her happy. "Not really. Mom and dad, plus a couple of brothers. And now sisters-in-law and nieces and nephews."

"Do you see them much?"

"As often as possible. My schedule isn't very predictable, but Richmond is only a few hours drive from Stone Valley, so I can get there whenever we have a slow day."

"So, let me play Mickey Spillane. 'How'd a doll like you end up in a place like this?' Stone Valley, I mean, not a bench in Central Park."

"Just like Mickey would expect. Restless, curious, not about to do what was expected. My dad was a school teacher, working in the poor section of Richmond. He said a Black man needed to do right for his community, so we lived there and he worked there. Mom stayed home, watching out for my two brothers and me. My brothers still live there, but I wanted more than Richmond."

"So you moved to Stone Valley?"

"No, the path was a bit more winding. After high school, I wasn't ready for college. So I joined the Marines and got trained as a military police officer. While I was in the service, I started going to college, taking courses whenever I could. In between a couple of tours in the Middle East, I got most of the way through a degree in criminal justice. Then, after I got out, I moved back to Richmond, signed on to the police department there. I finished my degree."

"So you conquer everything in your way, huh?" Remy asked. Maybe including me, he thought.

"Hardly. Those years working in Richmond wore me out. I kept getting promoted, but that just meant that I was working worse situations. Drugs, vice, major crimes. I knew I had to get out. That's when the opportunity opened up at VWU."

"But why Stone Valley?"

"Why not Stone Valley? Have you been there?" Remy shook his head. "If you visited sometime, you'd understand. Nice people, beautiful setting, fine university. The weather is mild. We get several months of autumn, just like today." The trees were alive with colors against a deep blue sky with occasional brilliant white clouds, birds flitting back and forth across the pond opposite their bench. "I can imagine our friend Fuertes painting this scene," Des said.

Remy understood that was all he was going to learn about her just then. "In fact, the scene that your stolen painting was part of was much like this. It depicted a pond, like this one, surrounded by woods and with marsh grasses in the foreground. It was summer, though, not fall. And, of course, the painting was filled with many species of birds, a few mammals and reptiles."

Des decided it was time for business. "Okay, let's talk about our stolen painting. Have any thoughts?"

"Quite a few, actually," Remy said.

"Don't keep me waiting, kiddo."

"First, I agree with Michele and you that the theft was a professional job."

"Why?"

"It seems carefully planned. All the details around the theft—taking advantage of a new staff member, no one around because the students were leaving for break, a story about taking a photo that fits with the upcoming transfer—all those details aren't something a kid trying to make a few bucks would think of. He'd have probably just grabbed the painting and run out the door."

"That's what my deputies think," Des said. "Makes sense. What else?"

"So, second, I'm pretty sure your painting hasn't gone far."

"Again, why?"

"A Fuertes painting is valuable and desirable, for sure, but it isn't something likely to attract an international buyer. They're after big names, art worth millions."

"How valuable do you think this painting is?" Des asked.

Remy considered for a moment. "About fifty thousand dollars."

"My friend at home thinks it might be worth a lot more, maybe two hundred thousand."

Remy frowned. "Maybe, to someone who knew and loved Fuertes. Like your dean who donated the work to the university. Maybe an East Coast sportsperson who really likes wildlife art. But I think on the general art black market, the value would be based more on the novelty associated with the museum display, not the art itself. Someone would want it because it was part of a composition that now would never be completed. Because he had the center piece."

"That's not much money, though. A stolen Porsche is worth that."

"Right," Remy said. "I suspect someone saw the publicity about the painting and decided he'd like to have it. Ordered it, more or less."

"And that means we need to be looking for a local guy who might have contracted to steal the painting for a client."

"Well," Remy continued, "your thief is obviously local, someone who could look and act like a student, knew the layout of the library, that sort of thing. Maybe a real student, who knows. But he would have to have a connection, a go-between."

"So we've got at least three people involved," Des said. "A thief, a buyer, and someone who worked between them."

"Right. Now, third point. I think the buyer is probably right here in New York."

"How do you know that?" Des asked.

"Well, first off, the stats suggest it. About sixty percent of all paintings stolen in the U.S. end up in New York City or the towns around here. This is where the artists live, where the galleries are, the museums, corporate collections, all of that. That's why I work here, right?"

Des had to admit that it made sense. "And then there is the local connection with the museum," she added.

"Right. So I'd raise the odds up to ninety percent that your painting is sitting right now in the private collection of some rich crook, maybe within shouting distance of us right now."

Des looked around at the ring of huge buildings surrounding the park. "That narrows it down to, what, about ten million people?"

Remy laughed. "About 9.99 million of them don't have the money or appetite for buying stolen art. Narrowing it down even more is what we get paid for."

Des looked at Remy, trying to decide if she should say what was on her mind. He caught her hesitation. "What's wrong, Des?"

"I've got to ask this question, and I hope that it doesn't upset you."

"Ask whatever you need to, Des. That's why I'm here."

Des shrugged. "Okay. So, we need someone who's got local knowledge to plan the theft, and someone up here who might want to have such a painting."

"Right."

"What if those are the same person."

"Who are you taking about?"

Des swallowed hard. "Michele Richards."

Remy first looked shocked, but quickly regained his composure. "Wow. That's quite an accusation."

"Not an accusation, really. But it is my job to consider everyone who could have committed the crime. Or planned it, in this case."

"I understand, Des. And I guess that I could see a motive. If she wanted the painting, she couldn't just buy it because it had been a gift to the university. So, the only way to get it would be to steal it. And she's got lots of places to display it that are very private. Like her penthouse at The Placide. She has some beautiful artwork in there. But it seems way out of character for her."

A red flag popped up for Des. She wondered how he knew about the decor of Michele Richards's penthouse. But she wasn't sure whether she saw red for personal or professional reasons, so she brushed away the thought.

Remy went on. "And why would she connect us, if she were the person behind the theft?"

"I don't know," Des said. "Misdirection, maybe. Get the two of us looking away from her."

Remy shrugged. "In The Thomas Crown Affair, maybe. But in my experience, art thefts are pretty straight-forward. If you don't want to be a suspect, you stay out of the spotlight."

"I'm sure you're right," Des said. "So, Michele Richards as art-theft-mastermind goes on the back burner. What's next?"

"Dinner."

Des was surprised. "Dinner?"

"Yeah, we've got to eat. This greasy sandwich isn't going to last us for too long."

Des looked at her watch. It was approaching two o'clock. "We've got a few hours before dinner. Can't we keep working?"

"Actually not," Remy said. "I have an appointment with another client this afternoon. So, I'll pick you up at seven at the hotel."

"Okay. Will it be another street vendor, or do I need to get decked out for an upgrade?"

"You look wonderful the way you are now," he said, his gaze not leaving her eyes, "but you might want to dress up a bit, just so you don't look too much like a cop." He smiled, and she felt her heart skip. "And maybe leave the badge at home tonight."

15

Ted Graham hated retreats. He especially hated them when they occurred during breaks. Breaks were the times when department heads, like him, got to catch up on work, maybe take a day off, or maybe, just maybe, work on that book they were always planning to write.

Time is what I need, he thought, not more poppycock about SWOT analysis or team-building or whatever was making management consultants rich this year. The Department of Renewable Resources didn't run itself, despite what the more cynical faculty liked to say, and Ted needed all the time he could get. He wasn't into strategic planning, either. Face reality, you management gurus, there isn't ever any free money, space or time to be strategic.

Despite Ted being skeptical of strategic thinking, an astute observer would see him as just that, without the labels. Maybe he wasn't going to create the next great innovation in university leadership, but he would wring every bit of good he could from the available resources, funds, facilities or people. Getting the job done, he liked to think, that's what I'm good at. And most of his department's faculty and staff, even the cynical ones, agreed and were glad he was there looking out for them.

But he knew that the higher you got in the university hierarchy, the more important it was to endorse the trappings of strategic this and that. So, even though he bristled at the thought of an all-day college leadership retreat, he played along like a good little mid-level manager.

And he appreciated the way the dean handled these nuisances. Ralph Vukovic was a good guy, for the most part. He held brief, well organized meetings; he didn't keep too much of the budget for his own purposes; and, most importantly, he let department heads run their departments. As long as the metrics—that's what management gurus called data, he had learned at a retreat about "metric magic"—of grants, publications and graduate students stayed high, he didn't get in the way. Not much, anyhow.

And the dean knew how to throw a party, disguised this day as a leadership retreat. He held the retreat at his home, a large federalist almost-mansion just off the edge of campus. It was more of a museum than a house, really, perfect for a bachelor dean who loved art, particularly art that featured animals. The walls were filled with paintings that Ted loved looking at on his occasional visit to the house, but he imagined a wife might soon tire of living in an art zoo.

They started at ten—so I did get a little time, Ted admitted— broke for a long lunch catered, thankfully, by anyone other than university dining, and finished at three. The guest leadership consultant was pretty entertaining, too. At least he avoided the usual letter scramble to diagnose personality types. He only had three categories, like three flavors of ice cream, vanilla, chocolate and strawberry. Ted was a vanilla, a "people-person" type who tried to keep everyone happy and did the best with what was available.

The dean pulled Ted aside at the end of the retreat, as others were leaving. "Comfortable about being a vanilla, Ted?"

Ted's antennae went up. He didn't know where this was going. "Sure," he said, "he nailed me."

"No, I don't think so. You've got a bit of strawberry in you, too. You like to think outside the box. Sometimes." Ralph laughed. "I'd say you're a strawberry swirl."

Ted joined in what he hoped was a joke. Strawberries, the consultant had explained, were folks who liked new ideas, liked to try things, even goofy things. Might end up being carried off the field on the team's shoulders, but also might get fired. Ted didn't think he was strawberry at all. "Thanks. I think."

The dean replaced the laugh with a more serious look. Aha, Ted thought, here it comes. "Yeah, you're a strawberry swirl. And, listen, my senior associate dean is getting ready to retire. He's my strawberry swirl right now. Has good ideas, but knows that most of them can't be implemented because we don't have enough time, money, or space. He tells me what he thinks, but he gets on board with whatever decision I make."

Ted understood that, for sure. "Peter is a good man. I'll be sorry to see him retire. We've always gotten along well."

"Yes," Ralph said, "we'll miss him. But, as they say, the senior associate dean is dead, long live the senior associate dean." Ted supposed he should laugh at this, but he just couldn't. "I'm thinking that you might be a good replacement for Peter. I'm a chocolate, you know, I like to follow the rules, keep everything tidy, establish protocols and stick with them." Right, thought Ted, that's why we're having a retreat when we could be working. "You know, a diverse team is a strong team." Ted had heard that several times today.

"I'm flattered," Ted said, but to himself he said, thanks, but no thanks. "I've never really thought about moving up. I like being department head."

"Well, it's just a strawberry-swirl kind of idea today," Ralph said. "Just think about it."

Ted was thinking about it. And what he thought was that the dean was a long way down the road on this already. His next thought was that maybe he better watch his step.

Ralph continued. "And Elena Bertoni might just be a good replacement for you as department head. How is she doing, by the way? Ready for promotion to full?"

"She's doing well," Ted said. "She really is a top-notch faculty member. She gets distracted easily, though, not producing results as fast as I'd like."

Ralph nodded. "Well, she's really helping the university, all of us, really, a lot with taking over the Drew Robbins mess. I'm sure that that would count in her favor for promotion, even if her publications and grants were a little light. I'd back her."

You haven't seen her resume since we hired her, Ted thought. But that's not what he said. "I appreciate that, Ralph. I was planning to encourage her to go for promotion next year."

"Great. But, listen, try to dissuade her from getting involved in the theft of the painting, you know, the Fuertes thing."

Ted's antennae were throbbing now. "Why would she get involved in that?"

Ralph shrugged. "I don't know, but it is her nature, isn't it? She was neck deep in the Robbins case. And she's leading the art and environment committee, or whatever it's called. And she's got that show about the painting coming up, with the students. She invited me. I don't know why really, but she did."

"Me, too," Ted said. "I'm sure she invited a bunch of the administration, hoping a few might show. And, yes, she is committed to the art and environment thing."

"Well, given what we've just been talking about, I'd hate for her to lose momentum because she got distracted about the painting."

"I'll be sure to warn her about not getting involved," Ted said, but knew that he probably wouldn't.

The dean smiled and slapped him on the shoulder. "Great," he said, and left Ted standing at the door.

I guess I've been dismissed, he thought, and headed to his car. Before he got in, he took a long look back at the looming front of the dean's house. "I wonder what that was all about."

16

Ralph Vukovic pulled into the driveway just as the sun was setting. He walked up to the white frame house, the last rays of daylight immersing the front porch in soft yellow light.

A thin woman dressed in a paint-splattered pair of overalls was rocking gently in the remaining sunlight. She smiled broadly when she saw him. "Hello, Ralph. Didn't expect you this evening."

"I hope it's okay for me to drop in. I needed some diversion."

"Of course, sweetheart, any time." Jennifer Haskins smiled as he climbed up the few steps to the porch, kissed her and sat in the adjacent rocker. "Bad day at the office?"

"Crappy, in spades. We had a leadership retreat at my house, all day. I know it's a good idea to have retreats every so often, but they do wind me up. And after you've been in the business for as long as I have, it just seems like the department of redundancy department, you know?"

Jennifer laughed and kept rocking. "Sounds just lovely. The cost of being the dean. You know, in crossword puzzles, when the clue is 'big man on campus,' the answer is always 'dean.'"

Ralph chuckled. "See, I knew you'd cheer me up. How are you doing?"

Jennifer signed. "Oh, fine, I guess. I painted for most of the day, more scenes from down the valley." Jennifer lived about fifteen miles outside Stone Valley, two small ridges away from town. It was a beautiful setting. The old farmhouse she lived in was about as picturesque as the paintings she made of the region. And the remodeled barn that she used as her studio often served as the focal point in many of her landscape paintings. "I was thinking, though, that it would be nice to get over to Montenegro in the fall for a change, rather than in the summer. I really need to expand my portfolio of Balkan landscapes to all four seasons."

"Sounds good," Ralph said. "Maybe we can take a trip over Thanksgiving break. It would be nice to get out of town."

They both rocked silently for a few moments, thinking about their summer home in the hills of Montenegro. Ralph and Jennifer had met soon after he took the job as dean of the College of Biological Sciences, some twenty years ago. Their mutual love of art—Jennifer as a painter, Ralph as a collector—had blossomed into a deep friendship and then a love affair. They had never married, but they were well known around campus and town as a couple.

Ralph had inherited a small villa and the adjoining farmland in Montenegro, handed down in his family for generations. Each summer, he spent a month there, partially as a retreat and partially as a base for studying the Balkan lynx, an endangered mammal. That work complemented his main expertise as a New World mammalogist and author of the definitive work on the taxonomy of North American quadrupeds. Jennifer usually traveled with him, using her time to paint landscapes around the eastern Adriatic—Montenegro, Croatia, Bosnia & Herzegovina, Albania. Her landscape paintings of southwestern Virginia combined with those of the Balkans to form the two portfolios that had made Jennifer Haskins a well known and widely sold regional artist.

"I would love that," Jennifer said, reaching between the rockers for Ralph's hand. "Maybe we could take Manny, too."

Ralph pulled his hand away, abruptly. "Let's not get too excited. He'd be bored, and neither of us would get to relax or get any work done with him around."

The biggest source of conflict between them was Jennifer's nephew, Manfred Kurtz, Manny as she called him. He was a student at VWU, in Ralph's college, and it seemed to Ralph that he was always pulling Manfred from the jaws of disaster. Bad grades, parking tickets, minor brushes with campus police. One reason he never married was because he didn't want the constant problems and anxieties that came with a family. He had grown up in a family with four younger sisters and two professional, type-A parents. So, he had been the de facto referee in their home. Raising one family had been enough for him. And it irritated him that Jennifer was constantly trying to paste her nephew into their relationship

Jennifer teared up, his verbal slap no less real than a physical one would have been. "It was just an idea. I'll go start dinner." She went into the house, a little sadder than when he had driven up.

Ralph stayed on the porch. He wanted Jennifer in his life, that was a given, but there were times when she was more needy than he could handle. And those times seemed to be coming more frequently. She fretted about the quality of her art, which, he assured her, had never been better. She grew lonely sometimes, wishing that she had more contact with her family, what little of it was left. Like wanting to take Manny to Montenegro. She often asked him to drive along with her when she went to see her sister in Lynchburg, but he usually found an excuse to avoid the trip. Once he consented to join her on a trip to Utah to see her brother and his enormous, Brady Bunch family. Only once.

He stayed on the porch until the sky turned from dark blue to deep gray and finally black. Then the aroma of a homemade pot pie came wafting through the door. He went in, thinking that he shouldn't have reacted automatically and negatively to Jennifer's mention of Manny.

17

Remy was waiting in the lobby when Des stepped out of the elevator. He turned to greet her, and then stopped. He had to tell himself to breathe.

Des was wearing a red dress, the kind that she might have worn to church on a special Sunday. Tailored, with a slightly flared skirt that stopped just above the knees, sleeveless with wide straps over her shoulders. Her short curly hair framed her face, her skin perfect and her dark brown eyes glowing. A double strand of pearls completed the elegant look.

Yes, she could have been dressed for church. But in Remy's mind, she was dressed to kill. She was, in fact, as Roberta Flack sang, killing him softly at that very moment.

Des walked to him, smiling. "I hope this is okay. It's all I brought with me."

Remy broke from his trance. "Perfect," he stammered, "just perfect." He stood still, looking at her.

Eventually Des took over. "Shall we go? We don't want to miss our reservation."

"Yes, of course," Remy recovered. "Do you mind if we walk? It's only a few blocks?"

She carried a white shawl over her arm, and now swung it across her shoulders. "Wonderful," Des said. "I wore my sensible heels."

Remy looked down at her shoes. They did seem sensible, not the spike heels that could have easily made her outfit unsuitable for church. His interest, however, was much more focused on the shapely calves above the shoes themselves. "Very sensible," he said, "very sensible indeed."

They walked north again, past Carmine's coffee shop, and then turned west. A few streets later Remy led her through the door of Delmo's Trattoria. The aroma of northern Italian cooking filled the room. Opera music played softly in the background.

The hostess smiled broadly. "Good evening, Mr. Tremblay. This way, please."

"Again?" Des said. "Do you know every one of the ten million?"

Remy laughed. "Aw, Des, give me a break. I wouldn't take you to someplace I didn't know was as wonderful as...." Then he stopped talking before he got way too far ahead of himself.

The hostess sat them at a table along one wall of the restaurant, angled so that when they sat next to each other they could look out across the room. The restaurant was busy, but not in the top-tourist-attraction kind of way. "Just a little neighborhood spot, right?" Des asked.

"That's right," Remy said. "They don't advertise, there's no website and the phone number isn't public. They are happy being who they are."

An elegantly dressed waiter who was obviously Italian came to their table. "Good evening, Remy," he said, "and good evening to you, also, mia bella."

Remy took charge. "I'd like you to meet my new friend, Des White. Des, this is Tonino."

Tonino bowed slightly. "My pleasure, Des. Remy is a man of exquisite taste, and he just proved it again. Please enjoy your dinner." Tonino then moved away.

"What dinner?" asked Des. "Doesn't this little neighborhood place have menus?"

"Not for us, Des. Let's just see where the evening takes us."

The evening took them to culinary heaven. Tonino brought several waves of glorious food. It began with tortellini in brodo, moved to the lightest, most flavorful Bolognese sauce that Des had ever tasted, over fresh pasta, cooked al dente, and finished with a breaded chicken cutlet, pounded whisper-thin, all accompanied by a red house wine that arrived in a dark green bottle with no labels.

"My god, that's wonderful," Des said, as she tasted the wine. She picked up the bottle to examine it more closely. "I'd love to get some of that back home. What is it called?"

Remy chuckled. "It's called red wine. I'm pretty sure they make it in the basement."

Changing the subject, Des looked around the room. Pictures of singers in operatic costumes covered the walls. "So the theme of the restaurant is opera, am I right?"

"Very good, Colombo. Delmo, the owner, is a devoted opera fan."

"How Italian," Des joked.

"You get the food—and wine—you've got to take it with a little opera."

Des demurred. "I have to admit my ignorance, Remy. Truth is I've never been to an opera." She waved her hand around at the photos on the walls. "I don't recognize any of the people in the pictures."

Remy pointed towards a photo directly across the room from them. It was a beautiful Black woman dressed as an Egyptian empress. "That is the important one, right there."

Des nodded. "She is beautiful. What is her name?"

"Angelique Tremblay."

"As in Remy Tremblay?" Des asked.

"Yes," he said, "she was my mother."

"Tell me," Des said, the wine and the ambiance taking control, "tell me all about her."

"My grandfather was an art dealer in Paris before World War II. However, he was also a Black man and Jewish. When the war started, he worked with the Resistance for as long as he could, but then had to leave. He went to St. Martin, where he met my grandmother, a native Creole singer in a nightclub. They married and had my mother, Angelique. When it became obvious that she had a special voice, they moved to New York in the 1950s so she could train. My grandfather started dealing in art again in New York. My mother's reputation continued to grow, and she sang opera all over the United States and Europe. By the time she met my father, who was also an art dealer, she was so well established that she kept her name. And when I came along, they decided that I, too, should carry her name."

"You said Angelique *was* your mother. Has she died?"

Remy looked deeply into Des' eyes, the pain showing clearly. "Yes, about ten years ago. The strain on her voice of all those years of singing led to throat problems. She developed throat cancer."

"I'm so sorry, Remy. I hope she didn't suffer terribly."

"No," he said. "She went very fast. It was a blessing, really, because she was devastated when she could no longer sing."

"And your father?"

"Oh, he's still alive, very much alive. He lives with me. And drives me crazy. The truth is, that's what I had to do this afternoon. I had promised him that I'd watch him play in a pickleball tournament."

Des laughed. "Why didn't you tell me? My parents love playing pickleball."

"It hardly seems like the sort of thing that should delay a criminal investigation, does it?"

Des shrugged, but what she really thought was, yes, it very much seemed like that.

In true Italian manner, their dinner progressed slowly, allowing them to savor the food, wine and atmosphere. In the meantime, the restaurant had come nearly empty. Remy signaled for Tonino to come over.

"I hope dinner was satisfactory, mia bella?" he asked.

"It was truly remarkable. Thank you so much."

Tonino beamed and started to speak again, but Remy held up his hand. "We have some business."

"Si, capo, let's talk business."

They quickly filled Tonino in on the stolen painting, and Remy passed him a small photograph of the two herons flying over the blue sky. "Nose around, will you, and let us know what the word is on the street?"

Tonino put the photo inside his jacket. "You got it. I'll let you know." He walked away.

"Care to explain?" Des asked.

"He knows everything that goes on in this town about the black market for art. If your painting is here, he'll find out about it." Remy brushed his hands together to signal an end to that topic. "Now, let's talk about tomorrow."

"Tomorrow?" Des asked.

"Sure. You said you weren't going home until Sunday. You don't think I'd leave you alone without a proper escort for a day in New York City, do you?"

Des's heart leaped. She wasn't quite sure yet what was happening between them, but she was willing to keep following the clues for now. "Of course not. Mr. Rembrandt Vincent Tremblay would never treat a lady that way."

"So, I'll pick you up at ten again tomorrow. When were you last in the Big Apple?

"At least ten years," Des answered, maybe exaggerating how recently she had been in town.

"Okay, so we'll go to the 9/11 memorial and then I want to take you to my favorite art museum."

"MOMA, I'll bet." she said.

"No, not at all. The Folk Art Museum. The art of the people is there, expressed without pretense or prescription." Des nodded her approval. "And maybe back here for dinner?"

"Sounds lovely."

They left the restaurant and walked back to The Placide. Along the way, he took her hand to guide her around a small construction obstacle along the sidewalk. When they had passed it, he continued to hold her hand. And she let him. She wondered if she were blushing. Are we in middle school, she thought.

At the door to the hotel lobby, he turned her and before she knew it they had kissed. Lightly, briefly. But a kiss.

He moved closer and put his arms around her waist. Des had to make a split-second decision that might change her life forever. Move closer into his embrace, or put her hands on his chest and back away. One decision would lead them both upstairs. The other would end one of the most remarkable days of her life.

She raised her hands and placed both palms on his chest. He backed away. "I'm sorry," he said, looking at his feet like a scolded schoolboy.

She lifted his chin and smiled into his eyes. "Don't be sorry. I'm not. But let's see how tomorrow goes and then try this again, okay?"

He nodded his school-boy head. "Okay, yes, okay. That's perfect. Perfect."

"See you at ten." The automatic door opened and she was gone.

18

Saturday

Remy arrived on Saturday morning a few minutes before ten. He sat in one of the over-sized lobby chairs directly facing the elevator. He wanted to see her immediately when the elevator door opened.

But after several trips by the elevator had not produced Des, he walked to the desk. The clerk recognized him immediately and apologized. "I'm sorry, Mr. Tremblay. I didn't see you at first. We've been very busy this morning."

"No problem. Could you call up to Ms. White's room and tell her I am waiting."

"Oh. Once again, my apologies. Ms. White checked out early this morning."

Remy stood still, rigid with his disappointment. His mind replayed the day he had spent with her. What could I have done to cause this? What had driven her away? He just stood, silent, utterly dejected. But the clerk continued, "She left this note for you."

He opened the folded paper. "Remy, I've been called back to campus. A student has died in questionable circumstances. I didn't want to text in the middle of the night. May I have a raincheck?"

19

Elena put on ancient sweatpants and sweatshirt from the University of Bologna, where she worked before coming to VWU. She slipped on a pair of long white socks and slid into a throughly worn pair of Crocs, their formerly bold red color faded to a pale pink. Thank goodness, she said to herself, for fashion-free Saturdays. She walked across her back yard to a small storage shed, grabbed a rake and began cleaning the flower beds that bordered her little house. Saturday had come around again, and with the crossword completed and in the recycling bin, she was determined to enjoy the therapy of yard work.

She had made good use of fall break, with no classes to prepare and few student appointments. She had sent one manuscript off to a journal for review, co-authored by Timor Madras, one of the graduate students she had inherited from Drew Robbins. She had corrected and returned the galley-proofs for two others that were ready to be published. Ted would be pleased, she thought, three in a week. The week of rapid progress had ended, though, and the distracting life of a busy campus would return when classes resumed on Monday.

As she raked, she heard the insistent honking of the Canada geese that moved from the small pond down the road into the park that lay just behind her house. She looked up as the honking grew louder and watched as a pair of geese flew by, barely clearing her roof and then disappearing through the gap between two maples at the end of the yard.

The geese reminded her of the painting. The stolen painting. She had had a couple of conversations about it with Des earlier in the week, over coffee. The police weren't making much progress, but at least they didn't suspect poor Hannah Maddox any longer. She wondered if Des's trip to New York to consult with an art specialist was yielding results.

And the university was allowing her project and exhibition to go forward as planned. There really wasn't any reason for the university to stop or delay the event, but that wouldn't matter if they thought it would get connected to the stolen painting. Aaron always told her that the university's unspoken motto was "sensus est veritas"--perception is reality.

Elena suspected that Dean Vukovic had a hand in keeping the project alive. It was obvious that he liked art, and he understood the relationship between art and environment. If perception were reality, then art was important for getting society to act more responsibly toward the environment. People loved wildlife art and photography, as evidenced by the ever popular books, calendars, and television specials about animals and national parks.

As she raked, she thought back on the reception that the dean had thrown for the American Museum of Natural History delegation when the loan of the painting was announced. It was held at the dean's home, which Elena had heard was like an art museum itself. So, Elena had needled Ted to get her invited, and he had made that happen (you owe me one, he had told her).

What people said about Dean Vukovic's home was true. He told the group that evening that he had been collecting animal-related art his entire life, and the walls proved it. Every conceivable space had a painting or sculpture. Not all of them were valuable, historically or financially, of course, but it was a far cry from the typical duck prints and antlers found over the mantles of most outdoor enthusiasts.

Elena had recognized many of the artworks. A Charlie Harper print of whimsical urban wildlife rendered in geometric shapes. A Beverley Doolittle hide-and-seek of horses on a snow-dotted mountainside. A whole wall of Audubon prints (surely reproductions she had thought at the time but she wasn't sure now). Several Ansel Adams photographs. But there were others, many others, that she'd never seen before. She had been mesmerized by the variety of styles and subject matters.

He had spoken at the event about his desire to make his collection more widely accessible. That is why, over his time at VWU, he had donated several artworks to the university, with the requirement that they be displayed in what was now called the Fuertes Room in the BSB library. And the opportunity to have one of the paintings—the center piece, as everyone had begun to cal it—on display at the American Museum was a dream come true.

He must be devastated, she thought, that the painting was gone.

More honking broke Elena's reverie. The geese were heading back to the pond, and it was time for her to get cleaned up for lunch at the cafe. She scooped the leaves into the compost heap at the end of her yard, and turned the pile over with a spade. As she walked away, several house sparrows flew down to find whatever partially decomposed treats Elena had churned up. We're just like them, she mused, the geese and the dickey-birds, flying back and forth between food and rest.

20

"Okay, fill me in." Des had gotten the earliest Saturday morning flight back from New York and had driven the twenty miles straight from the airport to the police station. Jessie and Jimmy were waiting for her when she arrived. Supplied with coffee, they were gathered around her desk.

"Sorry we had to call you back early," Jessie said. "How did it go with the art expert? Any help from him?"

"Fine. It went fine. But that needs to wait. Tell me about the student."

Okay, Jessie thought, down to business. "We got a call last evening about ten, from a student named, uh..."

Jimmy looked up from his notes and broke in. "His name is Howard Anderson, the deceased's roommate."

"And this was in a university dorm, right?" Des asked.

"Right," Jimmy said. "Fourth floor of Blanford." He looked again at his notes. "Room 414."

Jessie took over again. "He had just returned from break and found his roommate, Manfred Kurtz, on his bed. Anderson tried to rouse him, but he didn't respond. He called 9-1-1, and we had a patrol car and EMTs there in a couple of minutes. They tried to revive him, but it was obvious he had been dead for a while. They got Anderson out of the room, down the hall to a lounge, and sealed up the room. I was on call, and I got there at," she checked her notes again, "10:24."

"Then what?"

"I called Jimmy, and he got there not much later."

Jimmy said, "I got there as quick as I could. I was at Ara's, so it took a few minutes to get across town."

"We brought in the doctor on call as medical examiner, activated our forensics crew, and called the town cops to help with the crime scene and such." The town police worked well with the university, a relationship that Des and the town police chief, Frank Marin, had built over time. The town police usually helped with complex or extensive crime scene analysis, the analysis that went beyond fingerprints, things the small university forensics team wasn't prepared to handle.

"What do you think happened?" Des asked.

Jimmy spoke first. "There was evidence in the room that looked like he had taken cocaine, including a small vial that had traces of white powder in it. Forensics are testing it. We presumed he overdosed."

Jessie nodded in agreement. "We split up to talk with other students in the dorm, but only a few were back yet from break, and none of them could remember seeing Kurtz that everning. We had all the immediate steps taken by about one this morning, when we called you. Sorry it was so late."

"No problem," Des said. "You did right, both calling me and how you handled things here. What do you know about the student, ah, tell me his name again."

"Manfred Kurtz," Jessie said. "He's 24, been a student for six years, classified as a junior."

"Six years! Not making a lot of progress, was he? Major?"

"Botany."

"Botany? We actually still have a major called botany?"

Jessie nodded. "Yes, in the College of Biological Sciences. I looked it up."

"What else?"

"He got in a little trouble a few years ago for marijuana. Nothing serious. We just caught him growing a row of plants on his dorm window sill. Confiscated the plants and gave him a reprimand of record."

Des didn't remember the incident. Minor offenses involving marijuana made up the bulk of drug cases on campus, and these days no one took them very seriously. "Have you notified his parents?"

Jessie shook her head. "Not yet. They live outside Lynchburg. We thought we'd wait until we talked with you, knowing you'd be here right away."

"Okay, that's fine. Jessie, take the family-affairs officer who's on duty and drive up there right now. You can be there in an hour."

Jessie stood up to leave. "What do I tell them happened?"

"Just what we know. Tell his parents that we suspect a drug overdose, but that we will have to do an autopsy to be sure. Tell them it is standard procedure in unexplained deaths like this. And if they can handle it, ask them the usual background questions."

Jessie left, and Des and Jimmy headed to Manfred Kurtz's dorm.

21

Des parked the police car in the service vehicle spot next to the loading dock for Blanford Hall. The residence was relatively new, featuring two-bedroom two-bath suites with a common area, designed for two students, regardless of gender. Des and Jimmy attracted considerable attention from the smattering of students in the dormitory. They took the elevator to the fourth floor and walked down the hallway to room 414. The usual "police—do not enter" tape covered the doorway.

"What did you do with the roommate?" Des asked.

"He's staying with a friend who has an apartment off campus. We have his cell number."

"Good. Better to have him away from here until we're ready for him."

They unlocked the door and squeezed between the rows of tape. The door opened directly into the common area, which stretched from the doorway to the windows at the back of the suite, overlooking a lawn with a volleyball court in the center. There were unwashed dishes in the sink and some clothing strewn on the couch and chairs, but nothing that looked out of place for a student dorm.

"Kurtz's room is on the left," Jimmy said, pointing to a doorway in the middle of the wall. They walked into his room and found the same residue of student life—a few pieces of discarded clothing, textbooks and notebooks on the desk and floor, fast-food wrappers in the waste can.

"Where's his laptop?" Des asked.

"We took that with us last night," Jimmy answered, "along with his cellphone. We also took the drug-related items." He took his cellphone out and showed Des photos of the removed items.

"Good, again. Let's get our tech crew working on getting inside the phone and computer. Maybe there's something there."

Jimmy nodded. "We notified them last night to get into the office today and get started."

"Jeez, Jimmy, I could have stayed in New York. You don't need me."

Jimmy glowed at the praise from his boss. Des knew that pleasing her was at the top of his list, and it irritated her sometimes. Not today, though; she was genuinely pleased with how he and Jessie had handled things.

"Jessie deserves the credit, too," he said.

"No doubt. Now let's think what happened here. Sometime, maybe not yesterday, but not too long ago, Kurtz scores some cocaine and comes home to have a party. Is he alone, or does he share his prize with someone else? We need to find out who might have been with him. He takes the drug, lays down on his bed, and he never wakes up again. That about right, you think, Jimmy?"

"Yeah, seems right to me. That's the simplest explanation. Isn't that what they always tell us in investigative training—the simplest, most direct explanation is usually right?"

Des nodded. "That's right, kiddo. But we do have to get some facts together to confirm it. We need the autopsy results, and we need to talk with some possible witnesses. Jimmy, I want you to go room-to-room on this floor, talking to everyone. Students should start rolling back in again today, and tomorrow, for sure. Talk to the RA on the floor, too. And not just about what might have happened yesterday. Find out who Kurtz was. While you're doing that, I'm going to go talk to the roommate. What's his name again?"

"Howard Anderson." Jimmy punched a few keys on his phone. "I just sent you his contact information."

"Okay, Jimmy. Thanks. Now start knocking on doors."

Des called Howard Anderson and they agreed to meet at the police station.

Howard Anderson looked like he had been up all night. when he arrived at the station.

"How are you doing, Howard? Can I call you Howard?" Des asked.

"Howie, if you want. Everyone calls me Howie."

"So, how are you? It doesn't look like you slept much."

"Okay, I guess," he said. "It still seems like it didn't really happen. I mean, I never saw a dead person before."

Des sympathized, remembering the nausea she experienced looking at her first few brushes with death. "I understand, Howie. And just to let you know, you aren't in any trouble here.

Not if you tell me the truth and as long as you had nothing to do with Manfred's death."

"Thanks, Ms. White. And it's The Man."

"Excuse me?"

"The Man. That's what we all called him, called Manfred."

"Interesting nickname. Where did it come from?"

"I don't know. We've only been roommates since the start of the semester, and everyone else called him The Man, so I did, too."

"Did he seem like the kind of person to have a nickname like that? You know, was he especially strong, or smart, or domineering. Were people scared of him? Was he well liked?"

Howie looked uncertain as how to answer. Des sensed he was worried about telling the truth. "Listen, Howie, like I said, you're not in trouble, and probably won't be. But your friend is dead, and it's my job to figure out how it happened. I'm going to do that, one way or another. So you can help me, and everything will be fine. Or you can play around, and maybe it won't be so good for you. Understand?"

Des knew that talk generally loosened lips, and it worked on Howie. "Yes, ma'am, I understand. The Man knew his way around. If you needed something, he could get it for you."

"Drugs, you mean?" Des asked.

"Well, yeah, drugs, maybe, I guess, sometimes. But he told me he had gotten in trouble for drugs before, and he didn't like messing with them. He said the cops, pardon me, the police watched the drugs too closely. But that didn't seem to be the big thing. It was other things. Fake ID cards, booze. Copies of tests and answer sheets that aren't supposed to be out there. Keys for some of the buildings on campus where guys liked to take girls for, uh, you know." Des did know. The police had a running list of places where students snuck in to have sex. "And prescriptions for Ritalin and beta blockers, you know, things that help you study."

"So he really was The Man, huh?"

"Yes, I guess he was."

"Was he The Man for you, Howie?"

Howie's brows furled. "What do you mean?"

"Did he get things for you that you needed and shouldn't have?"

Howie shook his head violently. "Oh, no, ma'am, not for me. I don't use drugs or drink, and I sure don't need to cheat on exams and stuff. I have a 3.5 average in genetics."

"Okay, kiddo, good to know. Let's go to the other end of the spectrum, Howie. Lots of people liked him because he could get them things, but were there people who didn't like him?"

That stopped Howie. "First, I'm not sure I'd say that people liked him. He was useful to them, but he could be a real pr..., I mean, a real jerk."

"So, who didn't like him?"

"No one in particular. Kind of everyone, just a little."

"Anyone who might purposefully give him an overdose of cocaine?"

"God, is that what happened?" Howie exclaimed. "He OD'd in our room? Jesus."

Des put up her hand and shook her head. "We don't know how he died yet, Howie. I'm just thinking out loud, asking questions. Did he take drugs in your room often?"

Once again, Howie was searching for the right words. "It's okay, Howie. Just tell the truth."

"I know he smoked weed. I could smell it coming from his room sometimes,. But Bet didn't like him to do it."

"Who's Bet?" Des asked.

"His girlfriend. She stayed over sometimes."

"Do you know her full name, and where she lives? Phone number?"

"Bettina is her first name, I think, but I don't know her last name. She lives off campus, but I don't know where."

"One last thing, Howie. Classes don't start again until Monday, and most students won't get back until today or tomorrow. Why did you come back on Friday?"

"Oh, that's simple," he said. "I'm scheduled to work today and Sunday." He looked at his watch. "In fact, I'm supposed to be at work by one."

Des looked at the clock on the wall. It was just after eleven. "You better get going, then. We'll let you know when you can get back into your room. Take a shower and get yourself something to eat. And thank you for talking with us. If you think of anything else that might be relevant regarding Manfred's death, let me know." She handed him her card.

"Okay.

"By the way, where do you work?"

Howie smiled for the first time as he stood up. "At the Biological Sciences Library."

22

After Howie left, Des worked through the pile of normal police work that had stacked up on her desk while she was in New York. But she was distracted. I need to call him, she thought, now that I've got a minute to myself. I don't want to seem too eager, though. Cripes, it really is middle school.

She dialed Remy's phone, and he answered on the first ring. "Hello, Des. I'm so sorry to hear about the death. Are you doing okay?"

"I'm fine," she said, "but thanks for your concern. I'm just doing my job."

"Yeah, well, I can hear it in your voice. Stone Valley isn't so perfect today, is it?"

"No, not at all." She paused. "Listen, I'm sorry I had to take off so suddenly. I hope you understand it had nothing to do with us, I mean, with you."

"I know that, now that you've called," he said. "I wasn't too sure this morning. I mean, it could have been a really devious way to get out of seeing me again."

Des relaxed, and they talked for a long time, the conversation never dragging. It's like talking to an old friend, she thought.

Eventually, she looked at the clock and realized she was late. "Remy, I've got to go."

"Hot date?" he asked.

"Hardly, but, yes, lunch with a good friend. She's involved in the art theft a bit, so I need to check in with her."

"Suspect?"

"Heavens, no. Elena is a faculty member here, in wildlife conservation, but she also loves art."

"Sounds interesting," he said. "When can I meet her?"

That got Des's attention. "What?"

"You said I needed to visit Stone Valley to understand why you like it so much. And I'm thinking that I might need to see where the theft occurred, understand the bigger context, you know."

"You mean take a trip down here?" Des's middle-school heart was fluttering. "I thought you were heading out of town for work, on the West coast?"

"I can put that off for a while. No big deal. I could visit Michele, too. Ask her if she stole the painting." They both laughed. "It's nice down there, right?"

"Yes. Yes it is." Des smiled to herself. Even nicer if you were here, she thought. "I have an idea. Let me talk to Elena, and then I'll get back to you. You are serious, right?"

"Very serious, Police Chief White. Very serious indeed."

Des parked at the Scandia Cafe. She was late for the standing Saturday afternoon lunch group, but she assumed Elena had told the others that she was in New York. She was sure that her unplanned trip to the big city would be a subject of conversation for her friends. She stood near the entrance, hoping to catch Elena's eye.

Eventually Elena looked her way, jumped up and walked over to greet her. "What are you doing here, Des? You're supposed to be in New York!"

"I had to cut the trip short," Des said. "A problem came up on campus. Do you suppose we could sit together for a few minutes, just you and me? I need to talk, but not publicly."

"Sure. Let me get my drink." Elena returned to her friends, made her excuses, and came back to the table Des had chosen in the least busy corner of the patio.

"Thanks, kiddo," Des said.

"No sweat, Des. Whatever you need. So, what's up?"

Des told Elena that there had been a student death, but didn't reveal any of the details. "I can't say much. The death will be announced tomorrow. When a student dies, it really bothers me. We think it was a drug overdose, but don't tell anyone. I saw way too much of drugs in the military and in Richmond. When it happens here, it just brings back lots of bad old memories."

Elena reached across the table and took Des's hands in her own. "I'm sorry that he died, and that you have to deal with it."

"There's not that much to do, really. Jessie is up talking to the parents, and we've got to do due diligence around the events, but it'll be finished in a day or two. For us, that is, but not for his family and friends."

"If there's any way I can help," Elena said, "just ask. Now, how was New York?"

"Well, that's another interesting story." Des related her meetings with Remy, his suspicion that the painting was already gone from the area and now hidden in some crime boss's private collection. "We've seen the last of that thing, I'm afraid. But there's more." Des told Elena about what seemed to be developing between her and Remy.

"Oh, my god, Des," Elena said. "He sounds amazing. What are you going to do about it, I mean, about him?"

"Okay, I have an idea."

"I'm listening."

"He mentioned that he wanted to come down to visit. Visit campus, I mean, because of the stolen painting. He said he needed to get the full context."

Elena raised her eyebrows. "Yeah, right. Is that what he calls you, his full context?"

They both laughed, and Elena could see some relaxation in Des's face. "Here's the idea. I know you are having the art contest soon with your students. And Judith Heinz is going to be the judge, right?"

"Yes, along with Jennifer Haskins, a local artist that she's roped in."

"Well," Des said, "how about a third judge, a big-time art expert from New York City?"

"You mean Remy, right?" Des nodded. "That's a great idea. The kids would love it. I'd love it. And I'd get a chance to meet this guy. Done deal!"

"Well, hold on a bit. He's got to agree."

"I'll leave that to you, Miss Full Context. I'm confident you can arrange it. Get busy."

"When is it exactly?" Des asked.

"This coming Wednesday evening. Call him."

'What, now?"

Elena nodded. "Yes, right now. Call him."

Des dialed, and Remy picked up again, first ring. They talked for a few minutes, Des smiling the whole time. She hung up. "Okay, kiddo, it's all set."

23

Des left Elena at the cafe. She wasn't in the mood for joining in the Saturday afternoon merrymaking. She drove to the campus pond and parked at the far end.

Her first reaction to Manfred Kurtz's death had been all professional. Implement the correct processes. Isolate the scene. Authorize the autopsy. Inform the parents. Get the public affairs officer working on the news release. But telling Elena about it had led to her second reaction.

She relived her tour with the military police in Afghanistan. She had seen enough injury and death to last a lifetime, but it was the drugs that penetrated deep into her soul. Young men and women, far from home, unsure whether they would be alive or whole at the end of the day. Nothing to lose. So when they were off duty they ventured into the local village in search of, well, anything. Many found drugs. Afghanistan was one of the world's major producers of heroin, so it was cheap and available on every corner.

On most days, the military police raided known heroin dens. They dragged out American soldiers, nearly comatose from the drugs, and strapped them into the backs of their humvees for the drive back to base.

Military police in war zones didn't take soldiers to jail. They returned them to their commanding officers for punishment. The usual punishment was to just sleep it off. And the next week —or maybe the next day—Des and her colleagues would drag the same soldiers from the same drug houses.

But not always. Sometimes, much too often, the dispatcher would call them to the vicinity of a drug house because a soldier had been found dead along the street. Dead from heroin. Victims of the war as surely as those who died from an IED or a direct attack. And many who didn't die of an overdose came home crippled with addiction, the kind of ongoing, inescapable tragedy that she saw daily as a police officer on the streets of Richmond.

She was startled from her thoughts by a group of joggers running by her car, laughing and talking as they passed. Manfred Kurtz will never enjoy anything like that again, she thought, never. And she vowed that she would track down the vermin who had supplied his drugs and lock him up for as long as the law allowed.

Later that afternoon, Des met with Jessie and Jimmy again in her office. Jessie looked like she had been run through the wringer.

"Thanks for talking with the parents, Jessie," Des said. "I know it is hard."

Jessie looked like she might cry. "They were devastated. Manfred was their only child."

"Tell us what they had to say."

"He was a good boy at heart, they said, but he'd had his share of problems. He wasn't a particularly good student, and he didn't have a lot of friends. And he started drinking and smoking marijuana when he was in high school. They sent him to a special school for a year, and he seemed to get better. He got more confident, his grades improved, and he started going out more. He went to community college for a year in Lynchburg and then started at VWU. He has an aunt who lives here...." She consulted her notes. "Jennifer Haskins. She and the boy were close, and his parents thought it would be good for him to have a relative nearby."

Des was trying to place the name; she was sure she had heard it recently. But it didn't come, so she went on. "He'd been here for more years than typical. Did they say why? And why he still lived in a dorm?"

Jessie nodded, "Yes, we talked about that. They said he didn't really have an idea what he wanted to study, so he tried several majors. He also took a minimum of classes, so he could do better in each one. I looked at his records here, and that checks out. He was all over the place—business first, then communications, art and now botany."

"What about living in the dorm?"

"His parents said he liked meeting new people all the time, so he liked the dorm. And he didn't have to think about cooking meals or cleaning."

Des filled them in on what Howie Anderson had said. It all fit together, no discrepancies that raised a red flag. Manfred Kurtz liked having a pre-made social arrangement, one in which he could be the older, wiser person who younger students came to for help, legal or not.

"Does the university allow that?" Jimmy asked. "Staying around this long as a student, and living in the dorms with younger kids for that long?"

Des shrugged. "It looks like it. I've not run up against that before. Talk to someone in housing and admissions, okay, Jessie?"

"Sure. They came back to campus with us, you know, his parents, for the identification. I'm meeting them at the mortuary in a few minutes."

"Thank you for handling this, Jessie."

"That's okay, boss. They also wanted to know when they could bring him home. I said I'd let them know, but it would be a couple more days, at least."

"That's right. I haven't heard about the autopsy yet, so I'm figuring on Monday at the earliest. The same for laptop and cellphone, right, Jimmy?"

"Yes, boss. I checked with the tech guys just before I came in here. They are working on it, but aren't fully staffed over the weekends. They did tell me a call came in on his cellphone while it was charging. They didn't answer, but the phone showed the call was from someone named Bet, and they got the number."

"Cripes, Jimmy," Des snapped, "why didn't you tell me that when you came in? She's the girlfriend."

Jimmy looked hurt. "I was going to, right after Jessie finished with the parents' story. I thought we needed to hear that first. Sorry."

Des was sorry, too. "I didn't mean to jump on you, Jimmy. This death has me up-tight. It's the first one this fall, but you know it won't be the last. Sorry, kiddo. Give me the number, so Jessie and I can go talk to her."

24

Jessie had cross-referenced the name Bettina and the cell-phone number in the university's student database and learned that she lived in an apartment complex adjacent to campus.

Des and Jessie were greeted by loud barking when they knocked on her door. A young woman opened the door, pushing a large black dog into the background. "What?" she asked.

The police officers showed their identification. "We're looking for Bettina Pidgeon."

"That's me," she said, and opened the door wider. "Do you want to come in?"

"Yes," Des said, "if that's okay with you. And him." She pointed to the dog.

"He's all right. Just gets excited when someone comes by." Bet moved aside, holding the dog by the collar. "He's friendly. Too friendly."

It was a student's apartment, to be sure. Minimum furniture, all of the charity store brand. Lots of books and the usual electronic devices, but no television. Des suspected all entertainment came through a laptop or cellphone. The walls were decorated with travel posters from Europe, a few concert announcements, and several Olympic posters featuring weightlifters and gymnasts. Bet was a petite girl, with no evidence that fat had ever dared to seek a home on her body. Des guessed that she had probably been a gymnast as a girl, or maybe studied ballet.

"We can sit here." There was no couch, so Bet pointed to a small table with three mismatched chairs by the front window. She cleared away the books and papers that covered the table and two of the chairs.

"Thank you," Des said. "We believe that Manfred Kurtz is your boyfriend. Is that right?"

Bet nodded. "Yeah, that's right. Why?"

"I have some bad news for you, Bettina." She paused to give Bet a moment to process that idea before going on to the essential detail. "Manfred is dead."

Tears welled up in her eyes. "Dead? How?"

"We aren't completely sure yet, but it appears to be a drug overdose."

"Oh god," Bet cried out. "I told him not to."

"What do you mean? Not to do what?"

Bet started to speak, but caught herself. "I had nothing to do with that, I swear."

Des gave her a non-committal smile. "You aren't in trouble, Bet, so don't worry. We're just trying to find out what happened. So tell us what was going on."

"He came here last week…"

Jessie broke in. "When was that, what day?"

Bet stopped for a moment to think. "It was Thursday evening. I'd just gotten off work, and when I got back, Man was here."

"What time?"

"Uh, about six or so. I work at the coffee shop down the street. I get off at 5:30. I got my stuff together and walked home."

"Okay," Des said, "then what happened?"

"Man was here—he has a key—and he was all excited. He said he had just made a bunch of money, said the Ant-man had done him good this time. He took a big wad of cash out of his pocket. It looked like a lot of money."

"The Ant-man?" Des asked. "Who is that?"

Bet shook her head. "I don't know. Man talked about him every once in a while."

"So you have no idea who it is, no clue at all?"

"No, I don't. He never said his real name. Man was like that-- he had nicknames for everyone. Anyway, we didn't talk about things like that."

Des returned to the main topic. "So, he was here on Thursday when you got home. What then?"

"He wanted to take me out to dinner. Not just fast food, but a real restaurant. There's an Italian place next to the coffee shop, so we walked back there. He even ordered a bottle of wine, he was so excited about the money. We came back here, and that's when things got bad."

"How, Bet?"

"You sure I'm not going to get in trouble? I didn't have any-thing to do with this, I swear."

Des tried to reassure her. "If you didn't do anything wrong, you'll be fine. We're just trying to figure out what happened."

Bet relaxed a little. "He took out this vial of white powder. I'm pretty sure it was, you know…" She hesitated, and Des nodded to encourage her. "I'm pretty sure it was cocaine. It scared me, even for it to be in the apartment. He asked me if I wanted to do it with him. said it would be great for, you know...."

"For sex." Des completed her sentence.

"Yeah, that's what he meant."

"Did you share it with him?"

Bet shook her head. "No, no, of course not. I've never used drugs. And I never saw Man use them either. I know he smoked pot, because I could smell it in his room when I was there, but I never let him do it when he was with me. And never here and never anything like this. No, I told him I wouldn't do that and that he should leave. He got mad and stormed out."

"Had you seen him since then?" Jessie asked.

"No, that was the last time. I didn't have to work yesterday or today, so I went home to see my family. I live in Fairfax, up by DC. I just got back this afternoon. I called him a little while ago, but he didn't answer." She looked first at Jessie, then at Des. "Oh, god, he was already dead, wasn't he?"

Des nodded. "Yes, we think that he probably died soon after he left here on Thursday. He was found dead in his dorm room."

Bet started to cry again, as the reality of the death began to set in.

"Just a couple more questions, Bet, if you can manage it." She looked up and nodded just enough to be seen. "Have you and Manfred been going together long?"

"We met at the end of the school year, last spring. We went out a couple of times, but then I went home for the summer. We texted and stuff over the summer, and when we got back here, we got more serious. He's a lot of fun, and we do all sorts of things together." She gulped. "We did all sorts of things."

"Is there anything else you can tell us that might help us figure out what happened to Manfred?"

Bet shook her head, but then stopped. "There was one thing."

"Please tell us," Des encouraged.

"When I got home and saw Man here, I hugged him, and he pulled away and winced. I asked him what was wrong, and he said that he was sore. I asked why and he just shrugged it off, said he had started working out and his muscles were sore."

"That's it, just sore muscles?"

"Yeah, but it was sort of strange, because Man never exercised. But I dropped it because he didn't want to make a big deal out of it."

"Okay, listen. Is there someone you can call to stay with you tonight? This is going to sink in soon, and you shouldn't be alone. Do you have a roommate?"

Bet shook her head. "No, I live alone. But I'll call my cousin, she's a student here, too. We drove home and back together. I can stay with her."

"That's good," Jessie said. "Will you text me her name and contact information?" After a bit of tapping, the contact for Bet's cousin showed up on Jessie's phone. "Thanks."

"So, you're going to be okay?" Des said. Bet nodded, so Des went on. "Manfred's death will be announced tomorrow, so everyone is going to know about it. You'll be getting lots of questions from people who knew that you and he were linked. It will be a little nuts, I'm sure. So, I'm going to have a counselor call you in the morning to check on you. And here's my card, with my personal number on it. If you need me, for anything, just call. I'll be right over. Okay, kiddo, you'll call me, right?" Bet nodded again, but she looked less than certain about what was about to happen to her.

They got up to leave, and Jessie turned back and asked, "Last question. Did Manfred tell you how he got all that money?"

"Uh-huh."

"How?"

"He sold a painting."

25

Sunday

Judith Heinz was waiting for Elena when she walked into the student commons. "Hello, Judith, sorry to be a little late. The campus ecumenical service was a bit disorganized this morning, with students just getting back from break, and several wanted to tell me about their service trip to Guatemala."

"Not to worry," Judith said. "I actually got here early. I love to watch the students come and go. It's nice to know that some take the opportunity to spend their break helping others." She looked around at the passing students. "They're so wonderful, aren't they?"

"Oh, yes, they are wonderful," Elena granted. "As long as you don't have to grade their papers!"

Judith chuckled. "Amen to that. I miss teaching, but I sure don't miss all that nonsense. It is nice to get out and see them, though. We can get pretty isolated in the admin buildings. We seem to spend more time worrying about trustees and donors and legislators than we do about students." Judith had been an art instructor for decades before retiring. Now she filled in when some extra help was needed in the provost's office. She and Elena had become acquainted during the Drew Robbins mess, and their friendship had grown through Elena's interest in art.

"Let's get something to drink and then sit out on the patio. It's so nice today." They moved through the line at the coffee counter, Elena paid, and they found a table in the sunshine. The seasons were always mild in Stone Valley, with long springs and autumns. This October was no exception. The weather had been dry, with radiant blue skies and leaves turning gradually in a full array of fall colors.

"The leaves are really amazing this year," Elena said.

"Yes, they are. The provost got the media folks to send a drone up to take pictures of the campus. You should see how beautiful campus looks from the air right now."

Elena grinned. "I'll bet those views kept you busy painting all weekend."

Judith nodded and laughed. "Guilty as charged. And early this morning, too, before coming here." Judith's paintings were mostly abstract, large canvases drenched in rich, primary colors. Just the sort of work that a brilliant fall would inspire. They sat quietly for a few moments, until a pair of students on skateboards rumbled by, nudging them back into the present.

"And thanks so much for helping me with the art exhibition," Elena said. "Although I just realized it is like grading student papers. Sorry."

"Not the same at all, Elena. I'm more like a consultant. Drop in, give my opinions, collect my outrageous fee and take off."

Elena laughed. "But your consulting fee is pretty small. One mediocre cup of coffee."

"I'm happy to do it, excited about it really. So, you wanted to go over some details?"

"Yes, just so we're on the same page. The event is only a few days away now, so it's a good time to talk."

"Great. What do I need to know?"

Elena spent the next several minutes going over the plan. The pairs of students—one from art and one from the environment—would display a trio of artworks in a series. The first and third would be of their own making, but the middle one would be a copy of the Fuertes painting of two herons in flight that Elena was providing. The three paintings had to be a sequence, but that was about the only limit on the students' creativity. The paintings would be displayed around the Scandia Cafe, set up like an art gallery for the evening. All that Judith and the other judges had to do was choose the three winners.

"Let's talk about the judges," Elena said.

"I'm happy that Jennifer and I can do this for you."

"So, I need to talk to you about that. We've added a third judge."

"Oh," Judith said, raising an eyebrow. "Did you decide you needed a tie-breaker?"

"No, nothing like that. He's a friend of Des White's from New York. His name is Remy Tremblay. He's some kind of art expert, works on valuing art for insurance companies and the like. Des met him in regard to the theft of the Fuertes painting, and he's coming down to do some on-site work. He agreed to judge the contest."

"That's great," Judith says. "Add some big-city spice to our little down-home art community."

Elena laughed. "Yeah, Des is pretty high on him."

"As an art expert, or something else?" Judith asked, a sly grin on her face.

"Yet to be seen. Now, tell me some more about how you got Jennifer Haskins to be a judge."

"Jennifer is an old friend. We go way back."

"I have one of her prints at home," Elena said. "Her paintings are so realistic, almost like photographs."

Judith nodded with a sigh. "Yeah, that's really a problem. I think it has held her back as an artist. She works so hard to be representative that she doesn't let her own creativity come through. I think she could have gone much farther if she wasn't such a stickler for accuracy in her details. You know, people can just take photos if they want a copy of what they see."

"Like the drone flying over campus." They both laughed, but Judith's seemed to be tinged with a bit of sorrow, too.

The conversation was on the verge of melancholy, so Elena changed the subject. "So, you've been friends for a long time?"

"Yes. We were actually in school together here as under-graduates. But our lives went in different directions after we left school."

"You stayed here, I know. But Jennifer became a full-time artist?"

"I got busy, being an art instructor here. And I had to take care of my parents, who were getting older. I needed a secure source of income and a regular schedule. And, as you know, I loved teaching students about art. Jennifer has had it a bit easier. She lives out in the country, on a farm of sorts that her parents left her. They died when we were in our twenties, so she didn't have to worry about a place to live, that sort of thing. So she could paint full-time."

"Jennifer is really talented," Judith continued, "and I think she could have been a national figure in contemporary landscape art. When we were students together, she was experimenting with different approaches to representing the landscape, really innovative stuff. But she got into this representational groove and it was successful. I think her success has held her captive."

"Well, she's certainly successful. Her pictures are everywhere. I really like the ones she does of Europe."

"That's an interesting story, too. When your dean, Ralph Vukovic, came to town, about twenty years ago, they met through some art events. They became an item. Very discrete and all, but they started showing up everywhere together. They were both unmarried, so it was fine. She started spending time with him overseas and started painting those European landscapes."

"And are they still 'an item'?"

"As far as I know they are. But I'm not traveling in those circles anymore." Judith chuckled. "Well, really, I never did."

"She sounds fascinating. I'm glad that you were able to convince her to help with the judging. The kids will love getting to meet her."

But Elena wasn't really thinking about the students. Of course, they'd love the attention. She was getting nervous that three artists, two of whom she didn't know, might not play well together. She lived in a world filled with over-inflated faculty egos, and she suspected the art world was just the same. Times ten maybe.

26

Jimmy wondered why Des always seemed to give him these tasks. He didn't like them. He craved action, not sitting behind a desk, doing whatever.

She had called on Saturday evening and tasked him with going through Kurtz's cellphone and computer. Now that it looked like he probably stole the painting, they needed to know a lot more about him, sooner rather than later.

It's all part of the job, she told him, so you better get used to it and get good at it. Just like his father telling him he needed to get good at sanding wood if he wanted to be a carpenter.

His father had been a really good carpenter. Lyle Nesbitt built hand-made furniture from his shop behind the Nesbitt home, on a country lane not far outside Stone Valley. As a boy, Jimmy loved to be in the shop with his dad, lending the extra pair of hands that woodworking often required. Hold this steady, his father would tell him, while I join these pieces together. That a boy, he'd say, and Jimmy would glow with pride.

Until the day a drunk driver had run a stop sign down the country road from their home. At times like these, when he was stuck doing office work, Jimmy's mind often replayed the scene, cycling home from high school and coming upon the wreck, realizing that both his father and the drunk driver were dead. He could still remember the feel of his father's hand as he held it, the skin as hard and rough as an un-sanded board.

He had decided that day to become a cop, although in truth he had been leaning that way all through high school. He didn't like seeing some kids, bullies who didn't care about what others thought, take advantage of the kids who did care, the ones who wouldn't step on someone else to get their way. That's how he got in trouble in school, sticking his nose in other people's business. Arguments, fights, disputes about whose device was who's —those all ended up being part of Jimmy Nesbitt's somewhat dubious record at Stone Valley High School.

The banging of a door woke Jimmy from his thoughts. He punched the space bar of his keyboard to wake the screen up again and frowned at the download of Manfred Kurtz's cellphone. He had already been through Kurtz's social media and laptop and found nothing of interest, just a lot of crap (forgive my language, mom, he whispered to himself) about "The Man" and his exploits. What a jerk, Jimmy thought.

Now it was time to read through his cellphone calls and messages. As he worked backwards from the last day of Kurtz's life, certain patterns started to emerge. Messages went back and forth between him and Bettina Pidgeon regularly, but most were what you'd expect—meet me here, no I can't, why not?, I have to work—that sort of thing. A few other messages were interesting, including strings between Kurtz and his roommate, Howie Anderson, arranging for Howie to pick up or deliver various contraband. Other strings also revealed that Anderson wasn't the only courier for Kurtz. Jimmy picked up three other names who were supplying Kurtz with his stock-in-trade. He made notes about each of them for follow-up once they solved the murder.

When he had exhausted the messages, he went on to the phone records. Thankfully young people these days didn't make many calls; they communicated by text or social media. And, therefore, the few calls during the month before Kurtz's death were all easily accounted for.

Except for calls to and from one number. Kurtz had calls with that number repeatedly during a two-week period leading up to two days before he died. And the calls went both ways—Kurtz originated some, but others were dialed to him. Jimmy dialed the number and received the message he dreaded. "This number is no longer in service." For the hundredth time, he thought, this wasn't the way it worked in the cop shows on television. In those shows, about five minutes before the end of the program, someone unlocked a phone or laptop, punched a few buttons and found a suicide note, a signed threat letter or a confession.

On a hunch, Jimmy went to the evidence room and checked out Kurtz's phone. It was dead, so he found a charger in his bottom drawer and plugged it in. After the charge bar switched from red to green, Jimmy punched in the number, and the contact info popped up. Gotcha, he thought. But he was premature. The contact was listed simply as "AM," nothing else. No name, just initials.

Nonetheless, he'd have news for Des. Kurtz had been talking regularly with someone with the initials A. M.

27

Monday

Des met with Jessie and Jimmy on Monday afternoon to debrief. "So, if what Bet told us is true, it looks like we've solved the art theft. It was Manfred Kurtz who stole the painting."

"But that still leaves lots of questions, boss," Jessie said. "Like who got him to steal it and coached him through the process. It doesn't seem like the kind of thing a college student, even one with a criminal bent, would think of. Somebody had to have put him up to it."

Des agreed. "Right. But at least now we have someplace to start. We at least know some of the questions to ask."

"We also need to find out who he sold it to," Jimmy added.

"So, we've got our agenda for this week, eh?"

Just then, the desk officer knocked on the door, opened it, and handed Jimmy, sitting closest, a sheaf of papers. "It's the result of the autopsy."

Jimmy started reading, more intensely as he went along. Des was getting impatient. "Well, Jimmy, what does it say?"

"Wow. You're not going to believe this."

A note of irritation snuck into Des's voice. "Don't make me guess. What does it say?"

"Kurtz didn't die of an overdose. Well, maybe he did."

"Did he or didn't he?"

"Not a cocaine overdose. There was cocaine in his system, but not enough to kill him. He died of arsenic poisoning."

Des reached out her hand. "Let me see." He passed the papers over the desk to her, and she read quietly for a moment. "My god. He was poisoned, with sodium arsenate. Look that up on the web, Jessie. And he was badly bruised on his torso. Why didn't you two notice that?"

Jimmy held up his hand in protest. "He was fully clothed on the bed. We didn't disturb him. The EMTs had examined him and determined he was dead, and the medical guys took him away. We didn't see any evidence of bruising or cuts or anything, right, Jessie?"

But Jessie wasn't listening. She was reading her phone. "It says here that sodium arsenate is a white powder, odorless and tasteless. It is highly toxic when ingested."

Des rubbed her eyes with her hands. "So, it isn't an accidental drug overdose. Manfred Kurtz was murdered."

She sat quietly for a few moments. Her earlier anger about whoever gave Kurtz drugs was now replaced by a more general, but even more intense, anger over his murder. She leaned forward with a new sense of energy. "Okay, several things we need to do right away." Jessie and Jimmy were now on high alert.

"Jessie, take a photo of Kurtz over to the student who was on the library desk when the painting was stolen. What was her name?"

Jessie answered, "Hannah Maddox."

"Right. See if she identifies him as the person who took the painting. And contact the girlfriend, Bet, and set up a time to see her again. Jimmy, let's get the roommate over here again as well. We need to ask them both a lot more questions now that we know Kurtz was poisoned. Also, find Kurtz's car and get it to the town's forensics team for a complete work-up. While you are doing that, I'll brief President Crutchfield. We may have found the art thief, but that's the least of our problems. Now we have to find a murderer."

28

Howie Anderson arrived at the university's police station for the second time in a week, which amounted to the second time in his life.

He was conflicted. On the one hand, being involved in the death of his roommate was about the most exciting thing that had ever happened to him. Howie wasn't exactly the adventuresome type. He hadn't been a jock in high school, and he quit the boy scouts well before they started doing the riskier projects like backpacking and ropes courses. He knew people thought of him as Dull Normal, and pretty much he had always been okay with that.

But being The Man's roommate had already brought him a bit of notoriety. Kids were always coming to see The Man for one reason or another, and Howie got to play at least a walk-on role in the ensuing dramas of the deals being struck. And now that The Man had died and Howie was the one who discovered the body, he was center stage. Students were coming by to see *him*, pressing him for details, listening to his story. The death had drawn a line through Dull Normal and written Cool Dude next to his picture.

One the other hand, though, being called to the police station —again—stressed him out. They wanted the truth, the whole truth and nothing but the truth. Well, he thought, two out of three on his first visit wasn't bad.

The desk officer at the station led him down a hallway to the same small room he had been in the first time. Or maybe not. The first room had held a table and several chairs, but it had been cluttered. One wall had been piled high with new boxes of printer/copier paper. Other boxes, looking like they also held office supplies, had been scattered in smaller piles, filling the corners of the room. The room he was deposited in this time was empty, except for the center table and its surrounding chairs. He wondered if the first room was for casual talk, and this one for serious talk, the kind of interviews they always had in cop shows.

A few minutes later, Des and Jimmy came in and sat down. Jimmy introduced himself.

"Hello again, Howie," Des said. "Thanks for coming in to talk with us again. Today we're going to record this interview, just so that we have a record that we can refer back to. Is that okay with you?"

Howie wasn't sure. "I don't know. Is this something you can do, I mean, legally? Tape my conversation?"

Des nodded and smiled to ease his tension. "Yes, it is. But, this is still a voluntary interview, and we're not here to charge you with a crime or anything like that. It's not like on television. You can leave whenever you want, okay?"

"Okay, I guess."

"Good. So, we have some bad news about your roommates's death." Howie concentrated on her face. "He didn't die of a drug overdose, Howie, he died from poisoning."

Howie's face froze. "What? He was poisoned? I don't understand. How could he have been poisoned? Wait, are you saying someone deliberately poisoned him?"

"That's right, Howie. He was murdered."

"Oh, my god." A series of emotions passed across Howie's face. Surprise. Excitement. Confusion. Worry. Des could tell he was jumping from thought to thought. Eventually he spoke again. "But how could that happen? We don't have any poisons in our rooms." Then he thought some more. "Well, at least nothing that I know of."

"Do you know things about poisons, Howie?"

"No. Not really." But then he back-tracked. "Well, yes, maybe, a little. I took a botany course last semester on plants and humans. It was called something like plants, the good, the bad, and the ugly. It was one of those classes that satisfy the interdisciplinary requirement. We had a couple of weeks about dangerous plants, you know, poison ivy, that sort of thing. That's actually where I met The Man. He was taking the class, too."

Des continued. "So you know some things about poison, and so did Manfred. Is that something you two talked about?"

"Not much, not really. It was a fun class, and an easy A. But we just covered the basics, not anything in detail. The Man was interested, though, more than me."

"Why was that, do you think?"

Howie looked hesitant to speak, just like last time. But he figured he better start telling the whole truth. "The Man was always talking about growing marijuana plants. He figured that he would go into the pot business when he graduated. I'm pretty sure that's why he was a botany major."

So, Des thought, he hadn't learned his lesson from his earlier reprimand. "Was he growing pot in your rooms?"

Howie shook his head, vigorously. "No, not here. I told him I didn't want anything to do with growing pot. The other stuff was...". He stopped talking then, but it was too late. Des and Jimmy were both staring at him intensely.

"You were about to say that the other stuff was enough for you, am I right?"

Howie actually began to cry. At a signal from Des, Jimmy left the room for a moment. He came back in with a bottle of water and a tissue box. They let Howie sob for a while before they resumed.

"What were you doing with Kurtz?" Des asked. Time to stop calling him The Man.

"Nothing much. I was just a go-between. I'd run errands for him, delivering the things he was supplying to other students. He called me Bag Boy. Like I said before, cribbed tests, fake ids, that sort of thing. Or picking them up sometimes. Not often, but sometimes, when he was busy."

Jimmy was playing the bad cop. "Did you like that, Howie? Having a nickname like that, Bag Boy? Being part of The Man's gang? Huh?"

Howie was trying to stammer out an answer, but Jimmy kept talking. "What about drugs? Were you delivering drugs for him?"

Howie turned white. "No, never. I told you before, I never had anything to do with drugs. And as far as I saw, neither did The Man. Honest."

The good cop took over again. "Listen, Howie, we may have to come back to this errand-running later, but for now we've got a murder to solve. But, for the love of god, quit doing this. You've got your whole life ahead of you, and I hope it hasn't been untracked by trying to be the next big man. Understand?"

"Yes, ma'am," Howie squeaked.

"Now, we want to know everything. Especially if there was anyone who really had it out for Kurtz."

Howie nodded his pale face to show he understood. "There was one guy who he had me do all of the contacts with, so that might be someone that he didn't get along with."

"Who?"

"I only know him as Grinder. He works at the gym, checking IDs, handing out locker keys and towels. That sort of thing."

"Grinder?" Jimmy asked, wondering if anyone actually used names anymore.

"Yeah. That's all anyone ever called him. He is hard to mistake, though. He's huge, has a shaved head, and tattoos all over his arms and neck."

"Grinder is a term for someone who lifts really heavy weights, almost in slow motion," Des explained. Jimmy looked at her with a big question in his eyes. "You learn this stuff as a marine, Jimmy." Then she continued with Howie. "So what did you do with Grinder?"

"Like I said, The Man didn't want to go near the guy. So I went over to the gym often. It was usually for fake ID cards. I'd take the details over and leave them with him. And some money. Then, when he had something for me, I'd pick it up."

"What kind of money are we talking about?" the bad cop asked.

"Fifty per ID."

"Do you have any idea what the problem was between Kurtz and this Grinder?"

"No, Manfred never told me. He just said he was a bad dude, so I should just do the transaction and then get out of there. Grinder hardly even talked to me. About all he ever said was that he liked this arrangement so he didn't have to see that asshole. Those were his words."

"Anyone else that you can think of who might want to hurt Manfred?" Des asked. "What about the Ant-Man? What about him?"

Howie looked surprised that they knew about the Ant-Man. But he just shook his head. "No, I don't think so. Whenever he talked about the Ant-Man, it was in a good way. Sort of like a guardian angel. I really can't think of anyone else specifically. There were sometimes students who came in, complaining that what The Man supplied wasn't worth it. You know, the professor changed the test or the key that was supposed to get him and his girlfriend into the greenhouse didn't work. But none of that ever got serious. Too bad, he would tell them, and go tell your advisor that you got cheated cheating, try that. And then they'd leave."

Des switched off the recording device. "Okay, Howie, we're done. But let me tell you two things, and I mean both of them. First, if you think of anything else, you call us right away. And, second, if you get in trouble for anything else on this campus, even jay-walking, this recording is coming right out of storage and going to the student disciplinary board. Got it?"

He nodded and slunk out the door.

Jimmy said, "Well, I think we'll never see that guy darken our door again. You scared him pretty good."

"I feel sorry for him," Des said, "He got involved in something that made him a big shot for once in his life. He couldn't have picked a worse mentor, it seems, than our dead friend, Manfred The Man Kurtz. Now, Jimmy, find out who this Grinder is."

"Got it, boss." And he was out the door, not far behind a thoroughly rattled Howard Ain't-Never-Gonna-Be-The-Man Anderson.

Des and Jessie knocked on Bet's apartment door early Monday evening. It took her a moment to register that the police were back again. "Oh, it's you."

"Yes, it's us again, Bet," Des said. "Can we come in?"

"Yeah, sure, of course." She swung the door wide, once again collaring the dog before it could either bolt out the door or overwhelm the visitors with affection.

They settled into the same chairs as during their first visit, and Des started the conversation. "We have some news about Manfred's death." Bet looked down, as though she didn't want to hear anything more about any of this. "Your boyfriend didn't die of a drug overdose."

Now Bet looked up, her face expressing some interest. "He didn't? Then how did he die?"

"He was poisoned." Des stopped there, to watch how Bet reacted to the news.

She furled her brows and he mouth dropped open. "Poisoned? I don't understand? How could he have been poisoned?"

"We don't know," Des said, "but this changes the job we have to do. Before, this was an accidental death, and we were just filling in some details for a report. Now it is a murder investigation."

Bet sat up, fear cloaking her face. "You…, you don't think I had anything to do with it, do you? I didn't!"

"We don't know, Bet. That's what we have to find out. But we do believe you were the last person to see him alive, so that is very relevant."

"The last person? But he was fine when he left here. Mad, but nothing else. He wasn't acting sick or anything."

"Did you give him a drink or feed him?"

Bet shook her head. "No, nothing. We ate at the Italian restaurant, like I told you before. I was just going to the fridge to get a couple of beers when he asked me to take the coke with him. I stopped before I got there, and told him no and then we argued and he left. Just like I told you."

"Okay, let's change the subject. Did Manfred have any enemies? Someone who'd like to harm him?"

"No," Bet said, "no. He was just a regular guy, just a college student."

"Well, we've heard some different things about him."

"Like what?" Bet asked, but her composure was starting to slip.

"Like he sold fake IDs, and keys to tests and other things that he shouldn't have been selling. You know about that, don't you?"

She looked defeated and nodded her head. "Yeah," she said softly. "I did." Des and Jessie sat quietly, waiting for her to fill the silence. Eventually, she did. They always do, Jessie thought, they aren't smarter than the boss. "He'd brag to me about how much money he made doing this or that. It scared me."

"Why were you scared? Did he ask you to help him?"

"No," Bet said, "he never asked me to help. He had his Bag Boy to do his errands and that sort of thing. But he'd tell me how he had to make deals with people, people that didn't sound good to me."

"Okay, then, back to the original question. Might one of those bad people want to hurt him? Had he cheated them?"

Bet began to cry. "I don't know. Maybe. I wish I'd never gotten mixed up with him."

Des wasn't going to let her off because of a few tears "Too bad, but you did. And now he's dead. And you need to help us find who did it. So, keep talking."

"I don't know, I told you. I didn't know who he dealt with."

Des motioned to the posters showing weight lifters and gymnasts. "Interesting posters. Are you into that stuff, weight lifting and gymnastics?"

Bet wiped her eyes and nodded her head. "Yeah, I guess. I took gymnastics growing up, since before I can remember. My brothers lifted, so I was around them and their friends a lot. My whole family has always been gym rats."

Jessie broke in. "Is that how you got to know Grinder?"

Now Bet began to shake, and looked at Jessie and then at Des. "Grinder? How do you know about him?"

"It's our job to know things, Bet. So tell us about Grinder."

She was losing control. "Oh, god, yes, Grinder might have wanted to hurt him. Oh, god."

"Why?"

"I used to go with him. Last year. He's not a good guy."

"What do you mean? Did Grinder hurt you?"

She shook her head. "No, he never hit me or anything. But he'd get angry sometimes and yell. He scared me. That's why I broke up with him."

"And how does that involve Manfred?"

"Grinder saw us at a party one time, right after the semester started. Grinder and Man were talking, like they knew each other. Man saw me and waved me over. I didn't want to go talk to them, but Man came over and grabbed me, put his arm around me and dragged me back to Grinder. I could see Grinder getting upset. Man said I was his girlfriend, and Grinder went nuts. He started shoving Man and pushed him into a wall. A couple of other guys had to hold him back before he could start hitting Man. They told us to leave, and we did. As we were going out the door, Grinder yelled that if he ever saw him again, he'd kill him."

30

Tuesday

Des's cellphone rang as she was drying her hair the next morning. "Jimmy, what's up?"

"You're not going to believe it, Des."

"Believe what? What's happened?"

"Another painting has been stolen."

"You mean at the library? Where the other one was taken?"

"Right. Same place."

"My god. Are you there now?"

"Yeah."

"I'll be right there. Call Jessie."

"Right, boss."

Des was out the door in a matter of minutes and at the BSB library a few minutes later. It was just after seven.

She met Jimmy at the door to the library. "Jesus, what is happening to this place?" Jimmy looked like he was trying to think up an answer, and she stopped him with a pair of raised hands. "Just fill me in."

"This time isn't like the last one. Nothing subtle here. It looks like the thief must have hidden in the library when it closed last night. Then he went into the room with the paintings, picked one, cut it out of the frame—the frame is still there—then pushed open the door from the inside and took off."

"That's it? That simple?"

"That's how it looks."

"Who reported it?"

"The library supervisor, same one as last time." He looked at his notes. "Yvonne Michaels."

Jessie arrived, and they filled her in. "Yvonne Michaels, again? She's going to be a mess."

Des looked like she couldn't care less how Yvonne Michaels felt. "Jimmy, get the forensics team in here, pronto. Then look around outside and see if you can find anything. Jessie, come with me."

They walked into the library and found Yvonne. She looked like she might faint at any second. "I don't know what to do. What is going on? I can't handle this. I'm going to get fired."

Des took a few deep breaths to calm herself down, and then offered the same advice to the frantic librarian. "Just breathe, Yvonne. Breathe. It'll be fine. Nothing is going to happen to you. This isn't your fault." Des hoped she was correct, that Yvonne wasn't implicated.

"That's what you say, but it's my responsibility. How could this happen? Twice?"

"Well, that's my job," Des assured her, "and we'll figure it out. Now, tell me what happened."

Yvonne began to get the story out. Today was her day to be on duty at the biological sciences library, and she had arrived to open up a few minutes before seven, the usual opening time. She noticed that the outside door to the building was slightly ajar, but that didn't really bother her because some faculty members got in early. Probably the door was just sticking a little. Then she saw that the glass doors to the Fuertes Room were open, which they shouldn't have been. She went into the room and saw the empty space on the wall and the frame on the conference table. Then she called the police.

Des let her go back to her office, and she and Jessie went into the Fuertes Room. The empty space was about halfway down one long wall, a pair of empty brackets showing where the painting would have been. A frame was on the conference table. The ragged edge around the inside of the frame outlined where the thief had cut out the painting.

"I wonder what the painting was," Jessie said.

Des pulled out her phone, dialed a number and waited while it rang. "Hey, Elena. Are you in your office?" Apparently Elena was one of the early-bird faculty members. "Can you come down to the library, the room with the art exhibit?" Pause. "Yeah, right now. It's important."

A few minutes later, Elena Bertoni walked into the room. "Okay, I'm here, Des. But I've got class to prepare for. What's going on?"

"Another painting has been stolen. So, don't touch anything."

"You're kidding, right?"

"No. Dead serious."

"How could that happen? Again? Here, again?"

Des frowned. "Well, it did. Can you tell us what painting it was?" She pointed to the blank space on the wall. "You know what all these things are, don't you?"

Elena concentrated for a moment, trying to fix the arrangement of the artworks in her mind. "Yes, I do. It was a painting of a bald eagle, for savings bonds. From World War I."

"Valuable, right?"

Elena nodded. "Yes, pretty valuable, I guess. Probably more valuable than the Fuertes painting. It was the original artwork for a big series of posters." Then she noticed the frame. "Oh, my god, he cut it out of the frame!"

"Yeah, looks that way. That ruins it, doesn't it?"

"Jeez, I don't know. Maybe. But this painting had a large plain border. That's the way the paintings for the posters were made, so that other things could be printed around the edges. You know, slogans and such."

Des put gloves on and picked up the frame. All around the ragged edge where the canvas had been was just white paint, with no other colors or patterns. "Huh, you're right. There's nothing showing along the edges. So, maybe the thief had scoped out that this would be a good one to steal, easy to cut out of the frame without ruining it."

"I think you're right, Des," Elena said. "All of the other items in the room are designed as complete compositions, and parts of the art extend right up to the framed edge. But this one, like I said, was intended to become a poster with other information printed on it, like where to buy the bonds, how much they cost. That sort of thing."

Jessie looked up at the new camera installed on the ceiling inside the door. "Is that thing working yet?"

Elena and Des followed her gaze. "Let's go see. Maybe we got a break."

They went back across the hall to the library office and found Yvonne. "Is the video security camera working yet, Yvonne?" Des asked.

Yvonne looked up, as though they had roused her from a trance. "I think so. Let me call Will to be sure." She pressed a speed-dial number on her phone and waited. Eventually, she hung up. "He's not answering. I guess he's not in yet. It's still a little early."

Elena leaned over to Jessie. "Who's she talking about?"

"Will Morales, the branch library's IT guy."

"Okay, Yvonne, don't worry about it," Des continued. "We'll check the master back at our office. But the library needs to be closed today, at least until our forensic crew gets done with it."

"But the students and faculty need to use the library," Yvonne objected.

"Too bad. For the time being, it's a crime scene and that takes priority. Jessie, you stay here to monitor things and explain if anyone gets huffy. Elena, can you come with me for a while? When's your class?"

"At eleven." She checked her watch. "Sure, I can go with you for a little while, but I do still have some prep work. So, I need to be back by around 9:30."

"I promise to get you back in time. Let's go."

At the police station, Des took Elena into a secured section of the building. Two technicians were inside, each behind a bank of computer screens. They both looked up as Des led Elena into the room. "Good morning, Chief."

"Good morning, Sam. Good morning, Kate."

"Morning, Des. What brings you into the catacombs?"

Des briefly explained what had happened at the library and introduced Elena. "So, can you get us into the library camera and recording?"

"Absolutely," Kate said. "Give me a minute to find it." She clicked through a series of menus and screens, working her way down the access tree, department by department, building by building, room by room. "Here it is, Des."

The camera had been mounted on the front wall of the Fuertes Room, just above the entry door. It pointed to the back wall, but the camera's fish eye lens covered the entire room, except the corners just adjacent to the door.

"Nice work, Kate," Des said. "We need to see last night, from about... Elena, when does the library close at night?"

"On weeknights, at ten, I think."

"Okay, Kate, get us to ten last night and then let's fast forward until we see something."

The video was dark, because there were no lights on in the Fuertes Room. "Can you make it lighter, Kate?"

"A little, but not a lot." She fiddled with the controls and the room became lighter gray. "That's as good as we can do."

They watched as the clock wound forward until a figure appeared. "Stop, Kate," Des shouted. "Wind it back. That's got to be him."

Kate wound the tape back to when the figure first appeared. Then she pressed play. The figure walked into the room with his back to the camera. He moved quickly to the wall and took down the painting. He backed up to the end of the conference table and put the painting down. He pulled a box-cutter out of a pocket and cut around the inside of the frame until the painting was loose. He struggled to make the cut at several points, especially in the corners of the frame. He rolled up the canvas, closed the knife, put it back in his pocket and backed out of the room. The time stamp on the video showed 12:15 AM.

"Well, we certainly know when and how it was done," Des said. "Good work, kiddo."

"Can you identify the thief?" Elena asked.

Des shook her head. "Not a chance. He, or she, knew what to do. All black clothes, including a long-sleeved, high-necked shirt. A plain black ski cap with no hair showing. Black gloves. And he never showed us his face, or her face."

"Let's look at it again," Kate said. "I want to watch him cut the painting out again."

They rolled the tape back and re-played the part when the thief was struggling to cut the canvas, this time in slow motion. In one corner, the thief had to cut through the canvas several times. After one pass, he drew his hand back quickly and paused. "I think he cut himself, right then," Kate said.

They rewound the tape and watched again. "Jeez, I think you're right," Des said. "Maybe we really did get lucky. Maybe we have some blood on the frame."

"So, you can identify him from his DNA?" Elena asked.

Des laughed. "Only if we catch him, or her. It's not like on television. We don't have profiles of everyone's DNA. But if we suspect someone, then we can get a sample and try to match their DNA with the blood on the frame. If there is blood on the frame. Kate, please make a clip of this tape, the whole night, and put it in a separate file and send it to me."

"You got it, boss. Be on your computer in a few minutes."

Des and Elena walked back to Des' office.

"What's going on, Des? This is incredible. Not only does some guy steal one painting, but now he's got the nerve to do it again. This is crazy."

"It's worse than that," Des said. "There are two thieves, not one."

"What? You mean this isn't the same person who took the Fuertes painting? How do you know that"

Des filled her in that the dead student, Manfred Kurtz, was the first thief. "Besides the way the two robberies were done was completely different. The first one was carefully planned. Kurtz had to have had some help, or, more likely, someone who told him exactly what to do, when and how. This time, I think it was just someone who realized there was valuable art in the room and decided he could make some money stealing a painting, too. This time wasn't carefully planned or clever, like the last time."

Elena shrugged. "You're the detective, Des, not me. But obviously, the thief knew enough to conceal his identity from the camera. And that the camera was there."

"That's true, for sure. So, once again, we're looking for someone who knows enough about the university, and the library, to pull this off."

"And about art, too, Des. Someone who knew which painting to pick."

Des managed a smile. "That's right, Elena. So, tell me, where were you last night about midnight?"

31

Jimmy knocked on the door to Des's office. She looked up and saw the eager puppy look on his face. "What have you got for me, kiddo?"

"The guys are at the library going over the room. They're not finding anything of interest."

"What about the picture frame?"

"That's the good news, boss. There was a blood smear in one corner. The thief must have cut through his glove and nicked his finger."

"Great. Anything else?"

"No. Well, yeah, all kinds of old fingerprints, but nothing they think is new or would be connected with last night."

Des nodded. "That's what I figured. But if we can get a lead, the blood will help us."

"But that's not why I'm here. I need to tell you about that guy Grinder."

He had Des's attention, and she expected this was the reason for his tail wagging. "Oh? You've learned something?"

Jimmy nodded and grinned. "A lot. He's got quite a history."

"Don't keep me waiting, Jimmy."

"Okay. First off, his name is Bernard Havel. He's been working at the university for about ten years."

"Ten years? Handing out towels?"

"Yeah, seems so. Not much of a job, but apparently it suits him. He's a gym rat. Works out all the time, especially lifting weights."

"Right," Des said. "As we discussed, that's why they call him Grinder."

"Right. But he was a student here before he started working. He went to school for a couple of years, but then he dropped out."

"For a promising career as a cabana boy, eh?"

Jimmy frowned. "As a what? No, he just hands out towels at the gym."

Des laughed. "Never mind. Keep going. Anything else?"

"Oh, yeah. When he came as a student, he was a nationally ranked weight-lifter. He was recruited to be on the team here. There're lots of stories about him in the archives of the student newspaper. He was a big deal."

"We have a weight-lifting team? You've got to be kidding."

Jimmy backed off. "Not a team, exactly. A club."

The university had all sorts of competitive clubs, athletic and academic, and everything in between. Des remembered that Ted Graham, the head of the Department of Renewable Resources, was the advisor to the bass-fishing team. That's what's great about a university, Ted had told her. All interests are welcome.

Jimmy continued. "Havel was supposed to be the next star of the club."

"But I take it that it didn't turn out. What happened?"

"Steroids. He kept failing his drug tests and getting disqualified from competitions. Eventually, he got kicked out of the club."

"And," Des said, "I'll bet that did in his school work as well." One of Des's brothers had been a highly-recruited lineman out of high school and got a full scholarship to play at a regional university. But he got a pair of concussions in fall practice and couldn't play any longer. Without the opportunity to play football, he flunked out of school in one year. Fortunately, after a few years working, he went back, got a finance degree and was now a vice-president at a Richmond-based bank.

"You're right. He managed to squeak by for two years, but then he dropped out. Apparently the athletic folks felt bad for him, though, and gave him the job at the gym. He's been working there ever since."

Des leaned back in her chair. "And that job gives him the perfect position to be making shady deals on the side. Hundreds of people use the gym every day, and many of them are regulars. He'd get to know a lot of them. They pass their IDs to him, maybe with a little money, and he gives them a towel, maybe with a little something extra wrapped inside. Jeez, it's a perfect set-up."

"But there's more."

"More? Keep going, Jimmy."

"He's got history with the cops."

"For what?"

"Mostly minor stuff. Bar fights, drunk and disorderly, that sort of thing. A couple of possessions of stolen property. Maybe spend a night in a cell to sober up, but never anything major. And nothing he was ever charged and convicted of."

"What about drugs?"

"I talked to Frank Marin about him, and he referred me to someone in their street drug team. She said they had Havel on their watch list, and had picked him up a few times for being around when drugs were involved, but nothing ever stuck. Apparently he hangs out at Daddy's." Daddy's was a notorious bar. The only reason to go there was to get into trouble. "She also said that they're pretty sure he busts heads when someone needs a message delivered."

"Good work, Jimmy. Let's go see our buddy Grinder. Normally I wouldn't think that a guy like him would use poison, but mixing it with some cocaine, that's another story. We might just have our first murder suspect."

They got to the gym just as the lunch hour began, and the front desk was busy, especially with staff getting in a workout instead of eating. The big guy in the cage looked suspiciously at the two police officers heading toward him.

Des looked him in the eye. "We're looking for Bernard Havel."

"Never heard of him."

"That's not a good way to start, Bernard. We need to talk to you." They showed their police identification.

"I'm busy. It's lunchtime."

Des saw that there was another person behind the desk with him. "Well, your colleague is going to have to handle the rush today. We'll meet you outside at one of the tables in the picnic area. In two minutes."

They waited for five minutes before he came sauntering out, prancing in a typical body-builder gait, legs splayed out because his thighs were so thick. So was his neck, well, all of him really. He walked up to the table, and Des could tell he was fully flexed to look intimidating. "Whaddya want?" he croaked.

Des looked him steadily in the eye again. "We want you to sit down. Do it."

He did, but with all the attitude he could muster. "This is harassment."

"Just stop," Des said. "None of that is going to work with us. And, yeah, it is harassment. Our job is to harass criminals."

"I'm not a criminal. I haven't done anything wrong."

"We know all about you, Bernard. So, cut the crap."

"Whaddya mean?"

"Let's start with your fake ID business. How's that going these days?"

"I don't know what you're talking about."

"Fine, Bernard. We'll get to that in a day or two. We have a few officers taking statements from the students who you sold fake IDs to through Manfred Kurtz and Howie Anderson. And then they'll get to the ones you sold directly."

"It's not illegal to sell those old IDs."

Des shook her head. "We're not going to argue with you, Bernard." She could tell it irritated him to be called by his real name, and she enjoyed seeing his discomfort rise. It meant they were scoring. "Right now, we're here to talk about Manfred Kurtz. You know he's dead, right?"

"Never heard of him."

Des actually laughed. "None of that's going to work, Bernard. So, we'll just go on. We think you killed him. How's that?"

"What? I didn't kill anybody. You can't accuse me of that. I've got a lawyer. You're way out of line. Wait. I heard he OD'd."

Jimmy jumped in. "I thought you never heard of him."

Havel looked at Jimmy like he wanted to bust him in half. And like he could. "Well, sure, I knew him. He thought he was a big deal. But he was nothing. Couldn't have happened to a better guy."

"So, you didn't sell him the drugs that killed him?" Des asked.

"No. Hey, I do some, you know, some stuff, but I don't sell drugs. That's the fast track to prison or a knife in your back. The same thing, actually. No, I don't sell drugs."

"Have any idea who did sell him the drugs, Bernard?"

He actually sat quietly for a moment, perhaps even thinking. "Naw, no idea. As far as I know, Kurtz didn't do drugs. Not hard drugs, anyhow. Weed, yeah, but that's hardly a drug anymore, is it? Just beer that you smoke."

"When was the last time you saw Kurtz?" Des asked.

"I don't know. I don't see him anymore. He sends that kid Howie. That's fine with me. I hate Kurtz."

"Because he ended up with your old girlfriend? Still carrying a torch for Bet, eh, Bernard?"

"Jesus, how do you know about that?" He was beginning to wonder if maybe these two weren't as dumb as he thought initially. "Yeah, well, I wasn't too happy about that, was I? She dumped me and then took up with that nobody."

"Last time you saw him, you threatened to kill him."

"What? No, what are you talking about? Kill him? No."

"At the party, when he brought Bet over to you and told you she was his girlfriend. Remember now?" Des asked.

Havel was starting to give up. "Well, okay, yeah I guess maybe I said that. But it was just something you say, you know, when you're mad and maybe a little drunk."

"Funny," Des said. "I don't ever tell people I'm going to kill them. How about you, Jimmy?"

"Nope. Never."

"But you do, right Bernard?" He just sat there, quietly. "We're going to be back in a day or two to process you for selling ID cards." He was about to object again. "And, just to let you know, ID cards are university property. They don't belong to students. So, when you buy and sell them, you are trading in stolen university property. When we come back, it would be wonderful if you had some information for us."

He looked up now, with a can-I-make-a-deal look in his eyes. "What kind of information?"

Des leveled her eyes at him for the last time. "Where Kurtz got the drugs. Who's buying stolen paintings. That'd be a good start. Don't leave town, Bernard. You can go back to work now."

He slunk back inside the gym, no swagger this time.

32

Wednesday

Des was waiting at the airport when Remy walked out through security. She wanted to run to meet him, but took only a few controlled steps toward him. He picked up his pace once he saw her. They hugged, and Remy lightly kissed her on the cheek. Friends, Des thought, just friends.

"How was the flight?"

"Fine. A bit bumpy just before landing."

"Welcome to western Virginia. There's always some excitement from the air flowing down the mountains into the valley. You'll get used to it." I hope you get used to it, she thought.

"I'm starving," Remy said, as they reached Des's car and loaded his bags into the trunk.

"No problem," Des said, giggling. "I know a place, about twenty minutes away."

Remy grimaced. "I guess I can make it."

Des drove the back way back to Stone Valley, so Remy could enjoy the countryside up close and at slower speed than the interstate. "Wow," he said, "the trees are beautiful." Then he looked over to her. "Actually, everything here is beautiful."

Des didn't respond outwardly but inside her heart was beating as if she were running a 5K. It took all her discipline to focus on the drive. "Yeah," she managed to squeak out, "this is god's country."

She parked at the Scandia Cafe. As they sat down on the patio, Hans came out to greet them. "Hello, Des," he said. "Want your usual?"

A wide grin spread across Remy's face. "Trying to one-up me, are you, Des?"

"You know New York, I know Stone Valley. Same difference, right?"

Hans looked confused. "Want to let me in on the joke?" he asked.

"Hans, this is my friend from New York, Remy Tremblay. Remy, please meet Hans Kjer, owner of the cafe."

The men shook hands, and a light went on in Hans's eyes. "Oh, yeah, you're the art expert who's come to judge Elena's show tonight."

"Guilty as charged." He glanced at Des. "That's the right way to confess to the police chief, right?"

The three chatted for a few more minutes, and then Hans went off to bring two of Des's "usuals."

While they waited for their food, Remy said, "Now that I'm here, I can understand why you chose to live in Stone Valley. We could actually be sitting in a Fuertes painting. It's pretty much like the middle of paradise."

"You've been here about an hour, Remy. Maybe you ought to reserve your judgment until you've seen a bit more."

"You're right, of course. I'll keep an open mind." No I won't, he thought to himself, as he studied the woman across the table and realized that this case was pretty well closed.

A waitress interrupted his thoughts with two plates of Danish sausages, sliced potatoes covered in hot vinegar gravy and sides of red cabbage cooked in raspberry jam.

"It's not a Polish sausage from Joe's cart in Central Park," Des said, "but it will have to do. Dig in."

Remy caught the grin that Des was trying to hide. "Is this really your usual, Des?"

"No," she admitted and laughed. "I called Hans before you landed and set it up."

"You're a clever thing, Desdemona White," he said, and then devoted himself to a meal fit for a king.

33

The evening for the art exhibition had arrived, and Elena was as nervous as she could remember. It's just a student activity, she kept telling herself, stop worrying. But the reality that the stolen Fuertes painting was the evening's centerpiece plagued her like an unwelcome guest at a dinner party. The painting might have only been a pair of great blue herons, but it was also the proverbial elephant in the room.

And not just one elephant, but ten of them. No matter where you looked, those birds were flying into her anxiety.

Hans had transformed the cafe for the evening. The normal tables in the dining room were gone, replaced by a few stand-up tables at the center. Easels for the art exhibit were distributed around the periphery of the room, in groups of three for each of the ten student projects. The center easel of each trio held a copy of the Fuertes painting of the flying great blue herons.

"What do you think, my dear?" Hans asked Elena as he slipped his arms around her waist from behind.

Elena leaned into his hug as she looked around. "It's perfect, Hans, just perfect. Thank you so much." She turned and kissed him, with enthusiasm, a welcome surprise. She wasn't much for public displays of affection, and Hans had learned to tiptoe around his opposite need. But, then, the public wasn't there yet, just them and Hans' staff. He prolonged the hug until Elena tapped him on his arms and pushed away. "Plenty of time for that later, mister. I've got work to do."

Her students began arriving, hauling in their masterpieces. Elena got each pair to their assigned locations, while trying hard not to peak at what they had created. That would come later, and she wanted to have her first impression when everything had been set up. The room was now a flurry of activity, with twenty students absorbed in their tasks.

Hans showed up at her side again. "It looks like an explosion at a craft store! What a mess!"

"Not a mess," Elena chided. "Pure energy and enthusiasm. Not an ounce of inhibition or second-guessing. This is why I teach, Hans. Look at the fun they are having."

"Making shambles of my dining room!" But he was beaming as he said it. If it made Elena happy, then it made him happy. He drifted off again, chasing after a worker who was leaning against the wall, tapping a message into his cellphone.

She called the students to attention as the clock was approaching seven. "Listen up, people. The guests will start arriving soon. You need to be at your stations then, so finish up now and get yourselves put together. Remember, you have to explain your project to them, from both an environmental and artistic perspective. I want both of you to talk, not just one. And I'll be watching, so act...well, never mind! Just have fun."

Guests began to arrive and the room's energy switched to an even higher plane. Hans's staff began offering trays of little treats and soft drinks. Elena could tell they had to explain the lack of wine and beer to the crowd, but she was glad that she had maintained her—and the university's—standard: students present, alcohol absent. The room was rapidly filling, and Elena was busy greeting special arrivals—President Crutchfield, Dean Vukovic, and Michele Richards among them.

Judith Heinz caught Elena's eye just after she arrived. When Elena walked over, Judith frowned. "What's wrong, Judith?"

"I'm sorry, Elena. My friend, Jennifer, who was supposed to be a judge tonight. She called me to say that she couldn't come."

Elena frowned now, too. "I hope there's nothing wrong."

"I don't know. She said she just couldn't bear to be around young people tonight. I don't know what's wrong."

"Well, we can work around that. Thankfully, we have Des's new friend, who has agreed to judge, also. I thought we'd have three judges, but we can do with two. You okay with that?"

Judith relaxed and smiled. "Thanks for understanding, Elena. Yes, of course, I'm still in." She looked around at the chaos of students and art, and rubbed her hands together. "Can't wait!"

"Good. As soon as Des and Remy get here, we can get started."

Not much later, they did arrive. The chatter in the crowd quieted to a murmur as they walked in, the police chief they all recognized with an elegant man no one had ever seen before. In fact, they had never seen Des White accompanied by anyone, man or woman, elegant or not, at a university function.

Nor were they prepared for Des's appearance. She was generally in uniform at university events, but if not, she wore a plain business suit designed to blend into the background rather than to stand out from it. Not tonight. Tonight she wore a tailored gold dress that fell to her ankles in a slight flair. A brilliant green shawl draped across one shoulder.

As the crowd recovered and resumed their conversations, Elena walked to the door to meet them. "My god, Des, how about giving the rest of us a chance? You look beautiful!" In her mind, however, she went much farther. You look radiant, she thought, just shy of bursting out in a love song from My Fair Lady.

"Thank you, Elena. Let me introduce Remy. Remy, this is my good friend, Elena Bertoni."

"I"m delighted to meet you, Elena," he said, taking her hand.

"Forget that, Remy, it's hugs all around tonight." Elena smiled and gave him a warm hug before doing the same to Des. "If we had a society section in the local rag, you two would be on the front page, above the fold." Remy was perfectly dressed as well, in a charcoal gray suit and a light gray silk shirt. He knew how to be the perfect gentleman, Elena thought, dressed to complement rather than compete with the woman he accompanied. Hans walked up, dressed in a blue blazer, white shirt and camel-colored slacks. The two men shared a man-hug and were soon heading towards the kitchen, Hans extolling the virtues of his artisanal bread oven.

"Boys and their toys," Des said.

Elena looked confused. "Those two know each other? What am I missing?"

"Later," Des said, her gaze following the men.

They never got to the kitchen. The one other person in Stone Valley who did know Remy, Michele Richards, stepped into their path. She hugged Remy warmly, a bit too warmly, Des thought, and then shook Hans's hand as Remy introduced him. "I guesss they know each other, too, huh?" Elena asked.

"Yes," Des said. "That's how we got the connection with Remy. He's worked with her on other art projects over the years. She paid for my trip up to New York and for his time to help us on the theft." But alongside her words was the nagging idea that Michele Richards might just have something to do with the art theft, like Jimmy had speculated. Had Michele connected her with Remy with the idea that she could control him and, therefore, her?

Elena read her thoughts. "That's very generous. Too generous?"

They looked on, both noticing how Michele's hand remained tucked into Remy's side. Hans stayed for another minute and then excused himself, heading for the kitchen. Michele continued to talk with Remy. Des and Elena watched as she whispered something into Remy's ear and then took a slip of paper from her clutch and tucked it into the pocket of Remy's suit jacket, accompanied by an intimate tap on the pocket. Des shook her head as if to rid it of unwelcome thoughts. "No, I'm sure not. You know Michele is one of the university's most famous alums and biggest donors."

"Yeah, I know," Elena said, "but tonight she's trespassing on our turf. We need to get over there and dislodge the death grip she has on Remy's arm."

Judith Heinz was passing, and Elena grabbed her by the hand. "Come with me, Judith." They walked to Remy, and Elena interrupted the conversation with Michele. "Excuse me, Ms.

Richards, but I need to introduce our two judges to each other."
Michele stared at Elena for a long moment before relinquishing
the field of battle and walking away.

Des looked on with relief. That, she thought to herself, is the
definition of wing-woman.

Elena stepped on a small riser near the door, and clapped to get the crowd's attention. Gradually the noise settled down and the guests focused on the little stage. Elena switched on the hand mike.

"Thank you all for being here this evening. It is truly my pleasure to welcome you to the Art and Environment Student Natural Triptych Exhibition." A gurgle of laughter spread through the room. "Okay, now let me explain what that is when it's at home!"

"Last year, Virginia Western University began a new initiative called 'Art and the Environment.' It is my privilege to chair the faculty committee that oversees the project. Our goal is to unite two powerful forces in modern society—the fine and performing arts that so enrich our lives, and the ambitious goal of protecting our environment so that our lives, our world, will also be sustainable. As part of that project, I have been teaching a course with students from both the arts and sciences, working together to fuse these two great traditions."

"Tonight we get to share a bit of what our students have experienced by working closely together across disciplines. Around the room are ten projects, each created by a pair of students, one arts major and one science major working as a team."

"Their task was to create a triptych, built around one of the university's treasured art objects. You all know, of course, that that painting—a pair of great blue herons flying across a clear blue sky by Louis Agassiz Fuertes—was recently stolen from campus, a stunning disappointment to us all." Once again, a murmur ran through the crowd, as Elena paused to allow the gravity of the situation to set in and then dissipate.

Then she smiled and raised her arms in front of her, her outstretched palms and fingers swooping back and forth in the university's signature motion. "But in the spirit of the VWU Hawks, we will continue to soar, rising above our loss to new victory." A round of applause broke out in the crowd, composed largely of the university's leaders and alums, and many of them raised their arms and repeated her motions. Elena felt a little cheesy using this blatant boosterism, but she knew her audience.

"Now, let me explain exactly what we've done. A triptych is a three-piece artwork traditionally associated with an altarpiece. But we have adapted the idea for the theme of natural processes. So, each student team was charged with creating a triptych that used Fuertes' painting as the center piece of their own three-part representation of some natural process. So, around the room you see ten sets of easels, one set for each of our ten teams."

"A copy of Fuertes painting is in the center of each grouping, and the students' works are on either side. Together, the three works must depict a process that relates to the environment in some way, left up to the students' imagination and creativity."

"We are fortunate to have two outstanding judges for to-night's exhibition. Not that art is a contest, mind you, but I do have to give these students grades at the end of the semester— you all demand that, remember?" The crowd laughed again. "So they are here to help me out. Let me introduce them. First is Ms. Judith Heinz. You all know Judith, I'm sure, from her decades as an art history instructor at VWU and her continuing work in the provost's office." The crowd clapped politely as their old friend stepped on the little stage.

"Our second judge is Mr. R. V. Tremblay of New York City. Remy, as he insists we call him, is an expert art appraiser who works with major corporations and museums around the world to authenticate and value their acquisitions. We are honored to have you join us this evening, Remy." The crowd clapped more enthusiastically for him as he stepped up, the mystery of his presence now partially explained—but no less intriguing.

Elena went on to acknowledge several university officials, including President Crutchfield and Dean Vukovic, as well as Hans, for donating the venue and refreshments for the evening.

Hans beamed from near the back of the crowd. He was proud of his restaurant and happy to be part of the event. But he was even more proud of the woman with the microphone. Des may have hushed the crowd when she came in, but Hans, as the song goes, only had eyes for Elena.

For good cause. She looked the perfect combination of beauty and competence. Her dark hair and features oozed European sophistication. Combined now with the perfect-little-black-dress and a thick gold chain around her neck, she could have been a movie star or a corporate executive rather than an associate professor of wildlife behavior.

"Now," she finished, "please enjoy what the students have created. And if you have a favorite, don't be shy about telling me. Their grades may depend on it!" The three stepped down, and the event shifted into high gear.

The interest around the students' art projects lasted for well over an hour. Small groups of guests moved from triptych to triptych, listening to the students' descriptions. The decibels in the room made Elena happy—everyone was having fun.

Elena, who hadn't seen the students' work before the evening, was delighted with the imagination and effort that they had poured into their triptychs. After she visited with all ten groups and sensed that the room's energy was beginning to fall, she returned to the riser and again called the crowd to attention.

"Thank you again for coming tonight. Before we begin handing out awards, though, let me say that all of our students tonight are winners. I know you can tell from seeing their work and speaking with them that they have learned so much—and taught us so much, as well. Aren't our students wonderful?" The guests broke out into enthusiastic applause, along with whoops from the students and the less sophisticated art lovers.

"Now, it is time to pin some ribbons on a few of the projects. Let me call our judges, Judith Heinz and Remy Tremblay, up to join me and announce their selections."

The two judges once again stepped up next to Elena. "First, let's announce our white ribbon winner. Judith, please."

Judith took the microphone. "For the white ribbon, we have chosen the exhibit entitled 'Evolution of Flight.' Their exhibit features a three-dimensional model of a pterodactyl on one side of Fuertes's herons and a model of the lunar lander on the other. It asks us to think, 'where will our flights of fact and fancy take us in the future?' Please congratulate our white-ribbon team!" Applause again rippled through the cafe.

Judith handed the microphone to Remy. "For the red ribbon, we have chosen the exhibit entitled 'Feathers or Future?' Rather than a painting or sculpture, the students have developed an art performance. One student is dressed as a Victorian woman, wearing a massive hat festooned with white feathers. Artificial feathers, she assured me. As I'm sure she told every one of you, she represents the massive exploitation of migratory waterfowl for women's fashion at the turn of the 20th Century. The other student is dressed as President Teddy Roosevelt, our most renowned conservation president, who created the nation's first National Wildlife Refuge at Pelican Island, Florida, to protect those birds. We say bully for him, and bully for our red-ribbon team!" The crowd clapped even more enthusiastically this time.

Remy gave the microphone back to Judith for announcing the blue-ribbon winning team. "Before we award the blue ribbon, we want to thank you all again for your support of this wonderful art and environment project, and especially to our leader, Elena Bertoni. Hans, please."

The crowd was clapping politely for Elena as Hans stepped onto the riser with a bouquet of all blue flowers. He kissed her discreetly on the cheek and handed her the flowers. Now the applause launched into genuine appreciation.

"That's our girl," Aaron Schmidt whispered to Ted Graham at the back of the room.

"You bet," Ted replied. "That's our girl." And then he wondered where this effort would go on her promotion report.

Judith took over again. "And now for our blue-ribbon exhibit. There are two homonyms for the word 'triptych.' One, of course, is as Elena described earlier—a three-part art piece normally associated with religious iconography. But there is another, spelled slightly differently, but pronounced the same. The AAA Triptik."

The older guests in the crowd nodded and murmured among themselves. Younger guests were looking around for some hints. Judith laughed and continued. "Let me explain. The Triptik was a spiral-bound route map that the American Automobile Association would send its members on request, detailing how to get from start to finish on a road trip." When the confused looks didn't all go away, Judith tried again. "It's the 1950s version of GPS." Now the whole crowd was with her. "Remy, your turn."

"Most of you know the work of Claes Oldenburg," he said, "the American artist who makes massive sculptures of everyday objects. The most familiar may be the giant eraser in the sculpture garden of the National Museum of Art in Washington, DC. Our blue-ribbon winning team honored Oldenburg's style with a pair of six-foot tall Triptiks entitled 'Where are we going?' One shows the route from 'Eden to Endangered,' and its map shows how human civilization has changed the earth and endangered its creatures through the centuries. The second Triptik is entitled 'Endangered to Everlasting,' and is a homage to the environmental movement and a hopeful anticipation of a sustainable future. Please recognize our blue-ribbon team!"

Heart-felt applause filled the cafe for the winning team. As it began to wane, Elena thanked everyone again and closed the ceremony. The guests began to leave, reluctantly it seemed to a thoroughly delighted Elena. A photographer snapped all the exhibits and student teams and then everyone together—the students, judges and Elena.

Hans released his staff and locked the cafe's door. He brought out a bottle of champagne and five glasses for Judith, Des, Remy, Elena and himself. "It was a triumph," he announced as he raised his glass, "to my Elena!"

After a few sips, Judith excused herself. "I'm exhausted," she said. "You young folks carry on, but I'm off to bed." After another round of hugs, Hans unlocked the door and let Judith escape.

Remy and Des followed quickly after Judith. "I need to get this guy to bed, too," she said, grabbing Remy's arm. Elena smiled at her discretely, but Des gave her a scolding look. "He's staying at the university's hotel, and I've promised him a big tour of campus tomorrow."

"But before we go," Remy said, "I have a favor, Elena."

"Sure. What is it?"

"May I have one of the copies of the Fuertes painting? As a souvenir of the event?"

"Of course," Elena said, "just grab one on the way out."

"And one question. These are photographs of the actual painting, right? Of the original?"

"Yes," Elena said. "I actually took the photo myself a couple of months ago." It seemed like an odd question to Elena, but she was too elated and too exhausted to worry about it.

35

While the art and environment exhibit was winding down at the Scandia Cafe, the night was in full swing at Daddy's Bar. The small frame building stood in the middle of a pot-holed gravel parking lot, outside the city limits of Stone Valley and, hence, outside the jurisdiction of the town police. The county sheriff patrolled this territory, and odds were that his folks would be called in before the night ended.

The crowd was singularly unsavory. The place was called Daddy's not because anyone's father proudly declared his owner-ship, but because this is where shady business was conducted, often to the admonition to "remember who your daddy is." The bar's name changed frequently, but it had been called Daddy's for at least a decade. Not that anyone really cared.

The pool tables were all occupied, large, amply tattooed men wedging themselves into position for their shots between the narrowly spaced tables. The half dozen tables in what might be called the dining area were filled. A few couples were grinding against each other in a rhythm that never varied, regardless of what was playing on the jukebox.

The seats around the bar itself were taken up by regulars. Grinder was in his usual spot, tucked into the corner where he could see in all directions. Had he known who Wild Bill Hickok was, he would have agreed with him: never sit with your back to the door.

The bartender, John, noticed that Grinder was particularly quiet. "What's up, Grind?"

"Ah, nothing. I'm just tired tonight. I ain't staying long." He emptied his beer and signaled for another. "Time for one more, though."

John, as one would expect, was a conduit for the kind of business conducted at Daddy's. "I heard another painting was stolen from the university. You handlin' that one, too?"

Grinder shook his head. "Naw. I've got nothin' to do with that. And I wish I had never seen that first one, either."

"Why not? That was a sweet deal. We both made a wad of cash."

"Yeah, no problem about the money. It was supposed to be easy, you know, make the drop and the whole thing goes away. But it hasn't."

Whaddya mean?"

"The kid that I bought it from, that asshole Kurtz, he's the kid that OD'd at the university. Died about a week ago."

John now gave Grinder his full attention. "Jesus, *he* died? That was him?"

Grinder frowned. "Yeah, that was him. And the cops have been sniffing around, asking me about how I knew him and all."

John began to put up his defenses. "Hey, man, I want nothin' to do with any of that. I was just a go-between to get that painting out of town. You've got to tell 'em that."

"Don't be a pussy, John, for Christ's sake. I didn't have anything to do with the kid's death, either."

"What did you tell the cops?"

"Nothing." He took a slug of beer. "Nothing at all."

John moved away to serve other customers, and he didn't come back for the rest of the evening. The boycott was on. John didn't wanted the stink of a dead college kid to rub off on him. Grinder talked to a few other people who wandered over from time to time, but he waved them all off almost immediately. He wasn't in the mood for any business. Eventually he shoved one persistent pest a little too hard, knocking him to the floor and turning over a chair.

In frustration, he walked out of the bar, trying much too hard to figure out his next move.

36

Thursday

Elena awoke with Hans stroking her hair. When she turned to face him, he was smiling broadly. "I love dark hair," he said, "especially your dark hair."

She couldn't help but be amused. He was always so happy when she let him stay, like a child enjoying his first sleepover party. "What about all those blond Danish beauties?" she teased.

"That's the trouble. All those. They're everywhere, too much of a good thing." He continued to stroke. "But you, you're special."

He was right. Elena was a beautiful woman, her Italian-American heritage having blessed her with a full list of desirable attributes. Curves, check. Complexion, check. Subtle, musical accent, check. And hair, long wavy dark hair that Hans couldn't keep his hands off, check.

"I'll think you're special, too, if you leave me alone and make us breakfast." Hans took the hint and left the bedroom, his second-best room, for the kitchen, his best.

Elena lay back on her pillow and stretched in all directions. It had been a good evening, she thought, maybe a perfect one. Everything had come off as planned, except for the missing judge, and Des had come through with a more than suitable replacement. The students had been just right, a combination of youthful excitement and total absorption with their projects. The projects themselves were generally terrific, and she was pleased that the guests paid so much attention to the students. She had lived through—painfully—many student research exhibits where the guests stayed close to the refreshments and mostly talked among themselves, ignoring the students. But not last night. Last night everyone was engaged. Yes, she thought, darn close to a perfect evening.

Hans called from the kitchen. "Omelets are ready, my dear." And, she thought, the night and morning weren't so bad, either.

Across town, another couple was also having a late morning. Des was awake, Remy's head resting on her shoulder. She thought back to the previous evening. They had left the cafe, and walked to her car. As Remy held the door for her, he took her hand and pulled her close. "I believe I have a rain-check for this," he said, and kissed her. It was neither light nor brief.

After that, she drove them to her home, any thoughts of the university hotel long forgotten. They had made love, all the usual cliches about birds singing and earth moving fully in play. Never before, she had thought, never, ever before.

Des slipped out from under his head, causing him to stir. "You're not leaving me here alone?" he asked.

"Shower time," she said.

"Alone?"

"It's small."

"How nice," Remy said, and jumped from the bed.

Later, as they shared cereal and bagels at her kitchen table, Des asked, "What do you want to do today?"

"Be with you."

She laughed. "I promised you a campus tour."

"As long as I can be with you."

She smiled across the cereals bowls. "Of course. And we have work to do, too. Remember, you came down here to get the 'full context' regarding the painting."

"Yes," he said, "let's talk about that painting." He walked into the living room where they had left the photograph of the painting—and a good deal of their clothing—the night before. He brought it back to the kitchen and put it on the table, holding it so Des could look at it. "Tell me what you see."

Des stared at the painting for a few moments. "Sorry, Remy, I'm not sure I'm getting the point. I see a pair of great blue herons flying across a blue sky. There's nothing else to see."

"Remember when we were looking at the Fuertes mural of flamingoes in the museum?" She nodded. "Do you recall what we talked about, about how Fuertes painted birds?"

She nodded more. "Oh, yes, you called him a bird portraitist. He showed the personality of the birds he painted. Each one an individual, like a portrait of a person."

"Okay, now look again and tell me what you see."

Des studied the photograph more closely and carefully. "These birds don't have much personality. In fact, they look almost identical."

Remy agreed. "They are expertly painted, that's for sure, the work of a professional artist. And the style—thickness of the paint, blending of the paint colors, that sort of thing—looks just like the way Fuertes worked. But..."

"But," Des blurted, "those birds don't match what we saw at the museum. They look more generic, not individual."

"And why do you think that is?" he asked.

Des thought for a moment. "Well, Elena told me he painted this early in his career. Do you suppose he hadn't developed that portraitist idea yet? Or, maybe since this was just for a temporary exhibit, he didn't put much effort in."

"No, that's not what happened. The other panels for the exhibit are already assembled at the museum. I took a look at them before I came down—the curator is a friend." Of course he is, Des thought. "All the other birds in the other panels are painted as portraits. And seeing that this was the center feature of the panel, I'm sure Fuertes would have taken special care over these birds."

Des furled her eyebrows. "So, what's the explanation then?"

"Only one explanation possible. Your stolen painting is a forgery."

37

Judith Heinz knocked on the door of her friend's house. She needed to talk with Jennifer Haskins, to see what was troubling her. She had called earlier and gotten no answer, so she decided to take the chance that she was home, but ignoring her phone.

Besides, Judith loved the drive out to Jennifer's home in the country. The drive took her over the ridge that bordered the eastern edge of town, and down into the adjacent valley. The valley was picturesque, gentle rolling hills alternating between farmland and forest. Then the road curled up the opposite ridge and dropped down into a much narrower forested valley. The October colors filled her heart with joy. Color was the predominant feature of Judith's art, and the views she encountered as she drove along were salve to her worry about Jennifer.

At the bottom of the valley, she turned off the main road—not much "main" about it, she thought—onto a county road that skirted a small stream. The water ran clear under the canopy of oaks and hickories, punctuated by mountain laurel along the water's edge.

When she thought she was close to Jennifer's place, she slowed down. It was easy to miss the lane to her house, marked only by a plain black mailbox labelled J. Haskins. The lane itself was equally undistinguished, two dirt tracks with weeds growing tall between them. About a quarter-mile up the lane, the house and barn came into view. The house was beautiful in its country simplicity, with white clapboard siding, a covered porch that ran the length of the front, and a few small windows arrayed across the first and second stories.

The important building was the barn. Jennifer had converted it to her studio years earlier. Huge windows punctured the high barn walls, providing the light that all artists coveted. The barn still featured the original doors on both ends, so they could be opened when the weather was nice, but refitted with modern frames and hardware so the space could be sealed off from mid-summer heat and mid-winter cold. In reality, the air-conditioning and heat were more to protect the artist's work than to provide comfort to the artist herself.

Eventually, the door opened slightly and Jennifer peaked out. She looked ready to shoo away whoever was at the door, until she realized the visitor was her old friend. "Judith," she sighed, and swung the door open wide. "Oh, Judith." The two women hugged, and Judith thought her friend might never let go. "Come in."

They walked into the small sitting room and sat next to each other on the couch. "I brought us a little treat from Hans's place."

"Hans's place?"

Judith waved her hand. "Oh, sorry. I mean the Scandia Cafe. I'm sure you know it." Jennifer nodded and smiled. "Hans is the owner, and he's become a bit of a friend."

Jennifer brightened a bit when she saw the coffee cake that Judith unwrapped. The delicious aroma of almond filling took over the room. "I guess I need to make some coffee if we have coffee cake."

Judith smiled. "That would be lovely. Thank you."

When the cake and coffee were served, the pair settled down to talk. "I was worried about you, Jennifer," Judith said. "When you cancelled on last night's art exhibition. Are you okay?"

Jennifer frowned and looked at her hands. "I'm sorry. I just couldn't make myself come. I hope I didn't ruin things."

"Of course not." Judith described how the evening went and the addition of Remy Tremblay as a substitute judge. "It was a wonderful evening, really. You would have enjoyed it. And I missed having you there."

Jennifer shook her head. "No, I wouldn't have enjoyed it. Being around all those young people would have been too much."

"Why? What's wrong?"

"My nephew died a few days ago. I... I ... I can't get past it."

"Tell me about it."

Jennifer took a few deep breaths. "I'm sure you heard about the college student who died in his dorm room." Judith nodded. "That's my nephew, Manfred Kurtz.'

"Oh, dear. You poor thing. Were you close?"

Jennifer began to weep quietly. "Yes, his whole life. He used to spend summers with me here when he was a boy. He called me his other mother. And now he's gone. I just can't believe it."

Judith didn't know what to say, so she sat quietly. Eventually, Jennifer began to talk again. "He was a good boy, very loving and kind to me. But he made a lot of bad decisions growing up.

He got in trouble a lot up in Lynchburg where my sister, his mom, lives. We all hoped that when he came to VWU he would start over. You know, get away from the bad influences that were affecting him."

"And did that work?"

"We thought so, and my sister was so hopeful that he had changed. He lived out here with me for a couple of years, and he seemed happy. Then he went back to live in the university dorms."

"But it didn't last, I guess."

Jennifer shook her head. "No, I guess not. I just hate what happened to him. It's terrible. And I just couldn't get myself up to go to your party."

"I understand, Jennifer. I wouldn't have gone, either, in your shoes." She decided to change the subject. "Tell me about your painting. I see your prints all over town. They're so beautiful, so realistic."

Jennifer looked at Judith with tears in her eyes. "You know as well as I do that my paintings have no meaning. All I do is copy what shows on the surface. It's nothing. Today's cellphones do just as good as I do."

Judith felt as if Jennifer had been listening in on her conversation with Elena a few days earlier. But she was not about to let her friend suffer. "Don't be ridiculous, Jennifer. I feel like I'm living *in* your landscapes, not just looking at them. And that's why they're so popular. You transport people to places they remember from their youth, places they love. And places they've never seen, like the paintings you do of overseas. Where is it exactly that you go, someplace in the Mediterranean, right?"

"Montenegro."

"Sounds very exotic to me. I'd have to look at a map to locate it. Are you going back anytime soon?"

If anything, Jennifer looked even sadder. "I was hoping to, maybe later this fall. With Ralph and maybe Manny. But that can't happen now."

"Well, regardless, your work is wonderful. You should be very proud."

"Thanks, Judith. That is a comfort to me, for sure." Jennifer gave a half smile, all she could muster. But it lasted only a few seconds.

Judith tried again. She sat straight up and grinned from ear to ear. "Remember when we used to make those paintings of the great masters and sell them at craft fairs?"

"Of course I remember. That was so much fun." They sat quietly again for a few minutes, each absorbed in their memories of their time together when they were students. Eventually Judith broke the silence. "Are you working on anything special right now?"

Jennifer hesitated. "Yes. I've got a commission from a friend."

"Oh, can I see it?"

Jennifer looked alarmed and shook her head decisively. "No, no you can't. It's...it's...it's barely begun. And I'm not sure I'll ever finish it. There doesn't seem to be any point now."

"Nonsense! You just need some inspiration to get you going again. I tell you what—how about you come in to town for lunch later today. I'll try to arrange a meeting with this Remy Tremblay. I know you'll like him. It'll cheer you up. And you don't need to be around any young people. Just us old folks!"

Jennifer seemed to warm to the idea. "Well, maybe, Judith. That would be good."

"Okay, it's a deal. I'll get everything arranged, and I'll call you later this morning with the details."

Jennifer looked as though she might change her mind, so Judith got up and said her goodbyes. She waved to her friend and got in her car. As she started it up, she said to herself, "There's more to this than a dead nephew."

38

"Are you sure?" Des asked Remy.

"Well, of course, I haven't seen the actual painting. So, no, I can't say for sure. There are many indications that you can get from the painting itself, other than the work of the artist himself."

"Like what?"

"Age is main thing. The original painting is, what, 130 years old or so? The frame would be old, so would the canvas itself. And the stretcher that supports the canvas. How it was constructed, what kind of staples or nails were used to attach the canvas to the stretcher. Also, over a long time, the canvas shrinks or sags, pulling away from the nails. Anyway, lots of things."

Des was thinking. "Okay, so how sure are you, on a scale of 1 to 10?"

Remy considered for a moment, and smiled. "Pretty sure. Can I have fractions or just whole numbers?"

"C'mon, kiddo, this isn't funny."

He accepted her chastisement with a pout. "9.5."

"Grab your coat. We need to go."

As they were driving, Des had Remy call Elena. She agreed to meet them at the BSB library. Des took down the police tape on the door and let them into the Fuertes Room. Elena's shock at Remy's conclusion of forgery was, well, just that, shock. "How could that be? I've been looking at that painting for years."

"Are you a student of Fuertes' work?" Remy asked.

"Well, no, not really," Elena answered. "But I loved that painting, how realistic the birds were."

"There's no question that the forgery was done well, Elena. But there were some subtle things about it that don't match the details of how Fuertes painted."

"Something an art expert might catch, but not a casual observer?"

"Right," he said, "things that even a devoted art lover like you wouldn't notice. Don't blame yourself."

"Well, no, but I am feeling a little foolish for having drooled over those birds for so long. And how did a forgery get here?"

Des said, "That's what we need to figure out next, if we can."

"How?"

"First off, tell Remy and me what you know about history of the painting. Since it got here, I mean. We already know about Fuertes and how he worked."

Elena smiled and gave them both a playful glance. "Been studying a little art history, have you, Des?"

Des looked a bit like a schoolgirl whose father had caught her kissing the boy next door. But she recovered quickly and smiled at her friend. "I'm the police officer here, Dr. Bertoni. I'll ask the questions."

"Okay. I don't know the early history. I've only been here about five years, remember. The painting was hanging in this room when I got here. My guess is that it was hung just after it was donated by Ralph. Good lord, does he know it's a forgery?"

"Ralph?" Remy asked. Des didn't seem to mind if he asked questions.

"Ralph Vukovic," Des explained. "He's the dean of the College of Biological Sciences. Many of the paintings in the room were donated by him over the years. And, no, Elena, we haven't talked to him yet about this."

"So the dean's an art lover?" Remy asked.

"Oh, yes," Elena said. "You should see his house. It's like a museum for animal and nature art. He has an incredible collection."

Remy raised his eyebrows in mock surprise. "How much do deans get paid around here?"

Elena laughed. "They do okay, I'm sure, but I'm also sure that's not where his wealth comes from. He is author of one of the standard texts on mammalogy, and I'm sure the royalties from that are pretty good." Des put it on her mental list of facts to check.

Des took over. "So the painting was hanging here when you started working at VWU. And you took a photo of it for your art project?"

"Yeah. During the summer. That's when the announcement came out about the painting going on loan to the museum in New York. I thought it would make a great project."

Remy nodded. "It was a great project. Last night was terrific. The kids did a great job. And you must be some kind of teacher."

Now it was Elena's turn to be embarrassed. "Thanks. I love teaching." Then she frowned. "Maybe too much. That's what my department head says. Concentrate on the things you need to do for promotion, he always tells me, you can teach your heart out after you're a full professor."

"Back to the painting," Des said. "As far as you know, was it ever removed for any reason? Like maybe the room was getting repainted or some repairs had to be made to the lighting, or a leaky ceiling?"

"Or for the painting to be restored?" Remy added.

"Not that I know of. Rooms get repainted about once a century around here. But Yvonne ought to know. She's at the desk across the hall right now. Let's ask her."

Elena fetched Yvonne into the Fuertes Room. She looked around like she was scared to be there.

"Are you okay, Yvonne?" Des asked.

As usual, Yvonne looked on the verge of tears. "Hardly," she squeaked out. "I used to love this room. Now I hate it. I wish this was just a little library where nothing happened except books being overdue. I don't know if I can keep working here."

Des patted her on the shoulder. "It's okay, Yvonne. None of this has anything to do with you." Des hoped that those words were true. "We're wondering about the history of the room. Do you know about it?"

"Yes, of course. I've been a librarian here—and for the other two branch libraries, of course—for a long time. I was here before this was the Fuertes Room."

"So, how did it happen?"

Yvonne sat down at the conference table, and the others joined her. Des was hoping it wouldn't be that long a conversation, but she was doubtful. "It was about ten years ago. Actually, that plaque on the wall has the exact date."

Remy got back up and went to read the plaque. "Dedicated February 7, 2012."

"Yes, that's it," Yvonne said. "I remember now, that's Fuertes's birthday. Dean Vukovic made a big deal about having the dedication that day. The dean had donated a couple of other paintings in earlier years, and they were hanging in here when it was just an ordinary conference room. But when he gave us the Fuertes painting, he wanted a special place for all of them, and others, to be displayed." She almost managed a smile. "It was a wonderful occasion. President Crutchfield and Ms. Richards were both here, along with lots of others."

Remy asked, "I presume that the room was fixed up for being an art gallery."

"Oh yes. We had good lighting installed and some sort of changes to the ventilation system to make it good for the artwork. New carpet and paint, and this beautiful conference table and chairs. Ms. Richards paid for all that. She's a great art lover, you know."

Des winced at the fawning over Michele Richards. That woman keeps coming up, she thought. And her mind went to the note that Michele had slipped into Remy's pocket at the party. But she kept to the topic. "And since then, the painting has always hung here?"

"Yes. Always."

"Never taken out for a new paint job on the walls or any repairs to the room?"

Yvonne shook her head and sighed. "No, never. I'm sure the room could use some freshening up, but this is a library after all, and we're always last on the list for any repairs or improvements. Goodness, even the library director forgets we're here sometimes."

Des excused the thoroughly rattled librarian, and the three headed out the door into the bright October morning. Remy said, "I think we need to look into the authentication of the painting. How would that be done at a university?"

Des shrugged. "This is all new territory for me. Let me make a call and see if I can find out."

She walked away, leaving Elena and Remy sitting on a short stone wall surrounding the library's patio. The tables on the patio were all filled with students, alone or in groups, huddled over their laptops or textbooks. "What a beautiful place this is, Elena," Remy said. "I could get used to a place like this."

"It is wonderful to work on a campus like this." Just then, a pair of students walked up to ask Elena about their next assignment in her conservation of natural resources course. When Elena had handled their question, she turned back to Remy. "Of course, you're never far from The Madding Crowd."

"I live in New York City, tell me about it."

"At least you don't know everyone. But, wait, Des tells me you do seem to know everyone!"

Remy laughed. "Ah, a carefully curated mirage. I was just showing off to her."

"Well, it worked. She is quite taken with you."

Remy looked at her slyly. "Taken? What does that mean?"

"C'mon, Remy. You're much too astute an observer not to know what I'm talking about. But here's the real question, how taken with her are you?" Elena pointed her gaze across the patio to where Des was talking on her cellphone, and Remy's eyes followed. "She's a good person, and she doesn't deserve to be toyed with."

He paused for a long moment, watching Des. She finished her call, spotted them sitting on the wall, and started walking over to join them.

"Well?" Elena asked.

Never taking his eyes off Des, he answered. "All in, Elena, all in."

39

The group met for a late lunch at Greens, a new restaurant at the university's golf course. Elena's Thursday class, a graduate seminar on wildlife behavior that she had taken over from the disgraced Drew Robbins, went halfway through the lunch hour and then there were always students to talk with. One-thirty was as early as she could manage.

For a while, Judith thought Jennifer might not show up. She had been waiting with Des, Remy and Elena well past their agreed meeting time, making excuses for her friend. "She is pretty upset about the death of her nephew, so maybe she's changed her mind about coming." Finally, however, they saw her pull into the parking lot in her old pickup.

When she walked to the table, Elena thought that maybe Jennifer should have stayed home. She walked unsteadily, as though she were an invalid who had forgotten her cane and was barely able to stay upright. Her face was pale and drawn. But she made a brave attempt at smiling when she saw the group sitting under the canvas patio tent. "I'm sorry I'm late," she apologized. "You know what artists are like."

Judith introduced everyone, and took Jennifer in to order. The other three had gotten their food earlier, but Judith insisted on waiting for her friend. Greens was one of those trendy places where customers ordered the elements of a salad as they walked along, "greens-keepers" loading it all into a stainless bowl that they then mixed and chopped together and topped with the wicked organic garnishes chosen by the patrons. Elena could hardly keep from giggling as she had gone through the line, watching her personal greens-keeper scoop up her choices with spoons shaped like miniature hollowed-out drivers. The whole place was outrageously overdone, from the astro-turf on the floor to the irregularly shaped oval tables pretending to be greens.

But she did succumb to an Arnold Palmer—half sweet tea and half lemonade—as her beverage.

Jennifer sat quietly while they all ate and talked. She seemed timid to Elena, not what she expected from such a successful artist. She decided to address it directly. "Jennifer," Elena said, "I love your paintings of the landscape around Stone Valley, but I especially love the ones from Europe. I lived in Italy, as a girl with my parents, and it reminds me of our home near Bolobgna." Jennifer brightened a little.

Elena continued, "They are so realistic, almost like photographs."

That comment caused Jennifer to shrink again. "Some artists might find that comparison a bit, um, insulting."

"I certainly meant it as a compliment," Elena said.

Jennifer seemed to be settling into silence again, when Judith took over. "Art comes in all styles. Startling realism is no less artistic than startling abstraction, isn't that right, Remy?"

He nodded vigorously. "Absolutely. And I venture to say that realism may be the most difficult of any genre of painting. An impressionist or cubist or modernist can always retreat to the idea of 'what the viewer sees is the art, not what the artist painted.' But a realist is putting it all on the line. If the art doesn't look like what it represents, then the failure is obvious. Doesn't matter if it is a bowl of fruit where the grapes are too large, a portrait with a head like a basketball, or a barn that looks like a carnival crazy house. The skill is there or it isn't."

Des could feel herself falling deeper. She didn't know if Remy was telling the truth or driving a load of art manure down main street, but she knew that what he was saying was raising Jennifer's spirits. She recalled what she once heard as the definition of a gentleman: he keeps his eyes on all his company.

Remy went on, "Des showed me some of your work in a gallery downtown. It is remarkable. Some realistic art is just representational, but I find yours to have real depth, real feeling."

Judith jumped in. "See, Jennifer, that's just what I was telling you this morning."

Remy asked, "Have you always painted in this style?"

Jennifer rose to the question. "Basically, yes. Of course, I experimented a lot early on." She looked at Judith and smiled. "Judith and I did quite a lot of 'experimenting' early on, didn't we, girl?"

Judith laughed. "Yes, we were art students together here at VWU, in the sixties. We experimented a lot, indeed. But Jennifer is talking about our art. We had a business together for a number of years."

Elena asked, "Doing what?"

"Well, you know how art students are always sitting in museums, sketching and painting the artwork hanging there?" They all nodded. "We took it a step farther. We started making copies of famous artworks and selling them. This was before there were technologies to make reproductions look like real paintings. So there was some demand from people to have replicas of famous art works, something that looked more authentic than just cheap prints."

Des was intrigued. "You were that good that you could fool people?"

Judith shook her head. "Oh, no. That wasn't the idea. No one was going to believe that we were selling originals. No Van Goghs showing up at craft shows in western Virginia for fifty dollars each! But we could make a good enough copy that people could hang at home to appreciate. We'd go to flea markets and buy old frames and put them together with our paintings."

"And you made a living doing that?"

Now Jennifer actually laughed. "Heavens, no. But we did make some extra cash, and it was fun. We were full of ourselves back then. We actually named ourselves J2H2, and we stamped that on the backs of all the stretchers."

"Okay," Elena said, "I'll bite. Why J2H2?"

Des broke in. "C'mon, Elena. Use your detective skills. Two Js for first names, 2 Hs for last names."

Elena protested, "I'm a researcher, not Sherlock Holmes. I need more data than that to make a deduction."

Lunch ended with hugs all around, and Judith and Jennifer headed off to their vehicles arm-in-arm.

"Okay," Des said. "Time to get back to work. We have an appointment with Tim Worstall in a few minutes.

Tim Worstall was the university's director of material donations, in the advancement office. He worked in a tiny office in a one-story building in a seldom visited corner of the campus.

He greeted the trio as though they were his new best friends. "How nice to meet you all," he gushed. "It is so nice to have visitors!"

After introductions were made, Des returned his ebullience with her own. "And so nice to learn something about the university that is totally unexpected. I had no idea that an office like yours actually existed. Tell us about your work."

Now she actually was Tim's new best friend. "Oh, thank you for being interested. It is a bit of a lonely job, stuck out here. But I don't mind. My job is so interesting."

"I'll bet," Remy said. "I do a bit of work with museums and such. People are always wanting to give them treasures from their attics."

"Oh yes," Tim said. "Same thing at the university. Alumni want to give us things all the time. The rest of the building behind my office," he pointed over his shoulder, "is full of interesting items that the university has gotten and has no good use for. You wouldn't imagine the kind of things I have to evaluate."

"Like what?" Des asked.

"Well, just last month the development officer in business fielded a call from a corporate executive who is a big-game hunter. Shot animals all over the world. Disgusting, I think, but that's not my call. He's got mounted heads and even full-body stuffed animals all over his house. He just got re-married—another trophy, maybe?—and apparently his new bride put her foot down." He giggled. "Maybe her hoof? Anyway he wants to give his collection to the university. So, I have to figure out how to put a value on these things, can you imagine?"

Remy smiled. "I can imagine. I work with the American Museum of Natural History in New York, and they get this kind of thing all the time, because of their dioramas of taxidermy. Give me your card, and I'll text you the name of a person who can help."

"Oh, goodness, thank you."

They exchanged cards while Des looked on. There he goes again, she thought, keeping his eyes on all his company.

Elena, who had been observing quietly, now got into the discussion. "I'm sure that some of those taxidermy specimens might be useful in our department." Tim looked quizzical. "The Department of Renewable Resources. We work on wildlife conservation. There might be some specimens that would be good to use in class or display in our building."

"That would be great," Tim said, and handed her a card as well. "Send me an email so I can let you know when we get the donation here. What a good day this has been!"

Des got back to the topic. "So, we need to know about the authentication of the painting that was stolen a couple of weeks ago."

"What a terrible thing," Tim said. "What a loss to the university. Do you know what happened to it?"

Des shook her head. "Not yet, but we're getting closer. So, did you do the authentication?"

"Oh, no, not me. I can't do anything myself that is out of the ordinary. Regular things, things that aren't very valuable, that I can do. But if a gift is likely to be really valuable, like that painting, we have to have an expert's opinion. The IRS demands it."

"Do you keep records?" Des asked.

"Oh, of course. All computerized these days. " Tim picked up a file from his desk. "I dug these out after you called me. Everything is here." He handed the file to Des. "I made you a copy of it all."

Des smiled, genuinely. "Thank you, Tim, that is very kind of you. And efficient."

Remy asked, "Do you remember what expert you used?"

"No, not off the top of my head. But it will be there in the file."

Des opened the file and quickly scanned the first few pages. "Says a fellow named Grant Mullins, at the McGinty Museum of American Art , did the authentication."

"I know him well," Remy said. "He works with Michele Richards often, and she connected us a few years ago. We've worked together on several cases."

Tim's eyes got wide. "Cases?"

40

After the meeting with Tim Worstall, the trio broke up. They drove back to BSB, and Elena lent Remy her car so he could explore the town a bit more. After he drove off, Des and Elena sat in her police cruiser.

"This next step isn't going to be easy," Des said.

"What now?"

"I need to talk with the dean about his painting being a forgery. I can't imagine he's going to be pleased."

Elena agreed. "I'm sure not. Do you want me to go with you?"

Des shook her head. "No, better not. He's your boss, so you shouldn't be there when I confront him."

"Confront him? Do you think he had something to do with it?"

"Sorry, Elena, I shouldn't have used that word. But I am springing some unexpected news on him, and it isn't good news. Jessie is meeting me so we have strength in numbers. She'll be here in a minute."

They sat in Des's car while they waited for Jessie. "This is such a mess, isn't it, Des?"

"Yeah, it is. But that's police work. Most of what we deal with is straight-forward and easily tied up. But, then, you get something messy, like this. And the more you keep digging, the more mess you find."

Elena sighed. "First it's my advisee, Hannah, letting the student steal the painting. Then it's another student doing the stealing and ending up killing himself with drugs."

Des realized that she hadn't shared the news about Kurtz's death with Elena. "No, Kurtz didn't do himself in. Well, I guess, actually he did. He took the drugs. But what he thought was cocaine turned out to be mixed with a poison. That's what killed him."

"My god, you mean he was murdered?"

"Yes, he was. Poisoned with sodium arsenate."

Now Elena sat straight up. "Sodium arsenate? Are you sure?"

"Why?" Des asked. "And, yes, of course I'm sure."

"It's just that we have sodium arsenate here."

Now Des sprang to attention. "What do you mean by *here*?"

"In our building."

"Explain, kiddo."

"Sodium arsenate was traditionally used in taxidermy, to treat the inside of skins that would be kept in museum collections," Elena explained. "It works really well to kill insects that would get into the skins and eat them away."

"Like moths do to clothes?"

"Right, same kind of thing. A jar of sodium arsenate was on the laboratory shelf of every scientist who studied mammals, birds, even reptiles. And every taxidermist used it, too. The trouble was that it was toxic to humans. Eventually it was banned, and no one uses it anymore."

"So, why do you still have it here?"

Elena sighed. "This is a constant battle with faculty."

"What is?"

"Our chemical storage protocols. The federal government has a bunch of regulations about how we handle dangerous chemicals. Every lab that has any chemicals is supposed to keep an up-to-date inventory—which ones they have, how much they have, when they were bought, when they expire—all that kind of thing. And once a chemical expires, then you have to go through hell and high water to dispose of it, and if the labels are gone or just hand-written, then it gets really expensive and time-consuming. Faculty hate it."

"Faculty hate anyone looking over their shoulders, Elena. Nothing new there."

"But the chemical stuff is a real pain. Makes me glad that I just watch animals rather than killing them and putting their bodies in museum drawers. Anyway, faculty members are notorious for avoiding doing the right thing with out-of-date chemicals, including sodium arsenate."

"Like what?"

"I'm sure that all of our mammalogy and ornithology labs have some cabinets or drawers or closet shelves somewhere that aren't labelled for chemical storage where they keep small amounts of leftovers from earlier years. And as time goes by, it just gets harder to get rid of it and harder to explain that beloved old so-and-so hoarded the stuff in case he ever needed some.

You know, faculty hate change. So, it just sits there, hidden and ignored, decade after decade."

"And you think contraband jars of sodium arsenate are tucked away here?"

"I don't know for sure, but I'd bet on it."

"So, our murder weapon, sort of, could be sitting in any number of rooms in this building? Available to, what, dozens of people?"

Elena nodded, "And in several others buildings around campus, too."

'So, not dozens of people, but hundreds." Des lapsed into thought. They were jarred into the present when Jessie rapped on the window. "Jesus," Des said, "What a nightmare."

Dean Ralph Vukovic met with the police officers in the conference room that adjoined his office. The room oozed masculinity and power. The table was a single slab of oak with natural edges, no doubt cut from some ancient tree that was an acorn long before the university began. The chairs were formed of tubular steel in sleek modern design, wrapped in thickly padded black leather.

But the wall decorations were the focal feature. Each wall of the small room held just one large framed photograph of an animal. A rhinoceros with head low, staring ominously and directly at the viewer, an imposing horn framed perfectly between a pair of menacing eyes. A wolf trotting across an open field, carrying a snowshoe hare in its mouth. A walrus stretched on a rock with a rippling blue sea exploding into white foam behind it. And last a large, scruffy horse standing on a rolling plain, with several similar horses behind it and out of focus.

He gave them a minute to take in the artwork. "Beautiful photographs," Des said. "Did you take them?"

"Yes," Ralph said, not trying to hide his pride. "Yes, I did."

"Can I ask why the horse? It seems different than the others."

"Good eye, Chief White. But, you're wrong. All four photos are of wild species, including the horse. That's a Przewalski's horse, the only truly wild horse in the world. Highly endangered."

Jessie found her voice. "Wow. Where does it live? Is that Texas?"

"No, it's Mongolia. These are from a herd that was released back into the wild from captive animals bred at a zoo in Prague. They were extinct in the wild before being reintroduced just a short time ago. Magnificent, isn't he?"

Des and Jessie both nodded their agreement. "But so are the others," Des said.

"Sit down, please," the dean said. "I'm sure you're not here to compliment my photographic skills."

They sat, the leather cushions exhaling elegantly under their weight. "You're right, Dean Vukovic," Des began. "We have had some disturbing news about the stolen Fuertes painting."

"What news? Have you found it?"

"We have uncovered evidence that the painting wasn't genuine."

He looked shocked. "What? What do you mean? That's impossible!"

Des explained Remy's conclusion, but the dean just shook his head. "I'm sorry, but I just can't believe this. I bought the painting from a reputable source years ago. The provenance is exacting. And it was authenticated by an expert when I donated it to the university."

"Yes, of course," Des said. "And we've just been talking to Tim Worstall, who handled it all, and we have no reason to doubt that the painting you donated was genuine."

"Of course it was. So how do you explain your new expert's ridiculous opinion?"

"That's what we need to figure out. And maybe you can help us."

"How?" There was now a decidely unfriendly edge to his voice.

"Has the painting ever been out of your or the university's control? For cleaning, maybe, or display somewhere else?"

He shook his head. "No, of course not. It's always been right downstairs, hanging in the library." But then he stopped. "A couple of years ago, when the museum in New York was beginning to put the whole Fuertes puzzle together...you know, ours is one of nine panels?" Des and Jessie both nodded. "Okay, when they were working on it, they sent one of their people down here to check it out. I can't remember his name, but it'll be in the files somewhere."

"We'd like that information, please," Des said. Ralph got up and went to the door and spoke to his assistant. When he turned back to them, Des asked, "Did he take it away?"

Again Ralph shook his head. "No, but he did ask to take it down for a bit so he could examine it. He took it into a little seminar room down the hall across from the library and worked on it for, I don't know, a few hours."

"What was he doing?"

"I looked in on him once or twice. He had taken it out of the frame. He was taking detailed measurements, as I recall, of the dimensions of the painting. I guess he was making sure that it was exactly the right size to fit into the overall composition. He came up to my office to say goodbye when he was done. I asked him if everything was ok, and he said that it was. That the painting was definitely the missing panel. He said he had hung the painting back up in the gallery. I looked in as I was leaving for the day, and it was there, right back where it was supposed to be."

"But you didn't examine it closely?"

"No, I didn't. I just looked in as I was headed home. Besides, I had no reason to suspect anything. You don't think he could have changed the painting, do you?"

Des shrugged. "I don't know. But somewhere, sometime, the real painting seems to have gotten switched with a forgery."

The dean now showed another emotion, and red splotches began to color his face. "Wait a minute. You don't think I had anything to do with it, do you? That would be preposterous."

"No, of course not. But we have to figure out how a forgery got here, and what happened to the original painting."

"I think what happened is that your so-called expert is wrong. He's never even seen the painting, has he?" Des shook her head. "So this is just speculation. Your new boyfriend is just trying to impress you. There isn't a real painting and a fake painting. There's only one painting, and now it's gone."

"Maybe."

He got up, letting them know the meeting was over. "And I'm both surprised and disappointed that you are promoting this fantasy. You know better than that, Chief White. Forget this nonsense, and do your job. Go find my painting."

Des swallowed hard. "Good day, Dean Vukovic." On the way out, the dean's assistant handed Des a paper with the information about the museum's inspector.

41

Elena was waiting at The Hawk's Den when Des arrived. "How did he take it?" Elena asked.

Des had cooled down sufficiently that she could chuckle. "All thing's considered, pretty well." She reviewed the conversation with the dean, including his story about an inspector from the museum having had the painting in a room by himself to examine it.

"Do you think that man could have switched the paintings?"

Des scrunched her face. "Could have, I guess. But it doesn't seem likely. He would have had to bring a forgery with him from New York. Where would he have gotten one, and how could he know that he could pull off a switch?"

"You're probably right," agreed Elena. "But, I'll bet the museum has lots of records, early photographs, that sort of thing. Heck, he could have come down unannounced and viewed the painting, taken a picture. Then he could have painted the copy."

"Hadn't thought of that," Des admitted. "I suppose that an authenticator is the person who would know best how to duplicate something, right? Get all the details right, the canvas, those sorts of things."

"Right. And he probably does restoration work for the museum as well, so he'd have access to the right kinds of paint, brushes, all that. Aren't the best safe crackers the guys who designed the safes to be un-crackable?"

Des laughed. "Where'd you hear that? Sounds like something from Hawaii Five-O. We'll look into this. But let's change the subject a bit."

"Okay. Want to talk about Remy?" Elena asked and grinned.

Des frowned. "No, I don't want to talk about him. I'm serious. How do you feel about your dean?"

"Ralph? What do you mean?"

Des shrugged. "He just keeps showing up on the edges of all this. After you left Jessie and me, she told me that she had looked into Manfred Kurtz's record a little further."

"And?"

"Kurtz had gotten into trouble for growing marijuana in his dorm room a couple of years ago. I didn't remember it. But Jessie read the file, and Kurtz was given only a reprimand because a faculty member vouched for him."

"Is that unusual, Des?"

"It happens sometimes, but not usually for drug-related crimes. More for cheating on tests, that sort of thing. But this time the faculty member wasn't just any old faculty member. He was Dean Ralph Vukovic."

That got Elena's attention. "Why would Ralph do that?

"It's pretty obvious, isn't it? Kurtz is Jennifer Haskins's nephew, and Jennifer is Ralph's girlfriend."

"Oh, yes," Elena said, "of course."

"Yeah, of course. That makes sense, and we've got all these connections. The dean gives a painting to the university. Years later, the dean bails out his girlfriend's nephew. The nephew steals the painting. The girl who lets him steal it is being mentored by the dean. The nephew is poisoned with the kind of poison used by wildlife specialists. The dean is a wildlife specialist."

"When you put it like that...," Elena said, but she didn't know how to finish the sentence. "Did you ask the dean about all that when you talked just now?"

"No. I thought about it, but I don't know what it means yet. If it means anything. And we made the dean pretty upset by telling him his painting was a forgery."

They sat quietly for a few moments, letting all of this soak in. They each got another drink, a beer for Elena and sweet tea for Des. Then Elena gave her a sly look. "Did he turn bright red?"

"Yeah, he did," Des said. "How did you know?"

"I've seen it a few times, when he gets news he doesn't like. Ted calls him the thermometer because you can read how bad the situation is by the color of his face."

"He was medium rare when he told me that Remy, my new boyfriend, didn't know what he was talking about."

"He didn't care much for your art expert, eh?" Des shook her head and grimaced. Elena continued, "Speaking of whom, how are you and Mr. Tremblay getting on, anyhow?"

A smile replaced Des's grimace. "We're, uh, getting on just fine. Just fine indeed."

"I think he likes you, Des."

"I passed him a note asking him to check yes or no, at the end of algebra class. Of course he likes me."

But then a cloud passed over her face. Elena saw it. "What?"

"I'm wondering about his relationship with Michele Richards. At the party last night, I saw her put a note into his coat pocket."

Elena laughed. "Jeez, we are back in junior high. All the girls passing notes to the boys." Des didn't seem to think it was funny. "Did you ask him about it?"

"No," Des said. "There hasn't been an appropriate time to raise the subject."

"I thought you were the police chief, the one who asks the questions." She didn't give Des a chance to respond. "I'm sure it was nothing. Something about the work that Remy does for her, probably."

"That's not a very pleasant thought, either, Elena."

"Why not?"

"Jimmy thinks that Michele might be involved in the art thefts."

"What? That's ludicrous!"

"I don't know. It could all fit together. We're looking for a sophisticated art lover who is familiar enough with the university to have planned the thefts. The person who wanted the art needs to have somewhere to stash it that is private. And the money to pay for it all. Michele checks all the boxes."

Elena couldn't believe what she was hearing. "And then, what, she just gives us Remy as a red herring? C'mon, Des."

"Well, why not? We're relying on Remy a lot to lead us in the investigation. It would be the perfect dodge to have him pointing us away from the real thief. That's one reason why her slipping him that note is bothersome. And he could be playing me for the fool."

"Des, I've seen the way he looks at you. There's nothing false about that. Maybe Michele is an art thief, but Remy Tremblay isn't playing with you. He's into you big time. You know that."

"I want to know that, Elena, I really do. My gut tells me that what is happening between him and me is real. But it is happening fast. So fast that my cop alarms are banging like drums."

Elena certainly wasn't going to fault Des for wanting to walk carefully on the slippery slope of romance. She practiced it every day with Hans. "So? What now?"

"Remy is staying at the hotel tonight. He says he has a lot of work to do, including late-night calls to the West Coast tonight and to Europe in the early morning. And that will be good for me, let me get out of the whirlwind for the night. Maybe I'll just follow your lead and treat him like you treat Hans."

Elena took the bait. "And how do I treat Hans?"

"Like an umbrella. Useful when it's raining or the sun's too hot. The rest of the time, you leave it in the trunk with the jumper cables and spare tire."

They both laughed out loud, causing folks at nearby tables to look over. "Harsh, girl friend, pretty harsh." They clinked glasses, and downed their drinks, a beer in one hand, sweet tea in the other.

Des met Remy at the university hotel for dinner. "It's not Tonino's, I'm afraid."

"No sweat, Des," Remy said. "I just need some fuel." He looked at at the line of chafing dishes along the far wall of the dining room. "Buffet for two?

After they had fueled up, Des asked, "Did you enjoy looking around town this afternoon?"

"You bet," Remy replied. "You have a nice little downtown area."

"With an emphasis on little?"

"No, that's not what I meant. I liked it. Some good shops, and prices are cheap. I got my dad a new pickleball paddle for the cost of...."

"An overpriced Polish sausage?" Des broke in.

Remy held up his arms in mock surrender. "I did some work, too."

"Oh?"

"Yeah. I talked to Grant Mullins." When Des didn't seem to register the name, he added, "The authenticator for the Fuertes painting."

"Right. Sorry. What did he have to say?"

"He looked up his records, but he also remembered the case. Everything was legit according to Grant. Painting was pure Fuertes. He even texted me a photo from his files of the painting that he had authenticated. Take a look."

Remy handed Des his phone. She lay two fingers on the screen and spread them apart to enlarge the photo. "My goodness, even I can see that this isn't the same painting that Elena was using for her show. These birds are extraordinary."

"Yes, they are, just like the way Fuertes painted all his birds. So, whatever was hanging in that room was absolutely a forgery and had somehow been switched with the original."

They left the restaurant, and Des walked him to the elevator. "You're sure you want to stay here?"

"No, of course I don't *want* to stay here," he answered, "but I'm pretty sure that I need to. I actually have work to do, and I can't seem to stay focused on that when you're around."

"How nice." She kissed him good-bye in a way that assured he would regret his sleeping arrangements. "Now be a good boy and get to work."

42

Friday

Jimmy called Des the next morning. When she picked up, he started talking immediately. "I went to the gym this morning to check on Grinder."

"Bernard, you mean."

"Yeah, well that's not the important thing. He was supposed to be at work at six this morning, when the gym opens, but he didn't show. The supervisor said that never happened. He might show up still a little drunk, but he always came."

"Okay, Jimmy, pick me up at my house as soon as you can, and we'll go find him."

Classes were changing, and it took Jimmy several maddening minutes to get across campus. He was tempted to throw on the blue lights to move the students out of his way, but he knew Des wouldn't like it if she found out. She was waiting on the porch of her house when he arrived. "Took you long enough. I hope you got a donut for me too." He prepared to explain, but she waved his excuse away and got in. She directed him to the address she had gotten for Grinder off the university's personnel system.

Grinder lived in the attic of a used appliance store on the outskirts of town. A motorcycle was parked at the base of the wooden stairway that led up to the apartment. The motorcycle had a small trailer attached to the back, and the lid was open. While Des and Jimmy were getting out of the car, Grinder came out the door and headed down the steps. He was carrying a loose pile of clothes and other personal items, obscuring his vision.

Jimmy surprised him. "Going on a trip, Grinder?"

"What the...." When he realized who was waiting for him at the bottom of the stairs, he stopped talking for a minute. "Uh, no, just taking some stuff to the homeless shelter."

Des said, "Sure, Bernard, sure you are."

"What's it to you?"

"You didn't show up for work this morning. We were worried about you."

"Oh, yeah, I forgot. I thought I was off today."

"Tell you what, Bernard," Des said. "How about you lock up your things in your cute little trailer there and then come to the station with us."

"What for? I didn't do anything?"

"We'll be the judge of that. Jimmy will lock up your apartment for you." Jimmy climbed up the stairs and took a quick look around the apartment. "No one else up here, boss." He pulled the door shut behind him and headed back down to the parking lot.

They took Bernard to one of the interview rooms and sat him down. Des thought his bulk might overwhelm the cheap plastic chair, but it just creaked in protest and did its job.

Des started the questioning. "Last time we talked, I told you not to leave town. You aren't a good listener, Bernard, are you?" He didn't answer, just looked down at the table. "So, let's try again. When was the last time you saw Manfred Kurtz?"

This seemed to get his attention. "I dunno. Couple of months ago maybe."

"Let's try the truth this time."

He looked at her with scorn written all over his face. "I dunno. I don't write in my diary every night."

Des ignored the scowl and continued. "Well, here's some news for you. We've dusted Kurtz's car for fingerprints, and yours are all over the front passenger area—the door, seat, dashboard, everywhere."

"So what? I've been in his car, a long time ago."

"Well, that's the thing, Bernard," she said. "These fingerprints are new. We can tell these days. And that proves you were in his car recently, very recently."

"Yeah, okay, so what?"

Jimmy took over, allowing Des to watch Grinder's body language carefully. "Why'd you beat him up, Bernard? Didn't like your girlfriend being with that loser?"

Grinder was beginning to sweat, and veins were bulging on his bald head and down his neck. He looked from Jimmy to Des and back again, clinching and unclinching his pork-pie fists. "Look, I didn't kill him. Not even close. I just roughed him up a little."

Jimmy snorted. "You beat him black and blue. And all on his torso, where it wouldn't show, the way an experienced thug would do it. And then, what, you sold him some cocaine?"

"No, no, no. I didn't do any of that."

Des took back over. "Tell us in your own words, why don't you. We *are* good listeners."

"The day after the painting went missing, Kurtz called me and said we needed to meet. I told him to shove it. Send that kid Howie, I told him. It was a big deal, he said, that Howie didn't have the balls to handle. So, I agreed. We met in a parking lot by the stadium. I got into his car, and Kurtz told me he had the painting, that it was valuable, and he wanted to sell it. He wanted me to fence it for him."

He stopped talking, as though he were thinking if he wanted to go on or not. "Keep going, Grinder," Des said. "I think we're just getting to the good parts."

"Yeah, okay. I know this guy...."

"What guy?" Jimmy interrupted.

"Just a guy, okay? He's not important." They let it go for now. "He can get rid of almost anything. So I told him, and a couple of days later, he says that he can sell it. And for good money, too. He offered me ten grand for it. So I told him I'd have it for him the next day. He gave me five grand in advance."

"What day was that?"

"I don't remember exactly, but it was a day or two before Kurtz died."

"You're doing good, Grinder," Des said, feeding him by using his nickname.

"So, I told Kurtz to meet me back at the same parking lot that night and bring the painting. He got out of his car with the painting, and I took it and put it in my trailer. Damn thing hardly fit."

"Then what?"

"I gave him the five grand that we had agreed on. Then he started mouthing off, and I lost it."

"What did he say that made you so angry?"

"He said with the money he was going to take Bet down to Mexico for a trip, somewhere with nude beaches where he could show her off. So, I roughed him up a little."

"A little?"

Bernard shrugged. "Maybe more than a little. I left him laying on the ground next to his car." Then he looked up, wide-eyed. "But he was alive. I know what I'm doing with my fists. I didn't hurt him bad. Cracked rib, maybe, and some bruises, but nothing more than that. I didn't kill him."

"Not then, maybe," Jimmy said, "But the coke you gave him killed him later."

Grinder was shaking his head vehemently. "Oh, no, I didn't give him any drugs. I told you I don't do that. Truth is, he actually offered some to me."

Des took over. "We might even believe you, Grinder, so keep talking."

"The first time, when I was in his car. He said he had some coke and asked me did I want to share with him. He showed me the vial. I said no, and he put it away. He said, well, maybe I'll save it for payday."

"Did he tell you where he got it from?" Des asked.

"Yeah, he did. The Ant-Man."

43

Elena peeked into Ted Graham's office. "Oh, sorry, Ted, didn't know you had company."

Ted waved her in. "It's just Aaron. Join us."

"I'm not sure I like being 'just Aaron,' Ted," Aaron complained. But it was a good natured jibe. He knew that Ted appreciated having the eyes, ears and experience of Aaron Schmidt at his disposal. And for Aaron's part, he thought Ted Graham was about the perfect blend of managing what needed to be managed and staying out of the rest.

"You know what I mean. Good old Aaron. Reliable Aaron. Gentleman and scholar Aaron."

"Apology accepted, as long as a favor to be named later is included."

"Favor?" Ted said. "You're treated like a national treasure around here already. Favor be damned."

Elena laughed. "If you could put your bromance away for a bit, I have a problem I need to discuss. With both of you, if you've got the time, Aaron."

"Anything for you, lovely maiden-in-distress. Pray what is distressing you?"

She sat down. "Okay, so, do you think there are any old stashes of sodium arsenate hiding out somewhere in the BSB?"

Ted leaned forward in his chair. "Not a question I expected to ever come out of your mouth. Cripes, Elena, where is this coming from?"

"I'd rather not say," Elena answered. "Let's just say I was talking with someone official who might need to know such a thing."

Ted groaned. "You haven't been talking to the hazardous waste person again, have you? I told you to stay away from her. She just causes trouble."

Elena objected. "Get off it. Daniella has an important job. Imagine where we'd be if the NSF or NIH came through and we couldn't account for our chemicals. There'd go your precious grant funding. Anyway, no it wasn't her. Forget that part. Can we just accept that maybe I need to know this?"

"Ok, Elena, relax. Aaron, what do you think?"

"Absolutely," Aaron said. "I'm sure lots of labs have some squirreled away."

"Lots of labs?" Elena asked.

"Sure. Sodium arsenate is a great pesticide, and if you have valuable specimens, you want to keep everything from getting at them. Animal skins for sure, but herbarium collections, too. And even my wood samples."

"So, do you have sodium arsenate in your lab?"

Aaron shook his head. "No, not me. I'm a stickler for rules, you know that. I cleared that stuff out decades ago, after we weren't supposed to use it anymore."

Elena actually believed him. Aaron was a good university citizen. "What about our colleagues who aren't so interested in following all the rules, especially if it's inconvenient?"

"Oh, for sure." Aaron put on a mischievous grin. "I could make a list, in order from most to least likely to have ignored all the memos and protocols about toxic chemical disposal."

"Could you really? Do you mean it?"

"Sure, it would be a simple matter of making a dendrogram of yes-no branches, just like identifying a tree."

"Or a wetland plant," Ted interjected. He was a wetland specialist and never missed a chance to remind anyone who'd listen that he was a scientist, too, not just a paper-pusher.

"Right. It would be simple. Used in a lab in the past? Yes, no. Lab hasn't been moved in the last fifty years? Yes, no. Grumpy old professor has been in charge for a long time? Yes, no. Big enough name that nobody messes with him or her? Yes, no. Bingo, out the bottom drops all the most likely locations."

"If you do that for me," Elena said, "I'm yours forever."

"It was just a matter of time, my dear, before my gallantry won the day."

Now it was Ted's turn to object. "Oh, get a room, you two."

'Better than that," Elena said. "How about I make you both dinner tonight?"

"Italian?" they asked at the same time.

"Si. Seven o'clock at my house. And, Aaron, bring that list."

44

Des met Remy at noon for a walk around the campus pond. The day was less pleasant than recently, overcast with a chilly breeze. The water rippled with the breeze, generating an energetic rather than tranquil mood. The weather didn't bother the Canada geese that swam in several small groups around the edge of the pond, occasionally tipping their heads into the water to graze on the submerged weeds in the shallow water.

Remy didn't seem to mind, either. The crisp weather had put a glow in Des's complexion and a brightness in her eyes that he found irresistible. He tried not to stare at her continuously, but he was failing badly. Des seemed almost embarrassed by his unapologetic gaze, and she headed off any personal talk for the moment.

"Did you get your work done?" she asked.

Remy yawned. "Yes. Long calls to the West Coast and Japan. Thank goodness for melatonin, or I'd have gotten no sleep at all."

"Poor baby," Des teased. "I've been working, too."

"Progress?"

"This morning I contacted the man who did that inspection for the museum, the one the dean told us about yesterday," Des explained. "He says the painting was genuine, and he sent me a photo of it as well." They compared her photo with the one that Remy had gotten from his friend. They were identical.

Remy shook his head. "So the real painting was given to the university, and it was still hanging in the library a year ago. That can only mean the paintings have been switched relatively recently."

Des didn't quite buy it. "Don't you think someone would have noticed?"

"Not necessarily," Remy said. "How many people actually look, I mean really look, at the artwork on the walls of their offices or in the hallways?"

"I know, but this was a noted piece of art, hanging in something like an art gallery. Someone surely should have noticed."

"Only if they were familiar with the original, Des, and had studied it deeply. Elena didn't seem to have any idea that it was a forgery, and she was pretty captivated by the thing. None of the students or staff would know about the original."

Just then Remy's cellphone started buzzing. Des walked on a few yards so he could have some privacy. She found a bench and waited for him. She couldn't keep her mind from thinking about Michele Richards.

When he ended the call and joined her at the bench, Des decided she couldn't let this gulf grow between them. "Listen, Remy, I don't know where we are…"

"At the pond, and it's lovely. A bit chilly, but still nice."

"I'm serious, so just listen. I don't have any hold over you, what you do, who you do it with."

"Hang on, Des, what's going on?"

"Michele Richards."

A cloud passed over his face. "Okay. What about her?"

"I saw her slip a piece of paper into your coat pocket at the art exhibit. I need to know what that was about."

"Are you asking as the police chief or as something else?"

Des hesitated for a moment before answering. "Remy, look, these last few days with you have been wonderful. But I'm not a dewy-eyed teenager who can't face the truth. And whether I'm a police chief or something else depends on your answer. What was on the paper?"

Remy reached into his pocket and pulled out the note. He handed it to her. She unfolded it and saw two sets of numbers. She looked at him with questions in her eyes.

"Those are the entry codes to Michele's house. One for the gate at the driveway and one for the front door."

Des's heart leaped into her throat, and she looked at Remy with sorrow in her eyes. "Relax, Des. I didn't use them. Let me explain."

"Go on."

"There's nothing going on between Michele and me. She wants there to be. But I learned a long time ago that I need to keep my work and my personal life separate. I've told her that before, but I think you know that Michele likes to get her way." Des nodded. "She asked me where I was staying when I told her I was coming down. Then at the art exhibit, she whispered to me that I didn't need a hotel room. She slipped me the codes and said she'd be waiting for me."

"So you didn't go because it would be bad for business, huh?"

"Stop, Des. Just listen. Before last week, yeah, maybe I would have been tempted enough to use the codes. I don't know, maybe. But my life changed a week ago when I met you. You may not be dewy-eyed, but this guy doesn't know what hit him. He's just really glad it did. My decision wasn't about business. It was about Desdemona White and my future with her."

Des's face cleared in an instant. He reached a hand behind her head and pulled her to him. They kissed and held each other. "Remy," she sighed. "Remy. What is happening here?"

"Let's not worry about that yet," he answered. "Or put labels on it. Let's just..."

"Enough said," Des finished the thought for him. They sat quietly on the bench for a few minutes, enjoying the view. Maybe sitting on park benches together will be our thing, Des thought.

Remy's phone rang again. He checked the caller ID and then walked off a few feet to handle the call.

"Well, I have good news and bad news," he said when he rejoined Des on the bench. "Which do you want first?"

"Good news."

"That was Tonino. Remember he was our waiter at Delmo's?"

"Yeah, and your spy in the black market for art. Has he found the painting? Is that the good news?"

"Yes, he has found it. It was bought by a gang boss in New York, just as I suspected."

"That is good news. We can go get him, and get the painting back."

"Now the bad news. Two pieces of bad news, really. First, Tonino never names names. So, although he knows who bought the painting, he won't tell me. Never has, never will. I just live with that, and so do my clients."

Des understood how it was with informants. You couldn't push them too hard, or they'd go away, voluntarily or otherwise. "Okay, bad news number two."

"In a way, this is sort of good news, too."

"Make up your mind, kiddo. Either way, spit it out."

Remy thought Des was sounding a little too much like a cop. "The buyer discovered that it was a forgery and went ape. Threw the painting in his fireplace and burned it to ashes, canvas, frame, everything."

"I don't hear any good news in there. The university lost a valuable painting, and I have to explain to President Crutchfield that although I know that it got sold into the art black market in New York, it was destroyed because the buyer found out it was a fake. Where's the good news?"

"Well, we now know for sure that it was a fake. Whoever the buyer got to look at it came to the same conclusion I did. So, the university didn't really lose anything of value, did it? Nobody lost anything."

"But, you know, all of this doesn't help me much at all."

"Meaning?" Remy asked.

"The painting that was stolen a couple weeks ago was a fake, so no loss there. But the painting the dean donated was authentic. We still have a stolen painting. The only thing that has changed is that now I have no idea when or how it was stolen."

Remy put his arm around her and leaned back against the bench. "And then there's the other theft." Des looked at him with a question in her eyes. "Someone has stolen my heart."

Des sat behind her desk and frowned at her two colleagues seated in prison-made oak chairs opposite her. "Okay, let's review where we are. First the murder."

Jessie spoke first. "Manfred Kurtz was poisoned by sodium arsenate mixed with cocaine. There are several sources of the poisoned drugs."

"My top contender," Jimmy said, "is Bernard Havel, the infamous Grinder. He hated the kid, and he certainly had contacts from the bad side of the tracks. We caught him trying to leave town."

"Who else?" Des asked.

Jessie answered. "The girlfriend, Bet, is a possibility. Maybe she was tired of him, wanted to get back with Grinder. Maybe they were in it together."

Des shook her head. "Where was she going to get arsenic to spike the drug with? For that matter, where was Grinder going to get it?"

"That doesn't bother me," Jimmy said. "Grinder's the kind of guy who can find anything. He fenced the painting in a matter of days. He probably knows every drug lab in this half of the state. He's a bad guy."

Des moved on. "What about Kurtz's little buddy, Howie Anderson? Maybe he was tired of being the courier and wanted to be The Man. Replace Kurtz."

"Could be," Jessie said. "It's often the quiet ones, right?"

"On television, maybe," argued Jimmy, "not in real life. A guy like Howie would get eaten alive in a crowd of Grinder clones. You know who we really need to find?"

Des knew, but she asked anyhow. "Who, kiddo?"

"Ant-Man. Whoever the Ant-Man is, he keeps showing up. Kurtz told Grinder that's who gave him the coke, so he's most likely the one who laced it with poison."

"So, my detective friends, who would Kurtz have named his 'Ant-Man'?" Des asked.

Jessie looked stumped. "I've keep thinking about this, and getting nowhere. I thought it could be an entomology professor or student. I've checked the website for the entomology department, and we don't seem to have any ant experts on the faculty. I also checked the research data base for ant projects, and came up empty."

Jimmy said, "Maybe he's someone who is short, little, you know, like ants."

"And has six legs?" scoffed Jessie.

"Settle down, children," Des said. "Yeah, we do need to find the Ant-Man. Nobody seems to have a clue. But it is suspicious that the contact Kurtz had for A.M. is an unregistered phone. Jessie, do some cross-checking of staff names in entomology that have those initials, and students, too. Majors, etc. Also, see if there's an entomology club and go talk to the leaders. Someone has to know who the Ant-Man is. He's at the top of my list, even though we don't know what motive he might have. Now, about the painting thefts."

"Well, we know that Kurtz stole the painting," Jessie said. "The first one, anyhow. When I showed Hannah the picture of Kurtz, she positively identified him, and then promptly started crying again. Besides, Grinder told us he got the painting from Kurtz. I think we've got that nailed down, boss."

Then Des filled them in about the news from Remy that the stolen painting had been destroyed. "Even though we can't ever recover the painting, we can be as close to positive as possible that the stolen painting was a forgery, totally worthless."

"Good," Jimmy said, "that's that then."

"No, kiddo, that's not that."

"Why isn't it that that's that?"

"Enough thats. We still had a painting stolen—the real painting, the one that the dean gave, that two legitimate experts said was real. We just don't know when the theft happened or what has happened to the painting since."

Jessie shook her head like she was trying to knock the whole mess out through her ear and onto the floor. "Cripes. So anyone could have taken the painting since the expert from the museum looked at it, what, a year ago?"

"That's right, Jessie. But it was gone by this summer, when Elena took her photos for the art exhibition. And it seems to have disappeared since then. Remy is going to check with his sources again, but he's pretty sure his guy would have heard about the real painting being around when he was asking questions about what we now know was the forgery."

"So, let me get this straight." Jimmy said. "The real painting was stolen some time over the past year, replaced by a fake painting that no one seems to have noticed. And the original hasn't been seen or heard from since. Right?"

"Bingo, Jimmy."

"Boss, we've got about as much chance of solving this one as we do of winning the national football championship." The team had never been exceptional, but right now it was exceptionally bad, 1-4 at this point in the season.

Jessie, who was an unapologetic VWU sports fan, grimaced, but Des nodded. "About right, Jimmy. I think that goes on the back burner. But what stays on the high heat is the connection between Kurtz's murder and his theft of the painting. Presumably Kurtz didn't know the painting was a forgery when he stole it. But he very well could have been killed because he had made some connection that made him dangerous."

Jessie said, "He could have tried to blackmail the buyer. Well, not the buyer, but the middle-man."

"You mean Grinder?" Jimmy asked.

Des shook her head. "No, the timing doesn't work. Kurtz had the poisoned cocaine the first time that he met Grinder to talk about selling the painting. So chasing down the path of the forgery after Grinder got it is a dead end. I'll tell Frank Marin about it, but it is more a town issue than a campus one."

Jessie said, "We haven't talked about the second stolen painting. It happened after Kurtz was dead, so he couldn't have been the thief."

"I haven't really even had time to think about that one, Jessie," Des said. "Can I turn that over to you for the moment? Look at the tapes again and just toss it around in your mind. I think someone figured that if one painting was that easy to steal, he could get away with it, too. And that it would get blamed on the person who did the first theft."

Jessie nodded and smiled. "On it, boss." The idea that Des would entrust her with the lead on an investigation was a compliment that would motivate her out of sleep, food and any thought of a private life for as long as it took.

All three got up from their chairs, ready to end the meeting, when Jimmy held up his hand with a strange look on his face. Des sat down again. "What gives, kiddo?"

"I just thought of something," he said. "The real painting disappeared a while ago, but, according to your friend Remy, it hasn't shown up in the most likely place, New York. Actually, I'd say that was the second most likely place. The most likely is close to home, where it was stolen. Most crimes are committed by people who know the victim, right?"

Des nodded, "Yes, that's true."

"Well, we have a big-time art lover right here in Stone Valley, don't we?"

"Are you talking about Michele Richards again, Jimmy?"

"Yeah I am. Think about it. What if she wanted the Fuertes painting, or both paintings? What if she craved having them, but couldn't get her hands on them, because they belonged to the university? There was just one way she could get them—steal them. That is, pay someone to steal them."

Des played devil's advocate. "So, let's say that she did orchestrate the theft of the original painting and replacement with a forgery. Let's even say that there was some way she could have gotten the forgery made."

"She certainly has the contacts and the money, Des," Jimmy broke in.

"Yes, she does. But that leaves one big question that doesn't have an answer."

"What question?" Jessie asked.

"If she already had the original painting in her possession, why would Michele Richards steal the forgery?"

Aaron and Ted arrived promptly at seven, mouths watering for whatever Elena had prepared. A plate of bruschetta was waiting for them on the table in front of the couch. "Dig in, fellas. And pour yourselves a glass of wine. I'll be in in a minute."

They sat down, staring at the food and wine arrayed in front of them. They listened to Elena bustling around in the kitchen. "Should we be gentlemen and wait?" Ted asked.

"In this case, I believe a gentleman would follow the lady's wishes." Aaron answered. "So, no!" They pounced on the offerings.

Elena joined them, only to find only one slice of the appetizer left. "Well, thanks for leaving something for me!"

"It was Aaron's fault, not mine," Ted said through a mouthful of crusty bread.

Aaron deflected the conversation by examining the wine bottle. "Brunello. That's a fine red wine, Elena. Top shelf."

"I never heard of it before. It was a gift from Remy, for lending him my car yesterday." She poured herself a glass and took a sip. "My goodness, that is good. How do you know about it?"

"Ah," Aaron said, "secrets of my wanton youth. One of my early friends at the university was the oenologist."

"The what?" asked Ted.

"Oenologist, you cretin. Oenology is the study of wine. He taught me a lot about wines. Interesting thing about him..."

Ted groaned and interrupted. "No, not another Aaron story to make me feel stupid, especially on a Friday evening."

Aaron pouted, but Elena rescued the situation by moving them all to the dining room for dinner. Minestrone soup, followed by veal saltimbocca and a cheese and fruit plate. The Brunello disappeared quickly and was followed by chianti.

They moved back to the living room, where Elena served them coffee with homemade biscotti. As he dipped a cookie in his coffee and stuffed it in his mouth, Aaron shook his head as if in disbelief. "How a woman as talented, brilliant and beautiful as you and who can cook like this hasn't been taken off the market is one of the great mysteries of life, my dear. You solved the Drew Robbins murder, but can you solve that?"

Elena laughed, but couldn't let him off the hook. "Not sure I like the analogy of 'being on the market.' Maybe I just haven't met the right tree expert yet. Know of any?"

"If only I were, maybe, thirty years younger, I'd have swept you off your feet long ago." With that, Aaron grabbed his satchel from the adjacent chair and plopped it on the coffee table.

Of course, Elena thought, he carried a satchel. Not a backpack or a brief case. Never one to give Aaron a break, Elena poked him. "Nice purse."

"No purse, young maiden. This is a medieval packsack, used by knights to transport their essential materials."

"Pick that up at Goodwill?" Ted chided.

Aaron smiled. "Yes, more or less. I snagged this at a boot sale in the Cotswolds many years ago. Traded it for a Texas Instruments calculator. Fascinating, isn't it? The packsack is still as useful now as it was hundreds of years ago. When was the last time you saw someone with a calculator?"

Ted threw up his hands in mock defeat. "You win, as always."

Aaron opened the packsack and pulled out a sheaf of paper. "I have my report, as promised." He passed a copy each to Elena and Ted. "So, I did an analysis of the labs most likely to contain hidden stashes of sodium arsenate and put them in order of likelihood."

Elena scanned the list. "Yikes! Dean Vukovic is at the top of the list? Are you kidding?"

"Just the facts, ma'am. He's been here a long time and occupied the same lab all that time. It was the lab of an old mammalogist before him, a fellow named Jensen, who retired after an entire career in that lab. Then Vukovic took over. No one is going to question the dean or inspect his lab beyond the minimum needed. But he's just one on the list. Could be Samuels, the ornithologist, too. She's been here since the first dinosaur grew wings, and she has a reptuation as a confirmed traditionalist--doesn't like any new fangled ideas, techniques or, I presume, chemicals. And then there's the herbarium. The herbarium director has turned over recently, but that place is such a labyrinth that there could be remnants of the last ice age in there, and no one would know. And the last likely space is controlled by Milan Czarnatz, the entomologist. He is such a grumpy old thing that no one would dare cross him. Actually, if I could add a criterion for nastiness, I'd move him to the pole position."

"You've got too much time on your hands, Aaron," Ted said, marveling at his ability to pull this together in an afternoon. But it was just the kind of meaningless little puzzle that Aaron was fond of. "I may need to increase your teaching load."

Aaron ignored the threat and pulled another set of papers from his packsack. "That's not all, my friends." He passed the papers over to Elena.

The pages were yellowed with age and the ink was fading. "What's this?"

Aaron smiled. "I save everything, you know." Ted winced. He knew. He'd been after Aaron for years to clear out his lab. The wood specimens and such were valuable, he knew, but Aaron had a whole room full of file cabinets, and Ted knew there was nothing in the drawers that couldn't be tossed or at least digitized and stored in a fraction of the space. That room could be used by new faculty who needed space. "This is a report from 1965 of the hazardous chemical committee. They were charged with reviewing a list of newly designated toxic chemicals that had been in wide distribution before that time. Remember, Rachel Carson's *Silent Spring* had recently been published, and people had begun taking chemicals seriously."

"How did you get it?" Elena asked. "Even you aren't old enough to have been on the faculty then."

"Thank you for noticing, child. No, I wasn't on the faculty then, but in 1978, just after I came, I was made chair of the successor to that committee. No one else wanted the responsibility, so they gave it to the new guy. And I used a lot of chemicals on wood analysis, so it was logical. I inherited the files, and, voila, here they are."

Elena began to look through the report, but Aaron put his hand over it to stop her. "I bequeath it to you, lass. You can have it, and I'll bring you the rest of the committee files next week."

"And, Elena, when you're done with whatever nonsense you're about," Ted said, making sure he got the last word, "throw it all away."

47

Saturday

Des stared at Remy across the breakfast table. He was somewhere else. "Earth to Rembrandt," she challenged.

He shook his head, dislodging the cobwebs, and smiled. "Sorry, Des. I was just thinking."

"About who?"

"Who? Not about a who." Their eyes met and he smiled warmly. "You're the only 'who' that inhabits my world anymore."

"Okay, let's not get silly. I'll take being the only one who made you breakfast this morning. Breakfast that's getting cold while you're thinking."

He looked down at the bowl of instant oatmeal and chuckled. "Yes, I'm so sorry to be ignoring the quick Quaker. My apologies."

"So, what were you thinking?"

"Can we go back over to the Fuertes Room this morning? I'd like to look at all the paintings in that room that have been donated over the years. Can we get a list of those from Tim, the guy we talked to before?"

Des nodded. "Sure, we can do that. What's on your mind?"

"I'm wondering if the Fuertes fake is a one-off or a pattern."

"Of course. Let's get going."

As Des drove, Remy talked with Tim Worstall, apologizing for calling on a Saturday morning. As before, Tim was excited to be part of things. He told Remy that he would check his files and text him an inventory of all the paintings donated to the college and hanging in the Fuertes Room. "Shouldn't take much more than an hour or so," Tim said.

When they got to the library, Remy suggested that Des just leave him there, as his examination was going to take some time. "I'll call when I'm finished," he said and kissed her goodbye.

I could get used to that, Des thought, as she drove to the statiion--Remy and I going off to work together, then coming home to each other in the evening.

For the moment, though, ahead of her was every police officer's nightmare—spending her Saturday morning slogging through paperwork.

48

Elena was deep into the Saturday crossword when the ring of the cellphone broke her reverie. She was even more surprised to see Judith Heinz's name show up on the caller ID. "Hello, Judith. How nice to hear from you."

"Thanks, but maybe, maybe not."

"What's wrong?"

"You remember my friend, Jennifer Haskins, the artist?"

"Of course. We had a delightful lunch the other day."

"Elena, she called me a few minutes ago in an awful state. I could tell she'd been crying, and she kept going on about having nothing to live for. I'm really worried about her."

Elena understood. "She sounds like she's really hurting, Judith. Are you going to do something for her?"

"I offered to come out to visit, but after we talked for awhile, she seemed to calm down a little and said I didn't need to bother, that she'd be fine. But I'm very worried."

"I don't blame you," Elena said, but she was also wondering why Judith had called her. "What can I do to help?"

Judith sighed, perhaps with relief. "I knew you'd be willing to help. I am going to go out to her place this morning. I don't care that she said not to come. But I don't want to go alone. I was hoping that you'd go with me?"

"I'm not sure Jennifer would want me there. I hardly know her."

"It's not so much for her as it is for me. I want a friend with me, so if we need to intervene in some way, there'd be two of us."

Elena had no option. "Of course I'll be glad to go with you."

"Good. Can I come by your house in a few minutes?"

"Sure, Judith. See you soon." She quickly showered and changed into what her mother would have called a "visiting dress." Shirt-waist is what the catalogues called it, tailored on top and with a loose, flowing skirt below. A pink flower pattern on the white background produced a casual look that all women knew meant hi-friend-what's-up. After Judith picked her up, they stopped at The Scandia Cafe for a bakery treat.

The drive to Jennifer's home was the opposite of the drive Judith had taken a few days earlier. Today was overcast with light rain. The landscape looked sullen, like a toddler who couldn't go out to play because of the weather. The women rode in silence for most of the trip, their thoughts muted by the drabness around them and their uncertainty over what lay at the end of the journey.

When Jennifer answered the door and saw Judith and Elena, she seemed instantly embarrassed. "Oh, dear, you didn't need to come out to check on me. I'm so sorry. And Elena came, too. I've put you to a lot of trouble."

"No trouble," Judith lied. "We had planned to take a drive this morning anyhow, to look at the fall colors. Sometimes a gray day gives a different sense that an artist can use to advantage. You know that Elena is an art lover, and it was a perfect chance to get out of town."

Elena smiled and added to the lie. "And away from grading papers! No way to spend a Saturday morning, even a dreary one. Any excuse to put that off is a good excuse. And Hans made this for us." She held up the white box tied with a brown string.

Jennifer forced a smile. "Well, this is a cause for celebration then. Please come in."

She busied herself with preparing coffee and setting up the dining room table. "Don't use this much anymore," Jennifer said. "Not for just me." She put a hand on the back of a chair to steady herself, as though the idea of being alone was suddenly more than she could bear.

Judith put a gentle arm around her waist. "Do you need to sit down, Jennifer?"

But Jennifer shook it off. "No, I'm fine. You two look around while I finish setting the table."

They did as she suggested, walking through the living areas of the home and admiring the artwork. Most of the pieces were landscapes that Jennifer had painted, but one intrigued Elena. It was a copy of a Claude Monet scene showing a girl in a long dress standing on the crest of a small flower-covered hill, holding a parasol.

When Jennifer rejoined them, Elena asked about the painting. "If I didn't know better, I'd think that was a real Monet."

Both Jennifer and Judith grinned and laughed. "Well not quite," Jennifer said, "but it's not bad, is it?"

"It's better than not bad," Elena said, and then the light went on. "You two painted that together, didn't you?"

"Yes," Judith said. "That was one of our favorite scenes. We liked it because both the figure of the girl, which was my specialty, and the landscape, which was Jennifer's, were both equally important. I've got one at my home, too."

Elena then noticed a framed photograph on a small stand behind the dining room table. "Is that you, Jennifer, with Dean Vukovic?"

Jennifer looked at the photo and sighed. "Yes, it is. That was taken a long time ago, on one of our early trips to Montenegro."

They sat down for coffee and cake, five thin layers with alternating fillings of vanilla custard and raspberry sauce, and chatted about a variety of things. Eventually Judith said, "I'm worried about you, Jennifer. You don't look good, and you seem distracted."

"I'm sorry, Judith. I told you you didn't need to come all the way out here. I'm fine. Just still reeling from the death of my nephew. I feel like I let my sister down. I was supposed to be watching out for him. All of this," she pointed around the room, "is rather meaningless now that he's gone."

"Not true, Jennifer. You are a wonderful artist, and the community loves you. We need you, Jennifer, we really do." Then Judith switched tone. "So, stop talking nonsense about the meaning of life. Both of us made decisions long ago not to have a husband or children. We've been good with that for all these years, and Manfred's death, as tragic as it is, doesn't change that."

Jennifer stared off into space as tears ran down her face. "That all sounds so hollow now. Stuck out here with a bunch of paintings. Flat representations of life. Sometimes I think that I paint realistically because that's as close as I ever get to having a real life. Even Ralph and me. We've been together for decades, but 'together' is just an abstract idea." She reached back and picked up the photo of the two of them. "He lives his life and I live mine. We live like two balls in a pinball game, bouncing around off bumpers and flippers and springs, and occasionally making contact. And now Manny is gone. My ball just went down the hole and out of play. Meaningless, totally meaningless."

She paused and looked at her friends. She registered the concern on their faces and tried to back off her emotions. "Sorry, just a bit of idle psycho-babble. You live out here alone and sometimes your mind takes you on a journey that you hadn't planned for. I'm fine, really, just fine."

They sat wordless for what felt like hours, but was surely just a minute or two. Elena broke the silence. "Time for us to go. Much as I've enjoyed seeing you both, those papers of mine really do need grading."

At the door, Judith gave Jennifer a long hug. "I'll call tomorrow, to see how you're doing."

Jennifer gave a small smile. "My guardian angel. Okay, call me."

As they drove back to town, both women were silent for a long time. "Do you think she'll be okay, Judith?" Elena eventually asked.

"Sure. She's a resilient old bird, just like me."

No, Elena thought, she's not a bit like you.

49

Jessie had been over the tape of the second art theft so many times that she knew it by heart. And it had revealed nothing new. The identity of the thief was completely disguised, and he—or she—had been perfectly disciplined to never look at the camera.

That thought sent her in another direction. Only someone thoroughly familiar with the operation of the camera would know how to avoid being identified. Most crooks who tried to outsmart surveillance cameras just sprayed the lens with black paint. So, this thief had to be someone familiar with the camera system.

She looked back through tapes for several days before the theft. The room had been busy with meetings of university committees and library employees, but no one seemed to pay any attention to the camera. Lots of individuals and small groups came in to look at the paintings, but again, few gave more than a casual glance at the camera. One couple made sure to kiss and smile at the camera, and another looked up and gave it the finger.

So, no one was casing the room in preparation for stealing the painting. Jessie reasoned that the next most likely candidates were library staff themselves. She spoke with Yvonne Michaels, who was on Saturday duty at the library, and learned that all library staff swiped their identification cards to the office door lock when they arrived and swiped out when they left. Jessie asked Yvonne to compile a list of everyone who had worked the day of the theft, along with when they had clocked in and out.

It took Yvonne about an hour to organize the list, and she texted it to Jessie. Both Hannah Maddox and Howie Anderson were on the list, working together during the evening hours.

Jessie's phone rang, and she was surprised to see the librarian calling. "What's up, Yvonne?"

"Something doesn't make sense about the list. I don't know if it's important or not, but it is a little odd."

That's what witnesses always said, Jessie thought, but at least she called. "Let me be the judge of that. What did you notice?"

"Well, all the staff who checked in and out were on the schedule to be working that day. I checked the payroll program."

Jessie interrupted. "I noticed that Hannah Maddox and Howie Anderson were both working that evening. Is that what's bothering you?"

"I hadn't thought of that, really," Yvonne said. "Why would that be important?"

Maybe not important, Jessie thought, but maybe yes. She'd leave that for now. "Sorry, Yvonne, forget about that. What were you going to say?"

"The odd thing is Will Morales."

"Your IT guy?" Jessie asked.

"Right. He checked in in the morning, and he checked out at about five, when he should have. But I was working later that day, and he was still there working late, too. He didn't leave after he swiped out. Of course, I didn't know that then. I would never have noticed it except that you asked me to check the records."

"Can you remember when he left?"

"Well, no, I can't. I left before him. I do remember that he was fiddling with a couple of the computer terminals in the common area. He told me that they were misbehaving and he needed to get them back on line before he left."

"When was that?"

"I left at about eight, I think. Hannah and Howie were still there, working until closing and then locking up.

"When is closing time?"

"Ten. Anyway, I said good-bye and told them to be sure to lock up tight."

"Thanks, Yvonne. That's a big help. Please don't tell anyone about this right now, okay?"

"Of course. I hope I didn't get him in trouble. Good-bye."

Jessie immediately called Hannah Maddox. She was actually taking a walk with Howie Anderson. "Put me on speaker, Hannah, so I can talk to you both."

"Ok," she said and clicked the necessary buttons. "We can both hear you now."

"You were both working at the library on the evening before the second painting was stolen. Do you remember that?"

She heard them both say yes, but Hannah continued, "Oh, no, I really am in trouble now, aren't I?"

"Not if you didn't do anything wrong," Jessie said. "Did you do something wrong?"

"No, but it was me there both times."

Howie tried to be brave. "We were both there, Hannah. We didn't do anything wrong. We were just working."

Jessie stopped their worry. "I'm not really interested in you. I'm wondering about Will Morales, the IT guy. He was working that evening, too, right?"

Hannah answered first. "Yes, he was. He was working on the computer terminals that students use. We didn't really pay much attention to him, though."

"And did he leave before you locked up?"

It was Howie's turn. "Well, I remember that he finished working on the terminals and said he was leaving. Remember, Hannah?"

"Yes, I remember...wait. He said he was going to go out the back way, remember?"

Jessie asked, "There's a back way out of the library?"

"Yes," Howie said, "there's a door to the loading dock on the back of the building. It's where books and supplies get brought in. And, yes, now that we're talking about it, I remember that he told us goodnight and said he was going to let himself out the back door."

"Would you know if he actually went out that door?" Jessie asked.

Howie answered. "There's a light that goes on at the desk if the door is opened. I remember that just after he said goodnight, the light went off. I figured it was him letting himself out. But we didn't watch him leave, or anything. We're supposed to stay out front."

And flirt with each other, Jessie thought. "Okay, thanks. But listen, let's keep this between us for now, okay?"

She heard them both say yes, and then Hannah said the same thing Yvonne did. "I hope we didn't get him in trouble."

No you didn't, Jessie thought to herself, he did that all by himself. As soon as she hung up, Jessie hurried to Des's office and told her what she'd learned.

"Excellent, kiddo, just excellent. Do you know where he lives?"

Jessie had looked him up in the university database while they were talking. "Start the process for getting a search warrant. I'll call the town cops and let them know what's going on."

"Got it, boss."

In less than an hour Des, Jessie and Jimmy were knocking on Will Morales' apartment door. He answered, and then he blanched when he realized who they were.

"Will Morales, we have a search warrant for your apartment, car and any other properties that we might learn you control. Do you understand?"

He meekly nodded his head and stood aside to let them in. Jessie and Jimmy moved past him to the other rooms in the apartment. Des stayed just inside the door with Morales. "This will be a lot easier if you just give us the painting. Then we won't have to tear your house apart."

Without a word, he opened the door to the coat closet and pulled down a paper mailing tube from the upper shelf. He gave it to Des. She pulled out a rolled canvas. She spread it open on the back of a chair. It was, as she knew it would be, the missing painting of a bald eagle from the Fuertes Room. So far, Morales hadn't said a word. "Would you like to tell me about this?"

After a few tries, Morales found his voice. "I don't know what came over me. I just thought that I could get away with it. Someone had stolen the first painting, and I figured you would just blame this one on the same person."

"What were you going to do with it?"

"Sell it. I looked it up, and it was worth a lot of money. Thousands of dollars."

Jessie and Jimmy walked back into the front room. "Des, you need to see this."

Des followed Jessie back into the one bedroom in the apartment, while Jimmy stayed with Morales. She pointed to an open closet door. The floor of the closet was filled with books. She picked one from the top of a pile. It was an ancient veterinary anatomy text. A label inside said it was from the special collections of VWU's library. A quick look at a few other books confirmed they were all from the university library, some about art and others about animals and medicine.

They walked back into the front room and gave the book to Morales, his hands shaking so badly he almost dropped it. "Care to explain?"

He just stared at the book.

"Well, let me take a try," Des said. "You've been stealing books out of the special collections rooms at the art and veterinary libraries and selling them. You have access because of your IT position and you're able to disengage the exit alarms when you take the books away. People don't look for these old books often, so the chance of being caught is small. You sell them gradually."

He looked at her and slowly nodded his head.

"Jimmy, take him to the station, read him his rights, and charge him with theft. Jessie, you stay here and oversee the process of inventorying and removing these books and anything else that looks like stolen property. I'll call a patrol van and a couple of uniformed officers to help you."

"What are you going to do, Des?"

"Back to the scene of the crime." She rolled the stolen painting back into the tube and headed out the door.

50

In the Fuertes Room at the library, Remy checked the list that Tim had sent. The room had contained seven paintings that Vukovic had donated, including the two that were now missing. Remy studied each of the remaining five in turn, in some cases using a magnifier on his cellphone. Then he took each off the wall, turned them over and examined the back. He did the same for each of the other five paintings that were not gifts from the dean.

When he finished, he called Des. She answered from her car as she was driving to meet him. "Can you bring over the frame from the second theft?"

"Sure," she said. "But I can do better than that." She explained that they had just solved the second theft, and a great number of other thefts that no one even knew had occurred.

"That's great," Remy said, "but I need the frame, too.

"Got it, Colombo. I'll be there in a few minutes."

Des arrived after a short detour to the police station to pick up the frame, and she saw that Remy had pretty well dismantled the Fuertes Room. He had the pictures donated by the dean lined up on one side of the conference table, and the others along the opposite side. She handed him the rolled up canvas from Will Morales's house. "This completes the set. Well, except for the missing Fuertes painting."

Remy unrolled the painting of the bald eagle. He examined the ragged edge of the canvas, again with the magnifier. "Yep, this one's a forgery, too. I can tell from the cuts that it is a brand new canvas, no more than a few years old. Here's the bottom line. Five of the paintings donated by the dean are fakes. The other two are originals, along with the five not donated by the dean."

"Jesus," Des said. "Are you sure?"

"Absolutely."

"Okay, tell me how you know."

He brought Des to the end of the conference table, where he had put two of the paintings side by side, the study supposedly by Albert Bierstadt of deer wading in shallow water that was a gift from the dean, and a painting from another donor of farm animals by Francis Colomb, a lesser known painter of the Hudson River school.

"Both frames are old, so they're legitimate, but you can get old frames at antique stores for a few dollars." He turned both over. "But look carefully at where the canvas bends around the stretchers. If this canvas were 150 years old, the edges would be stiff and brittle. Little flakes of paint would have started coming loose. You can see with a magnifier that that is happening on the Colomb painting. But look at the Bierstadt."

"Nothing happening there," Des said after a brief look.

Remy nodded. "Right, nothing. There are other hints as well, technical things like how the canvases are attached to the stretchers. Whoever did the forgeries didn't worry too much about what was happening on the back of the painting, assuming, I suppose, that no one would ever look back there very carefully."

Remy turned the paintings over again and set the Biertstadt back in the line with the other fakes. "The paintings are excellently done. The artist is very good at copying, and I'm sure that he had the original painting with him while he was making each copy, or at least a full sized high-resolution photograph. But if you look carefully, you'll see certain idiosyncrasies in the style. We call that the stroke signature. It comes from the muscle memory of the painter's fingers." He held his cellphone magnifier over a small section. "See how each stroke ends with a slight curve?"

"Yes," Des said, although she wasn't sure.

Remy moved to the next forgery and again used his cellphone to highlight a section. "The same curve shows up here. And in all four of the forgeries. But the others, the ones not donated by the dean and the two smaller sketches he gave, all have unique and different stroke signatures."

"So, you're saying that not only are they all forgeries, but they were all done by the same person?"

"Yes, absolutely. And Tim's records show that the gifts were all made a few years apart, over a period of about twenty years. That's enough time between gifts so the forger could take his time doing each painting, letting it dry thoroughly, letting the varnish age a bit. That sort of thing."

"Only one person could have orchestrated such a thing, is that what you're thinking?"

"That's the most obvious conclusion."

The reality was setting in for Des. "And the most probable candidate is Dean Ralph Vukovic, right?"

Remy agreed. "Right. The dean must have paid someone to make the fakes, using his originals. He had the originals authenticated by an expert, like my friend, and then when he gave the painting to the university, he switched them, keeping the original and hanging the copy in this room."

"But who did the forgeries, I wonder," Des said.

"I think I know that, too," Remy offered. "That's why I wanted you to bring the frame from the second theft."

Des handed the evidence bag to Remy. "May I open it?" he asked.

"Yes. It doesn't matter anymore. We've recovered the painting and have a confession from the thief. So, go ahead."

He was already wearing white cloth gloves. He made a space on the table and laid the frame upside down on top of the evidence bag. He examined the remaining canvas that was still attached to the stretcher. "Yes, the same characteristics of the canvas are here, too."

Des checked Tim's list. "And it was a gift from the dean as well, and it fills a gap in the time line."

"Because the painting isn't attached to the stretcher anymore," Remy said, "I'm going to pry the canvas loose along the bottom edge. Okay?"

Des shrugged. "I guess. You're the expert."

"So, Ms. Police Chief, do you carry a pocket knife?"

She unsnapped a strap on her belt and pulled a tactical folding knife from its sheath. She pulled open the blade and handed it to him. "Perhaps a little more than that, but it should do. Be careful, it's sharp."

Remy used the point of the blade to loosen the staples that held the canvas along the bottom edge of the stretcher. After he'd freed a few inches, he stopped. "There it is."

Des crowded in. "What, Remy? What are you seeing?"

He used the light on his phone to provide some contrast. "Two initials have been punched into the stretcher. Can you read them?"

"Barely," she said, "but it looks like a J and an H. JH. Yes, that's it. JH. What do you think it means, Remy?"

"I know what it means. It means that Jennifer Haskins has been painting forgeries for Dean Vukovic for the past twenty years."

51

Sunday

Des heard the report crackle through her radio at 5 AM. A structure on fire, well outside town. The university fire brigade was requested to assist. Although it wasn't in VWU's jurisdiction, the university fire marshal sent a truck and an EMT unit. Des slid quietly out of bed, but Remy awakened. "What's up?"

"There's a fire outside of town, and our university fire crew has been called to help. That means I've got to get there, too."

"Do you want me to go with you?" Remy asked.

"No. I don't know what I'm going to find or what I'll have to do. Probably nothing. But you stay here and sleep." She dressed immediately and headed to the address given on the alert.

The location was obvious as she approached. An orange glow lit the pre-dawn darkness. She parked down the lane, trying to not clog the immediate vicinity with another vehicle that couldn't be of any help. She walked the quarter-mile to the turn-off to the property. She met Frank Marin as she approached the burning building.

"Hello, Frank." He turned and nodded. "Jeez, it is burning hot."

"Yeah, Des, it is. It's the studio for a local artist, and the place must have been full of paint and solvents."

"So it isn't a residence. Anyone in there?"

"We don't know yet. There's no one in the house. We've got to get the fire under control before we can go in. But the property belongs to Jennifer Haskins."

"My god, Frank, I know her."

"Yeah, she's pretty well known in the region."

"No," Des said, "I know her. I had lunch with her this week."

"Do you know how to get in touch with her? Cellphone number?"

"No, but I know who does." She dialed Elena.

A surprised voice answered. "Hey, Des, do you know what time it is?"

"Yeah, Elena," Des said, "I do. I've got an emergency here. Jennifer Haskins's studio is on fire..."

"Oh, no. Is she okay? What's happened?"

"I don't know, Elena. That's why I'm calling. Do you have her cellphone number? We need to contact her to make sure she's okay."

"Yes, I've got it here. Judith gave it to me because of the art show. Hang on." After a short pause, she continued, "Okay, I texted it to you."

Des's phone pinged. "Got it. Thanks."

"Can I do anything, Des?"

"Not now, Elena. We'll talk later." A definitive click ended the call.

Des called Jennifer's number, but the phone immediately went to voicemail. "Sorry, Frank," she said, "her cellphone isn't responding at all."

He stared at the still raging fire. "I've got a very bad feeling."

Later that morning, Des knocked on Elena's front door. Elena could tell by the look on her face that it wasn't good news.

"I have terrible news, Elena. Jennifer died in the fire."

"Oh, god, Des. That's awful. I hope she didn't suffer." Then she thought about dying in a fire, and tears filled her eyes. "That's a stupid thing to say. Of course she suffered."

"Based on their inspection of the site, the fire department thinks she died quickly, from the smoke. So, yes, maybe she didn't suffer badly. We'll never know, of course."

"I was just out there with her."

That was news to Des. "When?"

"Yesterday. Judith called me and said she was worried about Jennifer. That Jennifer had called and was very upset. Judith asked me to go with her to Jennifer's house. We were there in the morning."

"And?"

"We talked, and shared coffee and some cake that I brought. From Hans. The visit seemed to perk her up a bit, and I think that Judith was encouraged. At least a little. But Jennifer said she didn't have much to live for, after her nephew died."

"Did you tell her about the poison?"

Elena shook her head. "No, of course not. I assumed that you told me about that in confidence."

"I did, and thanks for keeping that confidence. Did she seem stable?"

"Stable?"

Des decided she had to be less subtle. "Do you think she was suicidal?"

"Oh, I see," Elena said. She thought for a moment. "Well, she was certainly down, that's for sure. I don't know her really, so maybe she was always kind of gloomy. You'd be better off asking Judith."

"Right, she's my next stop."

It took several rings before Judith answered the door. "Oh, hello, Des. Sorry, I didn't hear you at first. I was up in my studio. Come in. Would you like coffee, or tea?"

"A cup of coffee would be great. Thank you."

They sat in the kitchen. Judith could tell that Des was uneasy. "What's wrong, Des? You don't seem like yourself."

"I have bad news, Judith."

"Oh, no, what's happened?"

"There was a fire last night, at Jennifer Haskins's studio."

Judith's hand went to her mouth but it couldn't stifle a gasp. "Is she all right?"

"No, she's not." Des waited a few seconds. "She died in the fire."

Judith began to sob, tears streaming down her cheeks. Des sat quietly to let the news sink in. Eventually, Judith found her voice. "That poor darling. She's such a wonderful person, and artist. How horrible. Do you know what happened, how the fire started?"

Des shook her head. "The town police and fire folks are working on that. It doesn't involve the university directly, but they'll let me know what they find out. I just shared the news with Elena, and she told me you were out there yesterday."

"Yes, we were. Jennifer had called me, very depressed, and I was worried. I asked Elena to go out with me to check on her."

"And how was she?"

Judith looked concerned, the idea of suicide having occurred to her. "Oh, dear, you don't think she did this to herself, do you?"

"Don't know. Do you think she was capable of doing that?"

"I don't know, either. She was quite upset when she called me, but she seemed better when Elena and I were there. But she was still talking about having nothing left in her life, since her nephew died. I can't imagine that she would set fire to her barn and herself. It's unimaginable. Frightful."

Des saw the quizzical look on Judith's face. "What are you thinking?"

Judith frowned. "I know she was upset, very upset, about her nephew dying. But it seems like there was more to it than that."

"Like what?"

"I don't know. She talked about her relationship with Dean Vukovic, how it seemed hollow. Maybe they'd been having problems."

"So," Des said, "it's possible that she could have been desperate enough to take her own life?"

"I guess so." Judith shook her head hard, as if trying to knock that idea away. "It's just too horrible to think about."

52

Elena could barely concentrate. Sunday was an important day for her, when she got prepared for the coming week, getting ready for classes, scheduling out what she expected to accomplish on her research, planning whatever meetings she had to lead.

But the news that Jennifer Haskins had died in a fire at her studio knocked her into a tailspin. Jennifer was not only a lovely person, as Elena now knew, but she also had a remarkable talent. The thought of Jennifer dying in a fire kept shivers of grief coursing through Elena.

And the idea that Dean Vukovic might be involved was just as distracting as the fire. Elena's mind kept replaying the connections she had discussed with Des, and adding more. Dean Vukovic had a long-term personal relationship with Jennifer Haskins. Yesterday she had died in a tragic fire. Her nephew, Manfred Kurtz, had stolen a painting—a fake painting, she now knew—from the biological sciences library. Manfred Kurtz had been murdered with a poison that scientists once used to treat their specimens. The most likely spot for sodium arsenate to still be around, at least according to Aaron Schmidt, was in Dean Vukovic's lab.

As her mind traced through the connections again, she shuddered as she added a new thought. Des had found out that Kurtz told several people he got the drugs that killed him from the Ant-Man. What if he wasn't the "Ant" Man, but rather the "Aunt" Man. His aunt's man. Ralph Vukovic.

Now it all fit together for Elena. The dean had set Kurtz up to steal the painting. But he worried that Kurtz would talk, so he had to kill him. He had rewarded Kurtz with a vial of cocaine. Cocaine laced with poison.

She wanted to call Des with her conclusion, but she hesitated. Elena realized that Des would be skeptical about accusing him of murder based on Aaron Schmidt's analysis of who might have poison hidden in their lab. And there wasn't any reason for the dean to steal the painting he had given to the university.

Elena made a decision. If the dean were responsible for Kurtz's death, she had to find sodium arsenate in his possession. Fortunately, she knew right where to look, and Sunday was the perfect time to do so. Although some faculty might be working in their offices, catching up on paperwork and other chores, the chances were low that anyone would be working in the dean's mammalogy lab.

She drove to the BSB. Thankfully, the parking lot was almost empty. She went up to the third floor and used her key to enter Ted's office, for once glad that universities tended to skimp on costs by using the same lock for all the office doors on each floor.

Ted had told her once that all department heads in the building had a key card that would open all the labs in the building, in case of emergency. She went behind his desk and opened the center drawer. Based on where she hid things in her office, she lifted out the tray that held pens and paper clips. Beneath it was a key card, on which Ted had conveniently written "emer. lab key."

She could feel her heart beating in her ears as she walked up the back steps to the mammalogy lab on the fourth floor. No one was in the hallway and the lights had been turned off to save energy. The lab was in the old half of the building, but, like all the labs, it had been retrofitted with modern electronic locks. She touched the card to the key pad, the light turned green. She heard the lock click and the door cracked open. She took a deep breath, pushed the door open, and walked in. She relaxed, just a bit, when she was sure the no one was in the lab.

Fortunately, one wall of the lab was lined with windows, letting in more than enough light for Elena's purpose.

The lab was well maintained. The dean had an assistant who ran his research projects on a day-to-day basis, one of the perks of high position in the university. His work was also important, as he was always in the midst of the next revision for his book on the mammals of North America. So, specimens arrived regularly from colleagues across the continent, were catalogued, examined and then stored carefully in the long rows of cabinets. The cabinets all looked new, and Elena recalled that the dean had all the older cabinets replaced with modern versions, more customized to his needs, all with the latest in ventilation and specimen-friendly materials.

All the old cabinets had been replaced except one. The entire back wall of the lab had been set up like a museum display. The wall was covered from floor to ceiling with the original ancient oak cabinets, the kind of display cases one might see in an old-fashioned natural history museum. The upper two-thirds had glass doors and shelves so specimens could be displayed, while the lower third held large drawers.

When visitors came to the college, their tours often included the dean's lab, where they could see the modern work, but also pay homage to the ways mammalogists worked in the past. Occasionally Elena led the tours, so she knew her way around. The display shelves were full of old taxidermy specimens, mounted in life poses; each semester, she borrowed a stuffed pangolin for her lecture on endangered species. Some shelves had skeletons of small mammals in glass cases. Some held the huge bones of bison or bears or whales.

Today Elena wasn't interested in the specimens on display, but instead in the drawers beneath them. If something old were here that shouldn't be, this was where it would be hidden away. She searched methodically from top to bottom, left to right, across the wall of drawers. The thinner upper drawers were easy to dismiss, filled with old examples of glassware or dissection tools, ready to be shown as part of tours. But the lower drawers, taller and deeper, were cluttered and disorganized, over-filled with old tools, broken objects, even discarded specimens.

And chemicals. Elena found many small bottles of chemicals that have been used commonly in earlier days. Vials of mercuric chloride, DDT, ethylene oxide and strychnine, all previously tools of taxidermy and all currently illegal to have for those purposes. And, in the back of one drawer, she found what she was looking for—a small bottle of sodium arsenate. Aaron, she thought, you're a genius.

The bottle had been well hidden, covered up by boxes of label paper. It was about half full.

Elena picked it up, wondering what to do. Perhaps leave it where it was, undisturbed, until she could tell Des about it. But that would risk that the dean or one of his workers might notice that someone had been snooping around and take it away. Instead of leaving it, she decided to take some with her, but leave the jar there. She opened one of the upper drawers again and found an empty vial. She folded a paper label into a v-shape to make a funnel and carefully poured the sodium arsenate down the funnel and into the vial until it was nearly full. She screwed on the lid and dropped it in her pocket.

As she reached to return the jar to the drawer, she heard a thundering voice behind her. "What the hell are you doing here?"

She turned and looked Dean Ralph Vukovic in the eye. He bellowed again, as he approached her. "Tell me! What are you doing here?"

As he rushed forward, he saw the jar in her hand and the open drawer. He grabbed for the jar and it fell on the floor, shattering into little pieces. They both stepped back from the white powder that spread across the floor, knowing how dangerous it was. "Damn you," he yelled, his face a vivid scarlet. "Damn you."

Elena looked him in the eyes, every muscle in her body tensed. "I know what you did."

He jumped over the spilled poison, much quicker on his feet than Elena imagined. She turned to run away, but her hair flowed out behind her and he grabbed it. Her head jerked backward, and she fell to the floor. As she fell, she swung an arm backward and smashed her knuckles into his eye. He howled in pain, but held onto her hair. She tried to stand up, but he pulled her back to the floor. Recovering from her blow, he stood over her and laughed. "You don't know anything," he said, "and you never will. In fact you're only a few minutes from never knowing anything again."

He began dragging her towards the pile of spilled poison and shards of the broken glass jar. She clamped her legs around the leg of a lab table that was bolted to the floor. He kept tugging, and the sharp edges of the metal leg dug into her shins. She grabbed another leg with her hands, but he kicked her fingers so hard that she let go and nearly passed out from the pain He continued to pull on her hair as he walked backwards, dragging her closer to the poison.

Her grip on the table leg was slipping badly, and she was now holding on with just one foot. They both knew her strength was about gone. He stepped backward over the broken glass and spilled poison and prepared to give one last tug to dislodge her and drag her face the last few inches into the pile of sodium arsenate and a certain death.

"What's going on?" she heard someone yell. "Let her go, sir. Let her go, right now." The dean looked over his shoulder at the two police officers and did as they asked. "We received an alert of an unauthorized entry into this lab. Are you all right?" He looked from the dean to Elena and back again.

The dean growled. "I'm fine. I caught her in my lab. She broke in. She's not authorized to be here. She must be looking for drugs. Arrest her!"

The other officer, a female, approached Elena and helped her to her feet. "Please keep your hands where we can see them, ma'am. What is your name?"

"Elena Bertoni. I'm a faculty member here."

"Can I see some identification?"

"No," Elena said, "It's in my office. On the third floor."

Vukovic barked again, his face a flaming crimson. "Damn it. You know who I am. This is my lab, in my building, in my college. She broke in here. She's a thief. Get her out of here."

The female officer moved behind Elena and instructed her to put her hands behind her back. She cuffed Elena's hands. Elena caught the eye of the other officer and directed his glance to the mess on the floor. "Be careful of that white powder. It's not what you think. It's is a dangerous poison. Don't go near it." He backed away.

The dean glared at Elena as the first officer led her past him. "You're finished, Bertoni. Say goodbye to your career."

Elena returned his glare, but said nothing. Being arrested was a new experience for her. She couldn't have been happier.

53

"What the hell were you thinking?" Des had Elena in one of the interview rooms at the station. "I could hardly believe it when the desk officer called to tell me that one of our faculty members—you—was in custody for breaking into a laboratory on suspicion of stealing drugs."

"I had to get proof, or you'd never believe me."

"That's not your job, Elena, for heavens sake! That's my job. Your job is to tell me what you're thinking, not to try some Dirty Harry stunt that could get you hurt. Or worse. Do you understand how lucky you were that those police officers showed up when they did?"

In a way, it wasn't luck. Unbeknownst to Elena, an alarm had gone off in the police station when she used Ted's key card to enter the dean's lab. Because Ted's card was designated for emergencies only, its use triggered a protocol to call the responsible person for the room, in this case Ralph Vukovic, to see if the alarm was an error. When he told the police that no one should be in the lab, the dispatcher sent a patrol car to the room. At the same time, Vukovic had driven to the lab himself. He arrived first, but the police officers were only a few minutes behind him.

"But I got it, Des. I got the proof. Vukovic poisoned Manfred Kurtz. With the poison I found in his lab. I'm sure of it."

"How can you be sure? You told me this poison was hidden all over the building."

"I know," Elena said, "but the dean is the Aunt Man."

"What?"

"Yes. Kurtz didn't name him for the insect. He named him Aunt Man because he was his aunt's boyfriend. And he kept bailing Kurtz out. He was Kurtz's guardian angel."

That stopped Des's rant for a moment. "God. You might be right."

"I am right, Des, I know it."

"Yeah, well, maybe or maybe not." She was back to ranting. "Anyway, you realize that we can't use what you found? I can't present evidence that a witness stole from a suspect. Especially a witness who has now been charged with illegal entry. We just had to have a hazardous materials team in there to dispose of the spill."

"I'm sorry about that, Des. I really am. But you never would have been able to go after Vukovic. You told me that."

Des decided to give up. They weren't getting anywhere. She was mostly relieved that her friend was safe. "Okay, let's forget that for now. You can go home, but you still have an active case against you. I can't stop that, at least not right now. I'll drive you to your car."

Elena shook her head. "There's more."

"What?"

Elena pulled the vial out of her jeans pocket. "I have a sample of the sodium arsenate from the dean's lab."

"What?"

"I got it before the dean, and your officers, found me. I poured some of the powder into this vial. I figured you could get it analyzed to be sure it really was what the label said. I also thought, maybe, I don't know, that you could get a chemical profile of this stuff and the drug that killed Kurtz to compare them. That would be definitive, right?"

"Yeah, that would be definitive. If we could use it. And we can't, kiddo. That's the problem."

Elena accepted the chastisement again. "I know. I'm sorry. But, look, can't you just get it analyzed. Just so we know?"

"Give it to me, Elena." She handed the vial to Des, who held like it was, well, poison. "Now, let's get you, and me, home."

54

Monday

Des, Jessie and Jimmy met in her office first thing the following morning. They had a lot to review.

Several things had become clear. Manfred Kurtz was the thief of the Fuertes painting, and Will Morales the thief of the war bond painting of an eagle. Both paintings were fakes, however, and worthless. In fact, a series of paintings given by Ralph Vukovic over the years were fakes.

Based on Remy's discovery of the initials "JH" on the stretcher of the war bond painting, he had concluded that Jennifer Haskins had created the forgeries. With Des's permission, he had carefully loosened the backs of each of the other art works that Vukovic had given the university and Remy had determined were forgeries. There, in the same corner of the each stretcher, covered by the overlapping of the canvas or paper, was the same "JH" sets of initials, each punched lightly into the wood.

"How can he be sure that the initials mean Jennifer Haskins was the artist?" asked Jimmy. "They could mean anything, or anyone. Like Judith Heinz, for instance."

Des nodded. "Good point, Jimmy. Remy says it makes sense, artistically. Jennifer's fame as an artist is that she paints so realistically that her work looks like photographs. In other words, she has a talent for duplicating what she sees. Not for making things up, or abstracting something from a scene, but for representing it precisely as it appears. Remy says that is exactly the skill set for an art restorer, or an art forger."

She went on. "I also asked Judith about when she and Jennifer used to make copies of art and sell them, years ago. They used to punch their initials on the stretchers for the paintings. J2H2, for the pair of them. She said that when she quit doing it, Jennifer continued for a while. Instead of the J2H2 brand, they agreed Jennifer should use just one pair—JH. It all fits."

Jessie looked amazed. "This is pretty sophisticated stuff. How could she pull it off, I mean, copying the original, getting the fake in place, all of that."

"Remy thinks the dean is in on it, as well. The only way it could have been done is if he had the originals, so Jennifer could copy from them. Then, the university would have some legitimate art expert declare the originals were real. And then, somehow, the dean would switch them, giving the fake to the university."

Jessie's mouth fell open. "Wow. Could that happen? Wouldn't anyone notice?"

Des shrugged. "The dean had access to the entire building, including the library. So, he could go in some time, anytime, really, and switch the pictures. The fakes were good ones, remember, and no one from the university is going to be looking through a magnifying glass to study the brush strokes."

Jimmy pitched in. "So, the dean gives the university a real painting, gets an evaluation that puts a high price on the gift, takes a big tax deduction, and then steals the original painting back, replacing it with a fake. He's got a really good scam going."

"If," Des added, "if that's what's going on. We need to go talk to the dean. Actually, we need to get the dean in here, not on his turf. I'll call him and set up a meeting."

"One question, though," wondered Jessie.

"What?" Des asked.

"Where are the original paintings?"

"Remy thinks the dean sold them into the black market. Got the tax deduction and then doubled up with an untraceable sale."

Jimmy whistled. "Sweet. If I wasn't a cop, I'd be applauding this one."

55

Des kissed Remy good-bye at the airport. They held each other for a long time. Finally she broke the embrace. "C'mon, kiddo. It's not like you're going off to war or anything."

Remy smiled. "Feels like it. New York's a jungle, you know." In fact, Remy wasn't headed home, but to a task he'd just scheduled near Washington, DC. A painting that was supposed to be by Jackson Pollock had just been listed for an upcoming fine art auction in Fairfax, Virginia; one of Remy's clients was interested, but she needed him to authenticate the work. "Can't I just stay here with you?"

"I know. This has been wonderful."

"When can I see you again, Des?"

"Shouldn't we just wait and see?"

"Wait and see what? I can see pretty clearly that I don't want this to end, or have us just drift apart like the end of some bad 1980s movie. And I don't want to wait to move along to the next scene, either. I want you, Des, that's what I know. Wait and see doesn't enter into it."

In her heart, Des was ready to jump in the deep end. She was already well past where she could touch bottom. But her detective's brain told her that this situation, like all situations, was more complicated than it seemed. Two careers, two towns, two lifestyles, two families.

"The holidays are coming," she said. "Let's promise to get together again then."

He looked deeply into her eyes and pulled her close again. "All I want for Christmas is you."

"Cheesy, Romeo, real cheesy. Are you sure you're an art expert, not a composer of Broadway show tunes?" Des laughed and pushed him away with one last kiss. Then he was through the gate and out of sight, headed for the afternoon flight to Dulles Airport. I love cheesy, she thought.

There was a message waiting for Des when she got back to work. Frank Marin, the chief of the Stone Valley police, asked that she call him as soon as possible.

After several rings, Frank answered, sounding distracted and out of breath. "Sorry, Des, we had a little incident at the mall, and we just finished disarming a young man with a gun."

"Goodness, is everyone all right?"

"Yeah. Turned out to be a toy gun. But it had us going for a while. The local news will be pretty exciting this evening."

"I'm glad that it didn't turn ugly," Des said. She had been part of several active shooter events in Richmond while she was a uniformed cop there. You never knew how they might turn out. "I was just returning your call, but we can talk later if you want."

She heard him take a few deep breaths. "Naw, it's okay. The uniforms are taking care of things now. Let me walk to my car, and sit down." She held the line for a few moments, hearing a car door open, then close, and silence replaced the background noise of the shopping mall parking lot. "You need to go out to Jennifer Haskins's house and look at something that we found there."

"Okay, Frank. What is it?"

"It's a painting. Two paintings, actually. But I think you should take a look. And bring your friend, Elena something, right?"

"Elena Bertoni?"

"Yeah, that's her. She knows a lot about art, right?"

"Yes, she does," Des agreed, "but she's not an expert. She's a wildlife biologist. I just put our art expert on a plane back to New York."

"That's okay," Frank said. "I just think you'd like to have an extra pair of eyes on this. Get out there as soon as you can, because I need your perspective on this."

Des checked her watch and her calendar. "I can be there in an hour, and I'll try to get Elena, but I don't know her schedule."

"Up to you. I'll meet you there."

Des hung up and immediately called Elena. It was mid-afternoon, and Elena's class was over. Yes, she could be available, if Des really needed her. Des arranged to pick her up at BSB in fifteen minutes.

The ride to Jennifer Haskins's house was quiet. The late afternoon sunlight was slanting across the ridge tops, but didn't make it down to the shadowed road, another element to suppress their moods. Elena was embarrassed by what had happened in the dean's lab, but she still believed that she had needed to get the evidence of poison being there. Des was annoyed by Elena's actions, partly because she could have been hurt, but she was also intrigued by what the poison sample might reveal. She had sent it off to be analyzed, along with the powder that had killed Manfred Kurtz. Elena was right about that—the state lab told her they could make chemical signatures of both samples to see if they matched.

When they arrived at Jennifer' s house, the smell of acrid smoke was still almost overpowering. The sight of her burned out barn was as jarring to their emotions as the smoke was to their noses and taste buds. A talented artist had been destroyed by the very tools—paint, solvents, canvas and wood—that she used to create beauty. Sometimes, Elena thought, life is just cruel.

Frank was sitting in his police car talking on the radio. When he saw them pull up, he ended his conversation and got out of the car to greet them. "That was quick. Blue lights and sirens?"

"No," Des said. "Just wondering why you called this meeting. So we skedaddled."

"Well, come into the house." They walked past the remains of the barn, removed the police tape from the front door of the house, and Frank gave them both gloves and shoe covers. He began his explanation. "Our forensics folks went through the house, just to be sure there wasn't anything relevant to the fire in here."

Des frowned, knowing what he was talking about. "You mean a suicide note, right?"

He nodded his head. "We didn't find anything like that. It looked like she and someone else ate dinner, and then, probably, she went down to the barn to paint. Anyway, when the crew went up to the second floor, they found a locked room. We broke through the lock, and what we found inside is what I want to show you."

They walked up the stairs and along the hallway to a door that had obviously been forced. Frank went in first and said, "Ladies, be my guest." He pointed to a pair of easels with a painting on each. One was finished, the other, obviously a copy of the first, was unfinished. A gilt frame, undoubtedly the frame for the finished painting, had been placed carefully on a blanket in one corner of the room.

Elena exclaimed, "I know this painting." She pointed to the finished work. "It was hanging in Dean Vukovic's home the last time I was there. I loved it." The painting showed two dogs, lying together on a green surface, presumably grass, with a blue background. "The primitive simplicity of the forms just added to the sense of friendship between the two dogs. The dean told me it was from the mid-1800s, and, of course, the artist was unknown, as is the case with most folk art. But that doesn't affect the impact of the painting, or its value."

"And what about the other one?" Frank asked.

Des answered this time. "I'm afraid this proves what we've been suspecting. That Jennifer Haskins was painting a forgery of the original."

"Why here, not in her studio in the barn?" Frank asked.

"Because she didn't want anyone to see what she was doing. She did her regular work down in the barn, but this was secret, so she did it up here, in a locked room."

Elena added, "Not only that. Making a copy like this takes a long time, so the chance of it being seen in the barn would have been much higher than a painting that took maybe a week or so. And then it had to dry thoroughly and get several coats of varnish that were treated to look aged. It would be a long process. Months at least, maybe a year."

Frank wasn't done with his questions. "You see people making copies of paintings all the time in museums. Why hide this?"

"That's easy, I'm afraid," Elena said. "When I told the dean how much I liked it, he said that I'd have lots of opportunity to see it, because this was the next painting he was going to donate to the university."

"And?"

Des took over. "Frank, we've uncovered a long-time scheme to paint forgeries of valuable paintings and pass them off to the university as the originals. This proves that the pair who were doing it was Ralph Vukovic, the dean of the College of Biological Sciences, who donated the paintings, and Jennifer Haskins, who painted the forgeries, right here in her locked hideaway studio. We've suspected that was what was happening, but now we have the proof."

The light bulb went off in Frank's head. "So, he gets a huge tax-deduction for the donation, and he gets to keep the original for himself. Pretty clever." Then a brighter bulb went off. "No, wait, he sells the originals on the black market, so he collects twice."

Des held up her hand to slow him down. "We're trying not to jump to conclusions. Either explanation fits. Maybe he wants them for himself, but figured this was a good way to make some extra cash. Or, maybe he sold the originals. We don't know."

"Time to find the dean, isn't it?" Frank asked, but it wasn't really a question.

"Yes," Des said, "it certainly is."

"I might be able to help," Frank said. "I've got something else to show you. Downstairs."

They followed him down to the main floor. He led them to a desk that sat under a wide window with a view to the barn. He picked up a piece of paper from the desk and handed it to Des. "Take a look at this," he said.

It was a printout of a plane reservation. For two, Ralph Vukovic and Jennifer Haskins. The route showed IAD to LHR to TGD. Des handed it to Elena and asked, "You recognize these codes?"

Elena nodded. "IAD is Dulles in Washington, and LHR is London's Heathrow Airport. I have no idea where TGD is, but we can find out."

She unlocked her cellphone and entered the code. "It's the main airport in Podgorica."

"And where is that, kiddo?"

Elena punched a few more buttons. "It's the capital of Montenegro. Where the dean has a home. Des, the reservation is for tonight. The dean's planning to leave the country. Tonight."

"So, he's either driving up to Dulles or he took a commuter flight on a separate ticket. Either way, he's got a head start. Now is the time for blue lights and sirens, Frank."

Jennifer's house was a few miles from Interstate 81, so she called Jimmy and instructed him to get to the nearest exit and meet her. "Make it fast, Jimmy."

Then she called Jessie. "Listen carefully, Jessie," she said. "First get a search warrant for Dean Vukovic's house. Then get the officers who found him and Elena in his lab and take them back there. Have them show you where the bottle of white powder was dropped on the floor. Get the forensics team there to go over the floor and recover any powder that is still there. But be careful, because we think it's the poison that killed Kurtz."

"You got it, boss. Jimmy just tore out of here with a big smile on his face. What's up?"

"Let's just say we're late for a plane."

Des called to Frank as she was getting in her car. "Take Elena home, okay?"

"Of course, Des." She slammed the door and peeled out of the driveway. "And be careful," he said to the dust cloud where Des used to be.

56

Remy walked down the concourse of the local airport to the small seating area for the flight to Dulles. He recognized the man seated at the far end of the gate, looking out the window.

"Excuse me, you're Dean Vukovic, am I right?"

The man turned and stared as though he'd seen a ghost. "Yes," he stammered, "yes I am."

Remy extended his hand. "Remy Tremblay. I was one of the judges at the art show that your university had last week."

The dean took his hand, it seemed reluctantly. "Oh, yes, I remember now. Yes, nice to see you again. I thought you probably were long gone by now."

Remy shrugged and sat down next to the dean. You wish that I'd gone right back to New York, he thought. "Plans changed a little. I stayed on for a few more days. Stone Valley is lovely."

Just then, the desk agent made the first announcement that the flight was ready for boarding. The dean got up. "Excuse me, she just called my group."

"Mine, too," Remy said, and followed the dean to the gate agent, had his ticket checked and walked onto the plane. The dean was seated in the front row, what was euphemistically called business class on the small plane. Remy's seat was in the row just behind him.

The flight to Washington was so short that neither the flight attendants nor the passengers had the opportunity to unbuckle. Remy spent the time wondering about the dean's journey. The dean's good friend, Jennifer Haskins, had just been found dead in her burned out studio. Vukovic should have been staying close to home, helping out in whatever way he could. So why was he on a plane headed to Washington?

And why was he flying to Dulles? If you fly to Washington to stay there, or even transfer to another domestic flight, you flew to Reagan Airport. The only reason Remy was flying to Dulles was because the painting he needed to examine was in a specialized high-security warehouse adjacent to the airport. The usual reason for flying to Dulles was to catch a flight to some foreign destination. It just didn't make sense that the dean would be flying out of the country.

He couldn't risk calling Des, either before take-off or after the wheels touched down because the dean might hear him. And the whole situation was too complicated for text messages. So, he waited and thought.

When they deplaned at Dulles, the dean hurried off without acknowledging Remy. I understand, he thought, I don't like you either, but you're not getting away that easily. Remy got off quickly, too, but then he let the dean get considerably ahead of him in the concourse before following.

With more space between them, Remy called Des. When she answered, the road noise was so loud that he could barely hear her. "Des, we need to talk."

"I don't have time for that right now, Remy."

"No, no, I don't want to talk about us. I need to tell you about the dean."

"Vukovic? What about him?"

"He was on my plane to Dulles. I'm following him in the airport right now. It doesn't make sense that he's flying around. He should be back there mourning Jennifer's death."

"He's leaving the country, Remy. He's on the evening flight to London and then on to Montenegro." Des quickly explained what they had found at Jennifer's house.

"So what should I do?"

"Nothing."

"Nothing?" Remy interrupted. "You're kidding, right?"

"Let me finish," Des said. "Keep him in sight, but stay well away from him. And don't confront him. I'm on my way to Dulles with Jimmy, and we've been talking with the police there. But we've got to confirm several things with them before they can act. It's going to take a while to get everything set up."

Remy stopped in front of a video board showing departures. "The plane to London leaves in less than an hour, Des. Where are you?"

"We're on the way. Jimmy's driving fast, but we're still about two hours away. But don't worry, the police there will detain him. You just keep your eyes on him, okay?"

"Okay. Sure. But let me know what's going on with the police here, okay?"

"Yes, of course. Be careful, Remy."

Elena thanked Frank for the ride back to BSB and walked up to her office. Ara Sun, her teaching assistant, was sitting in a chair by the door. She looked at her watch and realized it was nearly four. "I'm so sorry, Ara, I got involved in something and lost track of time."

Ara stood. "That's okay, Elena. There were a few students who came by and I took care of their issues while I was waiting."

"You're an angel, Ara, you really are." She meant it. Ara was by far the best teaching assistant she'd had since coming to VWU. Conscientious and smart. And she seemed to love working with students. "You'll be a great professor, Ara. And how are things going with Officer Nesbitt?"

Ara blushed. "Just fine, I think. Jimmy's wonderful." Ara had begun dating Jimmy ever since they met during the Dew Robbins case. They were the epitome of opposites attract—the doctoral student from South Korea and the local kid who never wanted more than to be a police officer in his hometown. So far, it was working.

They spent an hour going over class administration details and discussing the next class. Ara was going to give the next lecture. They were covering protected areas—national parks and preserves—which was the subject of Ara's dissertation research. Lucky scheduling, Elena thought, given that her usual prep time had been spent chasing down a forger and murder suspect.

Elena checked the clock again. "Tell you what, how about joining me and Aaron Schmidt at The Hawk's Den for a drink? I'm supposed to meet him there in a few minutes."

Ara was delighted with the invitation and they were soon off to meet Elena's chief sparring partner. "I don't really know Professor Schmidt," Ara said. "Are you sure he'll be okay with me tagging along?"

Elena laughed out loud. "Are you kidding? Twice the audience? He'll be enthralled."

And so he was. He stood and bowed as they walked to the table he had secured on the patio. "To what do I owe this propitious circumstance, my dear?" he asked Elena.

"Go easy, you old reprobate. This is Ara Sun, my teaching assistant and Officer Nesbitt's, ah, good friend. So be on your best behavior."

Aaron smiled. "Wouldn't want to ruffle the feathers of the constables of Nottingham, would we?"

Ara looked at Elena for help. "Don't worry, Ara. He's like this all the time, and he's harmless. Just toss hm a quote from Shakespeare every so often, and he'll lie quietly at our feet." Ara smiled, but she still seemed a little uncertain what was going on.

"Yes, sorry, my dear," Aaron said. "Tell me about yourself."

Ara explained a bit about her background, her family in South Korea and her work on protected areas. Aaron listened intensely, ever the gentleman and scholar.

When she finished, he took over. "An important new tree was discovered there just a few years ago. The Ulleungdo hemlock."

Ara's eyes lit up. "You know about that? It is found on Ulleungdo Island, where I have worked on the marine nature preserve. I love that place."

For the next few minutes, Elena leaned back in her chair and watched her two friends talk about conservation in South Korea, everything from the endangered Korean fir tree to the chances of turning the DMZ into a biodiversity preserve when, and if, the two halves of Korea ever got back together.

Finally, when the conversation turned to the status of lynx on the Korean Peninsula, Elena jumped in. "Hey, you two, I'm the lynx expert around here, you know. Can I get a word in here somewhere?"

"My goodness," Aaron said, "I think your boss is a bit green with envy, Ara. We wouldn't want her to turn into the Incredible Hulk, now, would we?"

Ara giggled. "Sorry, Elena, we just got carried away. I know you've studied lynx all over the world. And Dean Vukovic, too, right?"

"Yes, he has," Elena agreed. Then her thoughts shifted to Des White speeding down the interstate to arrest him. She knew better than to talk about that. "I remember that he had a beautiful photograph of an Eurasian lynx hanging in the entry hall of his home."

"He is such a generous man, giving all that art to the university," Ara said. Now she and Elena talked art for a few minutes, leaving Aaron on the sidelines. "I've heard his house is like an art museum."

Aaron wedged himself back in. "Interesting house the dean has."

"How so?"

"I tried to tell you about it the other day, but Ted shut me down. Anyway, it's an old house, about a century, I think. The owner before the dean was a colleague. The university's first oenologist."

Ara frowned. "The what?"

"Don't encourage him, Ara," Elena said. But it was too late.

"Wine expert. Oenology is the study of wines, from the vines to the corks and the good stuff in-between. He was on the faculty when I got here in the 70s, and we got to be friends right away. He was interested in how the qualities of the wood in barrels affected the qualities of the wine aged in them. We published several papers together over the years. Most wine barrels are oak, but the grain pattern makes big differences in how thoroughly the elements of the wood interact with the wine to flavor it. Big wide grain, like most American oak used in barrels, gives bolder tastes. Tight grain, like most French oak, gives more subtlety. Fascinating."

Elena laughed. "Yeah, we could listen to you all day, Dr. Woodhead. But what about the house?"

"Ah, right. When Eliot—that's Eliot MacCumber, the oenologist. When Eliot bought the house, it had a swimming pool in the backyard. Eliot didn't need a swimming pool—he was a bachelor with a decided bias against exercise—so he had it dug up, deepened the hole, connected it to the house through the basement, and turned it into a wine cellar."

"Makes sense," Elena said, "I guess a wine expert needs a wine cellar."

Aaron continued. "Yeah, and a big one. He covered it with a couple feet of soil and planted grass on top. You'd never know there was anything there from the surface. Being buried, the wine stays at the perfect temperature."

"And you know what that is, of course?" Elena teased.

Aaron spread his hands to signify fake nonchalance. "55 degrees. A few feet underground, and the temperature is around that, all year long, regardless of whether we're steaming or freezing up here where mere mortals keep their wine."

"And so my education continues," she laughed.

"Wait, though, that's not all. Eliot had a lot of wine, and a lot of valuable wine. On a couple of occasions, students snuck into his house and stole some wine, fraternity pranks probably. Not valuable stuff, but he got more paranoid as the years went on. So, he had the door from the basement into the wine cellar concealed."

"A hidden door, Aaron?" Elena said. "Is this a medieval fantasy?"

Aaron nodded. "Not a fantasy, the real thing. The basement walls were concrete block, so he had a stone mason trim some blocks down to just thin sections. Then he mortared them to a board that could slide into the space right in front of the door. Eliot had a plumber come in and put an old hot water heater on a little platform on casters, attached to the moveable wall section. He had all the right fittings attached to the heater, you know, water pipes and an exhaust vent, all of which dead-ended in the fake door. He made a little wooden yoke that you slid behind the hot water heater and then pulled to move the whole contraption out of the way so you could get into the wine cellar. Ingenious. You just couldn't tell there was anything behind it but plain wall."

"Oh my god," Elena said.

"What's wrong, fair maiden?" Aaron asked.

"You're not making this up are you?"

"No. Scout's honor. Why?"

Elena jumped up. "I've got to go. Aaron, I think you just solved a mystery."

58

It was getting close to boarding time. Remy had his eye on Dean Vukovic sitting in the boarding lounge, but he was getting worried. There were no police around. Nothing looked in the least out of the ordinary.

He called Des again. "Des, there's nothing happening here. And we're only a few minutes from boarding. The crew went on board a few minutes ago."

"We're still far away, Remy. The traffic has been terrible since we turned onto I-66. Even with lights flashing and siren, we haven't been able to make good time."

"What about the police here? Aren't they supposed to be doing something?"

"Yes, they said they'd be there as soon as they were authorized."

"Well, they're not here yet. What should I do."

"Nothing. I told you. Don't do anything. This is police business, and you don't need to get in the middle of it. We'll get him at the other end if necessary."

"Ok," Remy said. "But hurry."

He rang off and resumed doing...nothing.

And no one else was doing anything either. No sign of police. No sign of extra airline personnel waiting for an intervention. The gate crew made an announcement for pre-boarding, and Remy made up his mind.

He walked up to the dean and yelled as loud as he could, "Hey, you stole my bag! Give it back."

He grabbed one of the dean's bags. The dean immediately grabbed back. "What are you talking about? Are you crazy?"

They began to tussle over the bag. Remy was acting crazy, grabbing and yelling. He backed up purposely and tripped over another passenger's legs, falling to the ground. "He pushed me! He attacked me! Somebody call the police! Help!"

The gate agents rushed over and tried to separate them, but Remy kept holding onto the bag and yelling, "He attacked me and he stole my bag. Call the police!"

A crowd began to gather, making things more chaotic. Remy was ricocheting from one person to another, falling over them and knocking them down. He grabbed the dean by the arm and never let go. In just a few minutes, one and then several police officers arrived and began to assert order. But Remy continued to yell that the dean was a thief and had attacked him. The dean was gasping for air, with a look of bewilderment on his crimson face.

Eventually, the police got control of the situation. A transport cart was brought in, and the police wrestled both men onto separate seats and handcuffed them to the railings. The dean was apoplectic. "I've got to get on that plane," he pleaded.

The officer in charge shook his head. "Neither of you are going anywhere on a plane until we get this sorted out. Right now, you are both going back to the security office with me."

Remy sat quietly in his seat, smiling to himself. That, he thought, is how Rembrandt Vincent Tremblay does nothing.

59

"This is Officer Hunt. Can I help you?"

"It's Elena, Jessie."

"Oh, hey, Elena. What's up?" Jessie looked up at the clock. It was past dinner time.

"Have you been to the dean's house yet with the search warrant?"

"No. I have the warrant, but I thought the search could wait until tomorrow. Why?"

Elena explained what Aaron had told her about the hidden wine cellar. "I think we ought to go now. I think that Aaron has just led us to the missing paintings."

Jessie agreed. "Meet me at the dean's house as soon as you can."

Ten minutes later, they met at the dean's front door. They expected the door to be locked, but it wasn't. "I guess he left in a hurry," Jessie said.

They found the stairs to the basement and flipped the switch at the top of the landing. The entire basement burst into light. The area was mostly unfinished, with just a couple of small rooms with doors. They worked their way around the stairs to the back wall.

There it was. A hot-water heater sitting by itself halfway down the wall. Elena looked around; in one corner, she found a long wooden board, about six inches wide with an arc cut into the center. She threaded it behind the hot-water heater and Jessie took the other end. As they pulled, the water heater began to roll away from the wall, taking an area of the wall with it. The whole unit slid away easily, revealing a door behind it.

"Good heavens" Jessie said. "Are we watching some old horror movie, with a hidden torture chamber? This is crazy."

"Crazy like a fox," Elena said, "or maybe a lynx."

A control panel next to the door lit when Elena touched it. The thermostat was set at 68 degrees. "Too warm for wine, but the prescribed temperature for long-term storage of oil paintings," Elena said.

She turned the knob and the door swung open into the hidden room. She felt along the wall and found a light switch. The room lit with a series of small LED spotlights.

"Oh my god," Elena said. "It's his own private museum."

The room was filled with art. Mostly paintings hanging on the walls, but some sculpture displayed on small stands. Each was highlighted by one of the spotlights.

Among them, Elena identified each of the pieces that had hung in the Fuertes Room in the library, gifts from the dean. The study of deer by Albert Bierstadt was there, along with the owl drawing by James Thurber, the alligators by John Singer Sargent, and the war-bond poster of a bald eagle.

"Are these the paintings that were supposed to be hanging in that room at the library? Where the fakes are hanging now?" Jessie asked.

"Yes. I'm sure these are the originals. All of them. they're all here, except one.."

"What's missing?"

"A pair of great blue herons flying over a clear blue sky."

60

Des and Jimmy walked into the small room within the security area at Dulles International Airport. They were exhausted from fighting through the traffic and then talking their way through the airport security bureaucracy.

Remy saw Des and jumped to his feet to embrace her. Two enormous hands grabbed his shoulders and pushed him back into his chair. "Sit still, buddy, and stay away from the officer."

Across the room, Ralph Vukovic had a different reaction. He blanched at the sight of the university's police chief and fidgeted uncomfortably. Des asked the security officer to record the conversation, and he turned on the device built into the table in the middle of the room.

Des quickly read the dean his rights and began her interrogation.

"We are charging you with fraud and theft of paintings belonging to the university."

"I didn't do anything wrong. I had nothing to do with that forgery."

"Forgeries, Dean Vukovic," Des said. "Not just one, but five And we found the painting that Jennifer Haskins was working on when she died."

He looked lost for a moment, but then recovered his bluster. "Yeah, so what? I like to have a copy of the paintings that I give to the university. There's nothing wrong with that."

"There is if you give the university the originals and then replace them with forgeries."

"I didn't do that, I told you that before. Someone else must have switched them."

Des stared at the dean. "We executed a search warrant at your home tonight."

He shrugged and continued the bluster. "Go ahead and look. I've got nothing to hide. You won't find anything there."

"That's where you're wrong, dean. We know about the hidden room in your basement." She watched his face drop and his shoulders droop as he seemed to shrink into the chair. "We found the originals of the faked paintings in there."

Vukovic sat silently and stared at the floor. Des knew from experience that suspects usually needed a few moments before they were ready to admit the truth. Eventually she spoke. "Want to tell us why you had to get Kurtz to steal the painting from the library?"

He looked up at Des and scoffed. "Really? You don't know?" Des waited. She wanted to hear it from him. "The forgery would have been discovered if it went up to New York. We could fool the idiots at the university easy enough, but not the experts. She was good, but not...". He stopped talking abruptly when he realized what he had said.

"Don't worry, Dean Vukovic, we know that Jennifer Haskins made the copies for you. You're not telling us anything we don't already know."

He looked at her, sadness now the only emotion on his face. "Poor Jennifer. I loved her. We could have been so happy."

"If you loved her, why did you kill her?"

"I didn't kill her," he said, barely louder than a whisper. "It was an accident."

"Tell me how it happened."

Vukovic sobbed several times before he could begin. "I went out there to tell her about us flying to Montenegro. To get her things together so we could leave. She told me she couldn't go, that she couldn't live like this anymore. I tried to reason with her that everything would be all right, we could leave all this behind. I've hid all the money I made on tax breaks from donating the paintings in a bank in Montenegro. But she wouldn't listen. I grabbed her so she'd listen to me, but she pulled away and fell. She hit her head on the corner of the table. Then she just lay on the floor, not moving. I knew she was dead."

"So you moved her to the studio and started the fire, right?"

Vukovic nodded, and then his face began to redden again. "And it was all about her worthless nephew. I bailed him out of trouble so many times, for her sake. He was just a waste of the air he breathed. I figured with him out of the way, everything would work out the way we'd always planned."

"So you got him to steal the painting for you."

"Yes," he barked. "I told him exactly what to do. That little fool Hannah would be on the library desk on the last day of class when no one would be thinking about the library. I told him to steal the painting and then destroy it."

"And then you gave him cocaine as a reward. Cocaine laced with sodium arsenate from your lab."

Now he actually seemed proud of what he had done. "Yes, I did. I did it for her. He'd hurt Jennifer so many times, and he was so worthless. This was the perfect answer. Use him to steal the painting and then get him out of our hair. The painting and Kurtz gone, just like that." He snapped his fingers with hatred. "Just like that."

"Okay, dean, there's only one more question. "Where is the original Fuertes painting?"

Remy spoke up from across the room. "Look in there," he said and pointed to a black plastic tube about six inches in diameter and four feet long that lay to the side of the room with the rest of the dean's luggage. "That's a specialized carry tube for artwork."

Des retrieved the tube and opened one end. She reached in and slid out a canvas, carefully rolled with a protective sheet of linen across its surface. She removed the linen covering.

"What's that?" the security officer asked.

Des answered. "A pair of great blue herons flying over a clear blue sky."

61

The fourth Saturday in November

The auditorium at the American Museum of Natural History was filled to capacity. The front row was occupied by the glitterati of New York art and culture, along with President Crutchfield. The row behind was occupied by lesser stars representing Virginia Western University—Acting Dean of Biological Sciences Ted Graham, Michele Richards, Elena Bertoni, Hans Kjer, and Desdemona White. Mr. R. V. Tremblay could have been in the front row, but he chose to take the seat next to his favorite police chief.

The program was mercifully short. A video biography of Louis Agassiz Fuertes was followed by the unveiling of a square painting, nine feet on a side, composed of eight three-by-three canvases encircling an empty space in the center. The museum director invited President Crutchfield to join her on the stage. Then, in a dramatic flair none of the guests had anticipated, the ninth canvas dropped slowly from the ceiling and came to rest in front of the empty space. The two dignitaries removed it from its harness and guided the canvas into place. Together they announced, "The Center Piece is home!"

The four friends skipped the formal dinner, leaving Ted Graham alone with the president and Michele. I'll pay for this later, thought Elena, knowing that Ted would be out of his element and feeling abandoned. They grabbed taxis to Delmo's Trattoria, where Remy's usual table was waiting for them.

Tonino greeted them. He kissed Des's hand. "Ah, mia bella, like the famous painting, you return." Then he turned his attention to Elena. "Due bellezze in una notte. Sono benedetto."

"What did he just say?" asked Hans.

Remy smiled. "Something about being blessed by seeing two such beautiful women in one night." Hans beamed.

Elena responded in Italian, and the pair were in deep conversation for several minutes. Tonino motioned expressively and hurried off to the kitchen. "What's up?" asked Hans.

"Oh, nothing," Elena said, "but it seems we are distant cousins. Both our families come from the hills around Modena." She smiled. "I think we are in for a special treat tonight."

And they were. The food was delicious and seemingly unending. The red wine in unlabeled green bottles flowed without interruption. The beautiful voice of Angelique Trembley played in the background the entire evening. Des could tell that at times Remy was somewhere else, thinking about his mother. At those times, she reached for his hand and shared his emotion.

The past month had seen the closure on many aspects of the case. Ralph Vukovic, of course, was in jail pending his trial for murder, theft, and tax fraud. The judge had refused bail, siting his attempt to fly to Montenegro as evidence that the man was a flight risk. He had been discharged from the university, and Ted Graham had been appointed acting dean while a nationwide search was being conducted. One of Ted's first actions had been to appoint Aaron Schmidt as acting head of the Department of Renewable Resources. Elena delighted in calling him "Dr. Falling Domino."

The infamous Grinder was in jail, too, and several students who had worked with Manfred Kurtz were placed on probation. The books Will Morales had stolen were returned to the library, and the ones he had sold—just a few, as it turned out—were tracked down and recovered. Morales was sent to a minimum security prison, where he was given the job of librarian.

Yvonne Michaels decided she had had enough of supervision and asked to be transferred to a back-office job at the library. She was now deputy assistant to the director for special projects, should any come along.

The original paintings that Vukovic had stolen were recovered and re-hung in the Fuertes Room of the biological sciences library. A replica of the Fuertes painting was hung in the position of honor at the back of the room. Each artwork was fitted with a motion-detecting sensor on the back of the frame, a glowing example of shutting the corral after the livestock had escaped.

The original Fuertes was reunited with its stretcher that Dean Vukovic had left in his secret art gallery, no visible harm done. The university made good on its earlier commitment to loan the painting to the museum. And so it went back home, the "Center Piece" completing Fuertes's now famous composition.

The four friends were finishing their evening at Delmo's. Hans raised his glass and toasted. "Here's to another success by the best pair of crime-fighting women in the entire universe!"

Elena laughed as she clinked glasses with her friends. "Let's not get excited, Hans. Maybe just the western hemisphere?"

Des took over. "Once again, Elena, we couldn't have done this without you." She looked at Remy. "Or you, Mr. Rembrandt Vincent Tremblay." He bowed his head in mock humility.

"Let's not forget Aaron Schmidt," Elena said. "Old Dr. Woodhead to the rescue again!"

"The interesting thing," Des continued, "is how it all came together in the end. Imagine, we solved this set of crimes by the two of you," she pointed her glass first at Elena and then at Remy, "getting arrested. I just can't get over that happening first to my best friend and then to the man I love."

The table went instantly silent. They all looked at each other, and then three said at once, "Love?"

Acknowledgments

This is a work of fiction. All aspects of the book--characters, places, events and situations--are fiction and any resemblance to individuals, places or events is coincidence.

I would like to thank my family and friends, who have encouraged me to continue writing as long as I enjoy it--and I do.

As always, I particularly thank Paul Gaffney for his insightful and detailed reading of an earlier draft, keeping me on my toes. Nonetheless, all remaining errors and weaknesses in the book are entirely of my making.

About the Author

Larry A. Nielsen is emeritus professor of natural resources at North Carolina State University. He retired as an Alumni Distinguished Undergraduate Professor in 2017. Along with more than 100 academic and professional writings, he is co-editor or co-author of three textbooks (*Introduction to Fisheries Science, Fisheries Techniques, Ecosystem Management*). He is author of four recent non-fiction books, *Provost--Experiences, Reflections, and Advice From a Former "Number Two" on Campus* (2013), *Nature's Allies--Eight Conservationists Who Changed Our World* (2017), *Wolfpack Ramblings--A Thousand-Mile Walk Across NC State's Campus* (2021), and *Speaking Skills for Graduate Students* (2022, ebook only). He hosts the website Today in Conservation (todayinconservtion.com), which includes stories from the history of conservation and the environment for every date of the year. Larry lives with Sharon, his wife of more than fifty years, in Cary, North Carolina.

The Center Piece is the second in his series of murder mysteries featuring Des White and Elena Bertoni (the first is *Dead Man on Campus*, 2022). His grandsons like to remind him that although he writes murder mysteries, he has never won a game of Clue in his life.